AN EDUCATED MURDER

AN EDUCATED MURDER

J.R. HULLAND

St. Martin's Press
New York

AN EDUCATED MURDER. Copyright © 1986 by J. R. Hulland. All rights reserved. Printed in the United States of America. No part of this book may be used or reproduced in any manner whatsoever without written permission except in the case of brief quotations embodied in critical articles or reviews. For information, address St. Martin's Press, 175 Fifth Avenue, New York, N.Y. 10010.

Library of Congress Cataloging-in-Publication Data
Hulland, J. R.
    An educated murder.

    I. Title.
PR6058.U3924E3   1987   823'.914   86-24820
ISBN 0-312-00122-3

First published in Great Britain by Hodder and Stoughton under the title *Student Body.*

First U.S. Edition

10 9 8 7 6 5 4 3 2 1

To H. M. L.
for time

1

It was a golden autumn. Already the tidy beech grove between the main building and the prefabricated lecture hall flamed like a contained forest fire, the leaves alight in shades of bronze and ochre, cinnabar and cinnamon. Lovely words to match the colours.

Kate Henderson stood alone and sipped her coffee as she gazed out of the Common Room window. The late October sunshine glowed along the length of grey beech stems, from that distance as smooth and sensuous as silk-clothed nakedness. Soon the thin grass at their feet would be crisply deep in the winter litter of copper; and then the spring again, with its unbelievably green leaf buds furled along whippy stems. Spring always came to Somerset and this was hers, Kate told herself. But she knew in her heart there was more encouragement than truth in the thought. You couldn't forever hop backwards and forwards through your life's calendar to avail yourself of seasons past simply because you were now ready. It was always the spontaneity that counted, for better or worse.

Kate turned her attention from the window to the room behind her and thought how predictable life was when one stopped imagining fresh excitements round every corner. Jeff and Gordon were as usual deep in the *Telegraph* crossword, entirely self-contained and exclusive. That pairing had been so immediate at the beginning of term that she wondered if they'd known each other before. But their friendship was understandable. They were both reserved and quiet, though their occasional questions and comments in tutorials and seminars were winning them a reputation for maturity. Kate wondered how that would survive the possible discovery that they were gay.

Jessica Nicholls would inevitably react badly, Kate suspected. She watched Jessica flicking over the pages of a pamphlet while covertly eyeing the two men. She'd at last learned that a direct, flirtatious approach got her nowhere with them.

Jessica had made her unsubtle interest embarrassing since term began, and not only to Jeff and Gordon. Was she genuinely interested, Kate wondered, or was it simply that she couldn't bear them to ignore her? Certainly both men were physically attractive, with their slim, dark good looks. Perhaps this attraction was intensified for Jessica by the elusive quality she hadn't yet defined. What would happen if she did, having made herself pretty singular by her unrewarded attentions?

Meanwhile she was repulsing the advances of Robert Denham, though she found him useful enough as a casual escort. Him and half a dozen others. Jessica gave the impression that she never moved without an attendance of satellite males. To be fair, there were plenty who'd gladly be singled out. Just unfortunate that the two she'd be delighted to honour weren't remotely interested in her.

The other women weren't as blatant, though Kate could see that Alice Jepson resented Robert's dangling attendance on Jessica. She was either more intelligent than Jessica – quite possible, thought Kate contemptuously – or less desperate, for her cool awareness gave little away. She hadn't Jessica's Burne-Jones prettiness but of the two Kate suspected Alice would prove the more implacable and more successful rival. If she really wanted him, she need only wait till he'd played himself out. She certainly had more steel than bumbling, well-meaning Robert. What was the attraction there? But Alice's interest wasn't obvious and Kate saw it only because she watched.

It wasn't an appealing trait in her character, she knew, but her age had pushed her into a ringside seat. Not that much of what Kate saw appealed to her, though it had a detached interest. And perhaps she even envied a little their energy in angling for – whatever it was. The usual, she supposed. Affection, possibly; friendship, even love.

Kate was assured of her own love and affection returned, though she knew that one day – perhaps even fairly soon – she would no longer have exclusive rights. Perhaps then she might abandon her ringside seat – but sufficient unto that day, she told herself, suddenly shivering in a stray emotional draught. Possession was an uncomfortable quest and unacceptable even when offered. Let there be generosity in love and a free release at its end. That much at least was owed for the happiness it gave birth to.

★ ★ ★

"'The proper study of mankind is man.'" Liz Jackson detached herself from a group by the notice-board and walked over to Kate. "We were just saying that when Armageddon comes, Kate Henderson will be found standing on the sidelines awarding points for artistic interpretation and degrees of difficulty."

Kate grinned, accepting Liz's slightly embarrassing perspicacity which nevertheless seemed not to affect her friendly tolerance. But Liz was a genuinely *nice* person, and with a fair share of critical appreciation as well.

"You can't go about not noticing what's before your very eyes, boring or not. Why do you think they do it?" Liz asked, unprompted, from the security of her engagement ring.

"Why who do what?"

"People like Jessica, who try to appropriate people." Because a comet's defined by its tail, Kate imagined. A few of her friends had followed Liz from the notice-board.

"Oh, but she's terribly pretty," enthused Barbara Jones. "You can't deny Jessica's got what it takes."

"No reason that should give her a Ghengis Khan complex," Liz reasoned.

"Why can't she see she's making herself ridiculous? If she was more likeable she'd be pathetic." Kate looked curiously at the girl who'd spoken. Elinor tended to utter blunt comments on what she saw.

"Why do you have to be likeable to be pathetic?" Kate asked her.

"Because otherwise you're plain irritating. Jessica's behaviour is nauseating and therefore irritating. Her vanity elbows out even her self-respect. She should hire herself out as a stomach-pump."

"You've answered your own question," Peter laughed, throwing a careless arm across Elinor's heavy shoulders. "Her vanity prevents her from seeing how ridiculous she is. Now you, little Nell, have so much self-respect no one's good enough for you." Elinor shrugged off the casually draped arm. "You see? Prickly as a hedgehog. But actually, listening to you female experts on the female psyche, I think you're missing the point. Surely the reason Jessica is as she is and can't know how foolish she appears – observe that not all of us men fall for her – is because she hasn't any girlfriends. You know, female confidantes."

"Cause or effect?" snapped Elinor, moving away, but Kate wondered if there was something in what Peter had suggested.

"Elinor as a girlfriend would depress anyone's vanity," he murmured, glancing after her.

"She's a good friend," Liz said staunchly. "But Jessica irritates her. She's all Elinor despises in women and she gives us a bad name, Elinor reckons."

Kate surprised a sardonic gleam in Peter's eyes, but when he saw her watching him his face lit in its ready smile and she wondered if she'd been mistaken. Peter shook back his cuff to look at his watch, a complicated gesture that always reminded Kate of someone shaking and throwing dice.

"Well, I'm free now, thank God, though my time'll be spent in riotous essay-writing. Anyone want a lift down into town? Kate? You're free too, aren't you? Anyone else?" But the others had tutorials or special option seminars after the coffee-break and only Kate took advantage of Peter's offer.

He was generous, with his lifts at least. And amusing, Kate reflected, as Peter spanked up the drive and aimed his new registration VW Golf between the vast, gateless pillars onto the main road. But he could be cuttingly critical – and quite possibly rather dangerous. Kate found it difficult to make up her mind about him.

"When is your essay due?" she asked politely, resisting the urge to shut her eyes and call upon her Maker as they sped through a set of changing traffic-lights.

"Last week," he replied carelessly. "Bunny gave me an extension in recognition of my inventive imagination. Where shall I drop you?"

"Oh – anywhere in the Centre, if you're going that way. If not, anywhere, thanks."

"Fine. I'm going on to the docks. There's a boat I'm interested in."

"Oh? Sailing? Fishing?"

"Not like you, dear Kate, to be so interested."

"Social convention, that's all. Though I can be more probing if encouraged."

"Fire away, then. Provided we establish a one for one basis."

"There's nothing you could want to know about me," Kate laughed. "But I was only going to say, as a statement requiring no answer, that I'm surprised to find you doing this fourth year. Perhaps writing, or advertising – even succeeding to the ancestral home – but not training to be an English teacher."

"My dear Kate! No one's ever said a nicer thing! But this'll do to begin with and then, you know, the world's my oyster." There couldn't be many career teachers who thought so optimistically, was her silent response.

Kate glanced down at the elegant grey suede sleeve beside her, the equally elegant hands on the wheel in easy command of the car. Peter Colebrook exhaled the oiled scent of money and expensive good taste in accessories, from his good but not racy car – with due allowance for the preposterous badge-bar all dazzling with chrome and enamel – to his good but not flashy clothes, as discreetly yet unmistakably as a rose gives off fragrance. But with a hint more of purpose. To what end Kate couldn't tell, since he didn't, apparently, aim to attract – though he had one or two small mannerisms that seemed to demand attention. He was popular enough among both the men and the women, if not intimate with anyone on the course. And only Elinor Purbeck appeared openly disenchanted.

"What about you?" Peter interrupted her thoughts. "Dear Kate, sweet Kate, but never cursed Kate, would you have me as your Petrucchio?" He'd quickly lost any interest in one for one confidences regarding her career and she answered him casually and with relief.

"Certainly not! She lost, didn't she? The shrew was tamed. Or was all that blarney at the end just tongue-in-cheek? I don't imagine you with a yen for older women anyway."

"No? But you're not old, Kate. You display none of the unattractive stigmata of age."

"You've never seen me without my teeth. And perhaps it's just that I've got a good memory of my distant youth."

"I can't picture you as an irresponsible juvenile. I think you leapt fully mature from the head of Zeus into the Styx and emerged unassailable. Or do you have a weak spot, honest Kate?"

"As is the leopard spotted," she countered lightly. "This'll do fine, if you'll drop me here. I can get the weekend shopping at the supermarket for a change."

"A modest ambition," Peter murmured as he slid the car into the kerb, ignoring the double-yellow lines. "Restful Kate." He smiled into her eyes as she leaned down to thank him through the open window, before vanishing into the stream of traffic. Kate was surprised to smell merely burning rubber and not sulphur in his wake. She trotted through the plate-glass doors; in one end of the supermarket and out the other.

She wished it was always so easy to shrug off Peter's attentions. Kate had the impression of being something on a slide, peered at by a monstrous eye through a lens. But perhaps it was merely that he was less diffident about showing his curiosity than the others. After all her presence among them must appear freakish.

* * *

Kate caught the bus from the Centre into the open country a few miles beyond the city. She preferred to use the buses to and from the Department, perhaps because it made her seem more like a real student. Though quite a few of them had old bangers if she were to proclaim her possession of the more important material things, a car, a house, it might make her training at this late stage appear even more improbable.

At nearly forty Kate could hardly hope to get very far in a profession that was frantically cutting down and off-loading in all directions. The wonder was that she'd been accepted onto the course at all. Kate couldn't believe she'd so convincingly sold the retraining line – at a time when qualified teachers were looking for alternative jobs – and her acceptance at her local university's Department of Education still seemed a small miracle.

It had made Vivvy happy, anyway, and amused to know they were both going off to college together, though at different universities. It would have made Celia happy too, but that was in the past.

Kate got off the bus where it stopped opposite a row of pale stone terrace houses. The houses were simple, unpretentious and identical; except for their front doors and tiny front gardens where a wealth of imagination and initiative was daily to be seen. One of them, number five, was home.

Today she let herself in through her front door – double-glazed, this one – without a glance at the little garden, and walked straight through to the kitchen at the back. Here was the refuge and nerve-centre now, even more than the study; though for real peace to dream over old memories the living-room at the front was Kate's favourite place and quietly cherished.

She made herself a mug of coffee and turned her chair to look out through the back door onto the small, paved rear garden, which was little more than a yard. White-painted tubs of fuchsias stood upon the flags and hung out the last of their brightly coloured, ballet-skirted blooms, and button chrysanthemums glowed like sombre jewels; garnet, amethyst, amber, carnelian. The yard, protected by its side and end walls of the same light-coloured sandstone as the houses, warmed quickly in the sun. But inevitably the frosts must come and put an end to all flowers, till the spring brought its early riot of bulbs. It was sheltered and private outside but Kate sat on in the kitchen, sipping her coffee and wondering what to do about lunch.

★   ★   ★

She hadn't been so conscious of her loneliness without Celia – not since she'd first heard the unbelievable, stupefying news of her death – until Vivvy left for college at the beginning of the month. Now, even with her own new course to provide new interest and keep her busy, the emptiness of the house pressed round her. And never was Kate so aware of her age, though that was something you lived with and grew up with after all, as when she came home from the Department to the empty house.

Not that Kate felt the individual years and their slow accumulation, but she was freshly aware each day of the distance in time and attitudes between herself and the other students. She'd never sensed it with her daughter, but then Vivvy was exceptional. By comparison her colleagues, if pleasant enough, were dull or childish or uncomfortable. Even their sophistication seemed an insult to Kate's maturity, achieved as it had been through the wounds and scars of experience.

When Celia was killed, one wet night two years earlier, Kate found herself willed the house and enough money to pay for her long-delayed post-graduate year at a Department of Education. Though stultified by legal phrases Kate could nevertheless imagine the well-loved, long-lidded smile that would have accompanied Celia's own words:

'In recognition of her kindness to me and her own ambitions I will give and bequeath the said sum to enable Katherine Rose Henderson to attend a recognised Department of Education and there to train as a qualified teacher.'

The crunch had come in the next paragraph in the worst of lawyerese, to the effect that should the said Kate fail to deploy the monies as the testatrix stipulated by the time she was forty, then the monies were to be divided among various societies. Furthermore, the sum of £2,000 to be bequeathed to Vivvy on the day that Kate should be awarded her diploma should also be so distributed. So, though the house and Celia's royalties were willed to Kate outright, poor Vivvy depended on Kate's fulfilment of the terms.

Kate smiled to herself. It was typical of Celia to force her somehow to do what was anyway in her best interests. Typically kind. And it had been her ambition once, long ago. Kate had known for two years that she'd accept Celia's challenge, not simply to do the Place-Names Society, the Sealed Knot *et al* out of their windfall, or even to enable Vivvy to come into her legacy; but because Celia wanted it for her.

Well, so here I am, Kate thought with another twinge of loneliness. In the empty house Celia had left her, she felt as hollow and as longing for her presence as she'd felt that hideous night two years before. The following day, the fourth Friday in October, would be the second anniversary of Celia's death. Two years ago today, thought Kate, dissolving again into her lonely grief, Celia had only twenty-four hours to live, and we none of us knew. None of us had warning to renew our necessary bonds and release others. She died and we didn't have the chance to show her for a final time how much we loved and needed her. Death should never come so, without warning. At least, not for the survivors.

2

The following day dawned more definitely on the side of autumn than late summer. The wind blew persistently, dispersing the scent of woodsmoke and garden bonfires over the city. As she walked up Carriage Hill to the Department, which was some way beyond the university proper, Kate found herself entering a mushroom cloud of damp mist from which her proud beeches emerged ghostly and drained of their colours.

She decided not to stop at the main building to drop off her sheepskin jacket but walked on past to the lecture hall, knowing that it would probably be as cold as a cathedral inside. One or two figures walked shadowily in front of her down the path and she could hear the voices of others following; but it was a strange, coffined sensation, like walking down the lane to the land of the dead.

Lights were already switched on in the lecture hall, fluorescent tubes that gave a white, dead light, and touched the atmosphere with the clinical sterility of an operating theatre – or morgue. It was a pity that their numbers were too many to be accommodated in any of the rooms in the main building for these compulsory lectures, Kate thought glumly.

She sat in the first available seat and found herself next to Peter. He turned to her with a scowl that would have stopped an Exocet in its tracks, but when he saw who it was his face broke into the familiar pleased smile, as if he'd been waiting only for Kate to make his day complete. Why, she wondered, did he go to such pains to charm her?

"How was the boat?" she asked tentatively, wishing old

Grundy had been more prompt and spared her the necessity for making small talk.
"Not at all what I'd expected," Peter replied almost sulkily. "Not very nice people either. In fact," he laughed carelessly, "when you strode in with such purpose I could almost have believed one of them had followed me up to continue our – haggling." Kate hardly liked to tell him that, contrary to any impression of purpose, she hadn't noticed or even cared who she sat by. Peter's vanity wasn't something one took lightly, she sensed, and wondered what had gone wrong.

The Growing Child, now aged seven, and subject of today's lecture, developed by one more psychological year during the next hour, and Kate dutifully noted down his interesting or less lovely characteristics. Peter, meanwhile, ostentatiously read the latest Harold Robbins. Had he been spanked too much? Not enough? His unusually bolshy assertiveness made Kate vaguely uneasy.

* * *

The hill mist had lifted by coffee-break and pale sunlight lay across the sculptured gardens terraced down the slope behind the main building. Kate decided to sit outside until the discussion seminar at eleven and write a letter to Vivvy.

She found herself a stone bench beside a small, irregularly shaped pool. There were glimpses of goldfish, glowing like fire-opals in the dark water and Kate sat and watched them for a bit. What did they do if the pond froze in winter? An artistically created rockery stepped down to the far edge of the pool, its little slopes and plateaux planted with miniature conifers and alpines in a Lilliputian garden. Some variety of tall pond plants, ornamental reeds or rushes, Kate supposed, grew out of the water at one end of the pond, using a curve of the rockery as a back-drop. There were water-lilies too, and no doubt the best effect was achieved in the summer.

Kate flipped over her note-pad for a clean page to start the letter. They'd agreed it would be better to separate for this year, each laughingly saying she had no desire to cramp the other's style; so Vivvy hadn't tried for entry to their local university. Kate had a morbid fear of being thought to be breathing down her daughter's neck anyway, but she missed her now. Missed her like hell.

Kate hoped Vivvy was as happy as her letters sounded. Thank God she was caring and articulate as well. Like Celia. Stiff upper lips and British reserve were all very well, no doubt, among people who couldn't speak your language – literally or emotionally – but as useless as a cough in a thunderstorm when you badly needed reassurance and verbal proof of continued love. Kate had learnt from Celia both to accept love and to give it herself, not lessons she'd found easy to learn, but with Vivvy it was different. A naturally more affectionate soul, she supposed, and hoped it didn't lay her open to vulnerability, hurt or rejection.

Kate checked her watch, took the top off her Biro but that was as far as she got. The squeak of gravel on the path made her turn round. She recognised one of the university lecturers in History of Art who visited the Department once a week. Miss Stanton's subject was vernacular architecture and her lectures were the sort attended because of the wit she managed to inject into the study of local buildings.

Kate smiled 'Good morning' as Miss Stanton approached, expecting her to walk by. Instead she came and sat on the stone bench beside Kate.

"Miss Henderson, isn't it? I was surprised to see anyone outside today – though Capability Brown would've been gratified. This is all his," she gestured at the sweep of the gardens around them. "Well, Capability's with modifications. Not an easy site. But I understand that the great outdoors is attractive these days only as long as it is hot enough to sunbathe in the pink. I rather like the autumn myself, as long as I'm booted and spurred in readiness. It's not so demanding as the heat. Morgan's Mount in winter, however, defeats even me. Knee-boots and long coats are the only possible wear then, even at the risk of looking like a refugee at the retreat from Moscow. How are you finding the course?"

The question came as a relief to Kate, who was beginning to wonder what there'd possibly be left to say about the weather when it was her turn to contribute.

"In a way I think I'm enjoying parts of it even better than I might have done in my twenties. I don't think I had an old enough head on my shoulders then."

"Will you use it, do you think? Your qualification, I mean."

"That's rather up to some discerning local authority, I imagine. I've joined the road near the exit after all. Er – I know who you are, of course – I've been to your lectures – but how do you know my name? And must I assume from your last question that I appear – past it?"

"Certainly not, and I realised straightaway that I might have sounded tactless. Sorry. As to the other – I knew Celia very well. Didn't she ever mention my name?"

"She never used surnames and we agreed long before she came here that it would be more – convenient if her home and university lives were kept totally separate."

There was a pause while Miss Stanton lit a cigarette. Kate wondered if she'd spoken too brusquely and offended the older woman.

"I saw you at the funeral," she said at last. "It was a terrible day for all of us – I can't tell you. Look, I'm doing this very badly. We all liked Celia, you know. It was our sorrow too, her death. Some of us wished we could have lightened yours. I know I did. But in the end we were afraid of intruding on your personal grief. We felt very – inadequate."

"I wish I'd known," said Kate quietly, wondering if the other woman remembered that this day was the anniversary of Celia's death. "It was I who felt inadequate. I might have known Celia's friends valued her as she deserved."

Miss Stanton glanced at her watch.

"Time I was making tracks. I only came to set up the projector for the slides after lunch but I saw you down here. Look, why don't you come round for a meal one evening? They do us pretty well in Hall. Tomorrow? It's not such a full High Table on Saturdays and there's room for guests. How about it? I'll leave directions in your pigeon-hole." She stood up.

"I'd like that. Thank you," Kate smiled back. The distant bell of the cathedral clock sounded its deep note up the hill and she remembered that she was due for the discussion seminar.

The two women walked up to the main building together.

"What have they in store for you now?"

"A group discussion, usually pretty uninformed on our part, of the lecture we had earlier – the psychological development of the growing child."

"Hm. Hold me back, someone. I'll take buildings any day. But what can you be expected to know, apart from this morning's chat?"

"We're supposed to have done some advance reading – conventional and controversial views. But I find it difficult to cover all the material. I must be rusty, I suppose."

"It is a knack that comes with practice, but even so you'd need the necessary interest. Shall we say seven for seven-thirty tomorrow, then? Reasonably formal, I'm afraid." Miss Stanton flashed Kate a smile and stalked off towards the car-park.

* * *

They were divided into groups for these post-mortem discussions and Kate's heart sank when she saw who'd be chairing her own group. Miss Welborne was dedicated, humourless and vulnerable. Her published work was recommended by Kate's own tutor and her lectures, where one wouldn't expect heckling, were interesting and full of enthusiasm; but she couldn't cope with personalities. In all but the most docile of discussion groups her defensiveness seemed to emphasise her nannyish manner. Kate felt sorry for Miss Welborne, but she set her teeth on edge.

Peter had already once displayed an unexpected cruelty in his suave treatment of her. It had at first amused and then embarrassed the others.

"There was no reason for you to have been so nasty to her," Liz had protested afterwards.

"But I wasn't nasty to *her*," Peter replied smoothly. "I merely demolished a couple of her fantasies. Miss Welborne's got to be able to back up what she trots out. She's supposed to be the expert, after all, and should be able to look after herself. She's been too long away from the classroom – where it really hurts."

But Miss Welborne wasn't able to look after herself, and

Kate suspected uneasily that that discovery had encouraged Peter. And now Kate was afraid for her again, remembering the uncertain mood Peter had been in earlier.

"Well, now," Miss Welborne began, with the air of one dipping into an exciting bran-tub on behalf of infant charges. "Mr. Grundy showed this morning how the innocent selfishness and possessiveness of the infant can lead to later aggression and really anti-social behaviour if it's not tactfully channelled. So where shall we start?" Kate wished she wasn't quite so twee and wished too that she herself had something riveting to kick off with. "Well, then. Let's look at it this way. Suppose you find Johnny pressing plasticine into Mary's hair – " She stood up and wrote 'Johnny' and 'Mary' on the blackboard. They all silently gazed at this terse visual aid. Chalk, thought Kate; the teacher's crutch and talisman. "Now, what would you do?"

"Stop him . . ."
"Distract him . . ."
"Send him out of the room."
"He'd get up to worse . . ."
"Make him apologise."
"How?" demanded a disgruntled voice.

Miss Welborne's head turned from side to side as if she were watching a centre-court rally; her specs beamed, her lips mouthed encouragement. At last, it seemed, she had a sensible discussion to chair.

"But all this is just so much nonsense." Peter's drawl pricked Miss Welborne's bubble. "One stinging spank, obviously, would settle little Johnny's hash and it would reduce the time before poor Mary herself is attended to. Or have we forgotten Mary? She could be in hysterics by the time you've all consulted and turned to page eighty for the answer. Miss Welborne should be asking why Johnny was able to go so far. What was the teacher about to allow it? If we're deprived of sanctions then we must prevent such situations before they have to be resolved. We need to be trained in the use of discipline, not second-hand theories about child development – and these seem to change from year to year even where you do find agreement."

"In other words you want a return to the rule of fear and orderly rows all facing front in dead silence?" Elinor asked belligerently.

"But what's wrong with that, dear Nell? Those are actually the conditions in which teachers are best able to teach. You surely don't think you're going to be a better teacher because you're prepared to be destroyed by some infant punk? In the end they have to face the discipline of public exams, and after that the discipline of a job. Where are they going to learn it? Not from their families any more. If they survive our remorseless fear of hurting or upsetting – "

"If you're interesting they'll want to listen to you." Robert Denham made a despairing effort on the side of the angels.

"Now I know you're just not thinking." Kate flinched on Robert's behalf. "Picture yourself having to contain a roomful of teenagers who'd obviously rather be doing something else. All you can use to keep them there – and listening – is the magic of your subject. History's your first subject, isn't it? You'd be better off teaching knitting."

"Well, thank you, Mr. Colebrook, but we must let others have their say now," Miss Welborne rather tittered. "Er – Miss – "

"Do forgive me for interrupting but I hadn't finished." Peter's drawl was becoming insufferable. Perhaps wisely Miss Welborne surrendered. "You see, I don't think Morgan's Mount is doing its duty by us. We're not taught the best methods of survival, only the best means of not upsetting our pupils. So I don't believe anything Miss Welborne has to say is valid for any but simple baby-minders. Or can have more claim on our time than – than a press release from the Flat Earth Society. We all know that teachers can be broken and I've seen it done. It's not going to happen to me. What we need to know is how – "

"You're talking about power, aren't you?" Gordon Watson interrupted.

"But of course. It's all a question of power. They have the power now to loose their natural beastliness and cut you down. We need the power to prevent this. So, what makes a teacher without sanctions powerful enough, and therefore successful enough to *teach*? How does he show who's boss?"

"Where does the teaching come in, Peter?" Liz protested. "You're advocating parade-ground instruction, not – "

"We could do worse than take a few tips from the army at that. Their success rate with what we call 'Remedial' or 'Ineducable' pupils is quite amazing. And it's all based on discipline. I don't believe teachers should resign themselves to being 'sowers of unseen harvests and reapers of thistles and weeds' when instant results *can* be achieved."

Kate wondered if Peter's argument was the result of careful thought or merely allowed to develop as he went along. He'd certainly entirely depressed Miss Welborne and left the rest of the group silent. Kate supposed some of them might be afraid to disagree, having seen Robert dismembered, in case that suave blade of a voice should be turned against themselves. Yet none uttered in his support either and Kate wondered why not. A breakdown in classroom discipline must be the secret dread of all but the most confident. Few would know how they'd cope with that until they were exposed on teaching practice the following term. And if any still doubted the power that could be wielded against classroom authority, they only had to look at the reduction of Miss Welborne herself.

The bell for the lunch-break split the silence and Miss Welborne left the room without a word. Kate didn't believe she could ever re-establish credibility with her particular group and hoped she'd be able to avoid chairing them again. She was probably perfectly effective anywhere away from Peter who had probably been right – at least to the extent that she'd be useless in all but the most well-disposed of classrooms. But that was no reason to try her to her modest limits.

* * *

"Peter!" Jessica Nicholls flew round the semi-circle of chairs, now mostly empty, and hung on his arm. "Marvellous! You really socked it to them! Just what I've been saying all along. Where shall we go for lunch?"

Kate kept her patience with difficulty. Jessica had never shown any interest in Peter before; partly, Kate suspected, because their two egos in competition could not have suited her domineering instincts.

She was not to be accommodated, however. Peter looked down into her pretty, beaming face as it snuggled against his arm.

"So precipitate," he murmured, and the glint in his eyes should have warned her. "Dear Jessica, you must strive to be less obvious and you really mustn't *maul*." He removed her hand from his sleeve and anxiously examined the suede. Red marks showed as she rubbed her wrist, gazing up at him in ludicrous dismay. "The best people," Peter was satisfied his jacket had sustained no lasting damage and he turned his attention back to Jessica, "the very best people wait to be invited. Kate? Quiet Kate, come lunch with me."

"I've brought sandwiches today," Kate looked back at him gravely, knowing he wouldn't believe her. 'No cock of mine, you crow too like a craven', she decided with finality.

"Cruel Kate!" Peter laughed lightly, but there was no smile in his eyes as he walked past her out of the room.

Kate took half a step towards Jessica but she needn't have done so much and Kate surprised herself offering even that little support. For Jessica saw the move, swung away and called out gaily to her attendant satellites.

"Wasn't he marvellous? Real charisma! Come on, fellahs! The last one to town buys the drinks!" She's got some self-respect after all, Kate thought admiringly, wondering if Elinor saw it that way. Kate knew that the sight of herself, dismissed as negligible these past weeks but apparently standing agog and witnessing her punishment, had stiffened Jessica's pride to a degree Kate found surprising. In her position Kate rather thought she'd have thrown herself to the ground and drummed her heels. Or lost her temper and simply thumped him. But – charisma? Generosity indeed.

"Have you really brought sandwiches, Miss Henderson?" Jeff asked as he and Gordon walked past to the door.

"For heaven's sake call me Kate," she snapped in reply, sickened by the whipping Peter had inflicted and even more by her own association with it. "And no, I haven't. I lied in my teeth. Jeff, what on earth has all this been about? It's even affecting me." And that's my most surprising admission to date, she thought, that I should feel any involvement on behalf of two such irritating women. Perhaps because Peter had won such easy victories. Well, he wouldn't over her, she promised herself.

"Then please join us. We've brought enough for three." Jeff ignored Kate's unusual curtness and her half apology.

"Oh – thanks. I'd resigned myself to doing without. But I don't think I can bear the Common Room just now and it's turned misty again outside."

"Lecture hall, then. No one'll be there till two-thirty." With good reason, Kate remembered the chill.

They walked down between the dripping rhododendrons and past the clump of beeches to the vast shed of the lecture hall while Kate wondered at their invitation to eat with them. They'd hardly exchanged more than half a dozen commonplace sentences since the beginning of term.

But Gordon spoke directly, without any beating about.

"We wanted to ask you to warn Peter – these are egg, those are cheese and chutney – as he obviously respects you – "

"Thanks, but hang on. Peter doesn't 'respect' me, though he does seem to enjoy playing the sides against the middle – "

"I did warn you, Gord," Jeff said quietly. "Mine are all sandwich spread, Kate. I've a passion for the stuff."

"It's ages since I had that. But what should I be warning Peter against? Apart from the possibility of getting his face pushed in if he grows too clever."

"More or less just that, but we seem to have mistaken the situation between you two so – "

"You're making our very casual acquaintance sound impossibly meaningful," Kate said uncomfortably. She couldn't produce the gay insouciance that Jessica had managed and nor could she feel amused by their mistake. "But why does Peter need any special warning?"

"The people he mixes with in the town. He could find himself in trouble. We thought if you just – "

"But if you know about it, why don't you warn him? He'd be quite justified in telling me to keep out of his affairs. I should think he's able to look after himself anyway."

"We can't do anything. I'm sorry we can't explain more, but he could stir up a whole lot of mischief as well as land himself in trouble."

"Well, don't risk your low profiles if you don't want, but I haven't any interest one way or the other." Kate was amazed by their reasoning.

"Peter's frightened, you see." Gordon looked up from his sandwiches. "That's why he's been so aggressive today. Physically afraid. Something went wrong at the weekend."

"If he's frightened that must be warning enough for him, I should have thought," Kate retorted. "Are you involved in whatever it is?"

"No," they shook their heads positively. "But we have a friend who – who knows things."

"Well, warn him to stay clear then," said Kate indifferently. "Let Peter find his own salvation. I don't see that we owe him anything."

3

It was at times an uneasy weekend for Kate, a mixture of extreme and counter-balancing emotions that she found hard to cope with. Her anger with Peter for trying to involve her in his latest unpleasant behaviour was matched by her incredulity that Gordon and Jeff should expect her to involve herself even more deeply with him. Why were people so intent on making use of her, she wondered with resentment. Good God, at her age she might be expected to have outgrown that sort of petty intrigue – or was it perhaps because of her age? They saw her as an elderly referee, maybe? Yuk!

What little the two men had said about Peter's affairs seemed the height of melodrama anyway, and surely not to be taken seriously. What, after all, might Peter be in to – pot, perhaps? Blue movies, even. She felt he might be capable of worse, but how was one to know where to set the limits to one's imagination? Kate was prepared to admit that she had rather less real understanding than someone half her age. Than Vivvy, for instance. Though she hoped with motherly concern that Vivvy was well out of anything like pot or blue movies.

In her new-found anxiety, Kate wrote and posted the letter she'd intended to start beside the ornamental pond on Morgan's Mount. She made it a quiet, peaceful letter that would please Vivvy and reassure her that all was going smoothly in her absence: that May of the paper-shop sent her best wishes; that next door Mrs. Harrison's kittens were born at last, three ginger and one tortie exactly like her mother; that she herself was continuing to enjoy the course and making friends – Liz, Elinor, Barbara. That she had been invited to dinner in Hall and would tell Vivvy about that in her next letter.

By the time Kate had posted it, on her way to the village churchyard with a mixed bunch of chrysanthemums – where she recognised with her usual silent gratitude Willy's careful tidying – she was on an even keel again. And the prospect of hearing and talking about Celia cheered her so much by Saturday that she felt there could have been nothing more seriously wrong with Peter than a cracking hangover.

★   ★   ★

Kate dressed carefully in a dark suit for her dinner in Hall, manoeuvred her mini out of its cramped space in the row of street parking outside the house and set out for the university. In spite of Celia's years there, Kate hardly knew her way about the campus and had to rely heavily on Miss Stanton's directions. The evening had drawn in early, damp and foggy with a rising river mist, and the quadrangle lights glowed dim within their haloes of fuzzed fluorescence.

Kate walked up the staircase looking for Miss Stanton's rooms in the staff block and found her outer door left hospitably open. She rang the bell and waited, hearing an outburst of warning barks and stern admonitions to 'comport himself more seemly, do'.

Miss Stanton ushered Kate through a tiny hallway into her sitting-room, where fawn velvet curtains, drawn against the night, and shaded lamps welcomed with an invitation to comfort and security. A gas fire flanked by shelves of books and deep armchairs on either side of a goat-skin rug seemed to set the seal of civilised living at one remove from the naughty world.

"Sit down and relax while I get you a sherry. How do you like it?"

"Dry, please." Kate felt suddenly shy. How old was Miss Stanton? About Celia's age? Only a few years older than herself; yet Kate felt a constraint. She bent to make a fuss of the dog, a black dachshund. Perhaps she ought to get an animal of some kind herself.

"His great advantage is that his hairs don't show on dark

suits and gowns. All right, Hermann. Time's up. Bed!" The dog trotted obediently to his basket beside the chair across from Kate and peered beadily at her over its rim.

"It must be fun to have a dog," she remarked, as Miss Stanton moved up a small table and put Kate's drink beside her. She then sat in the chair beside Hermann's basket.

"He keeps me amused, but they have their own disadvantages. Luckily Hermie's very amenable and he's lovely to come home to. Now, I hope you won't mind, but I've invited a few friends – just one or two – to drop in for a sherry before Hall. I've only told them that you were a friend of Celia's. They won't be coming back here afterwards, though I hope you will. Or do you have to get home? I'm sorry, but I didn't even ask if you were mobile. Will you have to rush for buses?"

"No, I've got my car. But thank you, I'd love to stay on." Kate had felt momentarily dismayed at the thought of meeting any of Celia's friends outside the protected formality of the dinner table, but she perked up at the prospect of returning for more private conversation now that she had greater need than ever to see Celia alive and whole.

"Good. I'm glad you don't have to hurry away. I've been looking forward to this evening. May I call you Kate? And I'm Ruth. That'll be them." Miss Stanton got to her feet as the doorbell rang and Hermann darted briskly out of his basket, ready for anything. Kate stood too, nervously taking a swig at her sherry. It seemed that she was to be scrutinised. Well then; let them look.

"Come in. Hang up your coats if you need. Shoo, Hermann! Basket!" Ruth reappeared with the three women who'd arrived together. "Now, Kate – meet Margaret O'Hare, Chris Lowther and Dee Travis. Kate Henderson, people. Sit where you can while I see to the drinks." Kate exchanged polite murmurs with the others as they settled themselves. "Margaret belongs to Morgan's Mount, strictly speaking." Ruth crossed the room with three sherry glasses on a tray. "She's Mrs. Robert O'Hare. You know him, don't you, Kate?" Bunny, of course. Peter's subject tutor.

"Oh, yes," Kate smiled at Mrs. Bunny. "We have him now

for History of Education, but I think he'll be my second subject tutor when we get round to our second strings."

"Good heavens, I didn't realise you were a student! Ruth, you never said! I might have made a fearful blunder! But now I come to remember, Robert did say there was a very mature one. So it's you?"

"Er – yes, actually. Though you've made me feel like an elderly chicken or a ripe Stilton," Kate laughed in embarrassment.

"My dear, I simply shouldn't be allowed out! Let's start again. How brave of you to take this up so – so – "

"Late?" Kate queried amid general laughter.

"Give up, Margaret. You're only wallowing deeper," Ruth advised. "What she means, Kate, is that students are all very well in themselves, but at our age we'd find it difficult to get right in among them. As it were."

"It's all right. I know it must look pretty odd," Kate grinned across at Margaret. "And they find me short of an appropriate pigeon-hole too."

"Why did you decide to do this course now?" Dee Travis asked curiously.

"It's only now that I've had the chance to. But it's an old ambition come home to roost, really."

"You brave thing. Do you think you'll survive?"

"I certainly expect to last out the course, but whether they'll be satisfied enough to hand over the diploma at the end is another matter. Continuous assessment, instead of staking everything on final exams, is a mixed blessing for us poor post-grads. But I hope to have the stamina at least." Or bang goes Vivvy's legacy, Kate reminded herself, and heard Celia's laugh.

"Robert was saying you're a pretty bright lot this year. He's positively overawed by one of his tutorial group."

That must be Peter, Kate supposed, as the conversation grew more general. Mrs. Bunny quoted her Robert's views with an authority that would have surprised that formal, rather diffident man, while Ruth listened politely.

Meanwhile Dee and Chris Lowther compared notes on those of their undergraduate students who intended to take the fourth year course. Before Kate had become friendly with Celia she had assumed, together with most of her friends, that undergraduates were somehow like the anonymous shadows thrown on the walls of Plato's cave; barely distinguishable to the teaching staff. She wondered if Dee's students believed the same. They would have been unnerved to hear just how much they were noticed, noted and assessed.

"Ruth says you knew Celia." Chris took advantage of a lull in her conversation with Dee and the room suddenly paused to listen. But that's why they've come, Kate reminded herself, because they knew her too. She braced herself to be as open yet as non-committal as possible. Celia wasn't to be remembered as if she had something furtive to hide.

"Yes, we met during my own undergraduate days," Kate replied.

"That was a terrible thing!" Margaret O'Hare's whole person conveyed a distress still acutely felt. "Such a gifted woman and so genuinely *human*. She had that brilliant mind but never made me feel stupid. I still miss her terribly, you know," she said, looking round at them. "And Robert, of course, was simply desolated when it happened. They used to have such fun. He always said she could've been a professional musician, not just playing duets with him to amuse the students at the Music Soc. concerts. A true Renaissance mind, he said. A complete person." Kate warmed towards Margaret as she spoke.

"I remember you at the funeral," Chris continued quietly and then smiled. "Your hair." Celia used to laugh at it – 'The Burning Bush' – and weave ridiculous stories about the Raging Red Hendersons and Kate Flamehead, who'd led her monstrous regiment through the night by the light of her hair. It had lost its fire now, as she had herself, but it was still distressingly distinctive. "You had someone with you," Chris reminded her. "She was so very upset. I wondered – " Chris looked away.

"Vivvy." Kate felt the prickle of tears behind her eyes at the memory. "She wanted to be there. Vivvy never takes the easy way." It was a kind of arrogance Kate half recognised and even sympathised with, though it made her feel uneasy. Slapping your cards down on the table was all very well but you needed the aces.

"It must have made it doubly distressing for you," Ruth said. And no one asked who Vivvy was.

"She was only sixteen," Kate explained. "It was her first close tragedy when Celia died." And her stormy grief had served to turn Kate's own mind from wishing herself dead with Celia; forced her to play her own cards in support of Vivvy's hopelessly grand gesture. It had brought Kate almost to her knees.

"I thought at first it was one of Celia's students. Celia could do anything with those kids," Dee said gruffly.

"Oh – now I know who you must be!" Margaret squeaked. Kate's heart sank. The others probably knew too, but had the tact not to announce the fact. "Of course! You're the secretary Celia raved about."

"Secretary, housekeeper and general bottle-washer," Kate acknowledged lightly, wondering what else Margaret knew.

"She kept you very dark – except to tease Robert. Robert used to threaten to lure you away. He's always in a fearful muddle with his manuscripts, poor lamb, and I'm no earthly help to him. But Celia produced all those books and articles and still kept sane. And now you're a student again. Robert's student. Life's amazing!" And death the final blow. For all that Celia had forced her to open another door.

"More than time we were moving down, people," Ruth warned. She'd sat quietly while Kate coped with what might have been an awkward turn in the conversation. It would have been even more awkward if any of them had openly made the obvious connections. Kate wondered how far their deductions had led them and what effect their conclusions might have on their memories of Celia. None, she hoped. She'd been very touched by their affection. And when at High Table she was introduced to others of the academic staff as a friend of Celia Rowland's, and saw the same spark of interest and remembered fondness, Kate felt glowingly well disposed towards the entire world.

"Don't lose touch with us," Chris said after the meal as they went their separate ways. "I'll ask Ruth to bring you to my rooms for an evening."

* * *

Back in Ruth Stanton's sitting-room Kate fended off Hermann's exuberant advances while Ruth made coffee and brought it through.

"I thought you'd prefer coffee here rather than in the SCR. They don't force port upon us these days and you've probably had enough of my colleagues, great though they are. But I wanted you to meet them." Why? Kate wanted to ask. For her pleasure in hearing them talk of Celia as they did, or because something was expected of her? And had it been a conspiracy of four or was it only Ruth Stanton's curiosity which asked to be satisfied?

"It's been very pleasant altogether," Kate replied. "I don't know when I last went out for an evening."

"It must've done you good, then. So, when did you become Celia's general factotum?" Ruth asked, sipping her coffee thoughtfully.

"Oh – well, I did a shorthand and typing course after I graduated and offered myself as her PA. Celia lived in college when I was a student, but she'd just been appointed to an Assistant Lectureship at Reading – her thesis had not long been published. When I first knew her she was on a research grant with some lecturing and tutoring thrown in. She was good – great – at that. But what she wanted most was to research and write. Anyway, she thought my offer was a good idea and I helped with the occasional project for her colleagues too. So she lectured, researched and published until she became a big enough catch to be offered the Senior Lectureship here. I was enormously proud of her. There seemed to be no stopping her until the accident." And that, thought Kate, is a fair enough review for anyone.

"You still miss her." Miss Stanton was nothing if not direct.

"Very much. She wanted me to do this, you know – the Dip. Ed. course. It's what I would've done if – things had been different."

"And she never mentioned me?"

"Oh yes, now I know your Christian name – unless there are other Ruths in the Fine Arts Faculty. And I know you were very friendly with Celia." Kate remembered the occasional unease when learning of friendships in which she had no part. "I'm glad to know you personally at last," she smiled. Ruth lit a cigarette and studied the tip.

"I wonder what she said about me? I knew about – you." Kate's coffee-cup paused on its way to her lips. "That you existed and your name. Not much else, though to me you were always more than a backroom assistant." Kate was suddenly confused by the expression on Ruth's strong-featured face. "Celia wasn't secretive about her private life, for all she kept it separate. She told you if you asked outright, but of course she never volunteered anything and she didn't give reckless openings for very personal enquiries. I suppose we're all like that in this kind of set-up, really; reserved after a certain point both in what we want known and what we want to know about each other. It's not an 'all girls together' thing. In fact I think the live and let live attitude is one of the more attractive qualities of our sort of community – among us single people, anyway. But Celia's friendship was immensely important to me and she knew it. I'm glad if she let you understand that. *Tout passe, l'amitié reste* – because we're human and if we're lucky."

"Nothing more certain," Kate agreed. "Though if I keep you up to unsociable hours *l'amitié* may be strained beyond repair." She stood up and buttoned her jacket. "Thank you for giving me such a pleasant evening. Would you like to come round to our place one day? It's the same address. But perhaps it won't be long before we meet again, socially I mean. Chris Lowther said she'd be in touch with you about a foregather at her rooms."

Kate's chatter had brought them tactfully to the door, accompanied by a sleepy Hermann, where she said good night to Ruth and walked down the stairs to the car-park.

★ ★ ★

As Kate undressed and got ready for bed her mind ran over what she'd heard about Celia that evening, and again she felt the warm comfort of knowing how they remembered her.

She lay in the dark and recalled her own early days of commitment to Celia, based as it was on admiration and then gratitude sparked off by blatant opportunism. Kate remembered the relief of Celia's lectures; something, they'd all agreed, you could follow logically and get hold of. Not like the Talking Heads and Walking Dead you were otherwise forced to bear. Celia wasn't much older than her students and they'd felt she appreciated their difficulties. Or that she ought to. She was ready to laugh with them and tease them – not slaps on the back and swapping hats, but quietly. Kate smiled into the darkness at the memory of her own first experience of Celia's gentle wit. She'd yawned rather too obviously during a morning lecture which had followed a night of late revels:

"My dear Miss Henderson, I'm not keeping you awake, am I?" Celia had enquired solicitously.

During her famous tutorials Celia would talk about the 'divine spark' and persuade her students that they might even be gifted with it. The ensuing discussions reached a level of intellectual maturity they hadn't known they could achieve, while Celia sat slumped in an armchair, her long legs sprawled out, and listened with a smile. One or two she invited on their own, Kate among them, and those were the evenings Kate really loved. Under their influence she felt there was no star she couldn't ride.

Then had come Finals and the night of the June Ball, and Kate passed out. Not *magna cum laude* but with alcohol. Chaste Kate, who spoke so pompously and ignorantly about chivalry and virtue and whose sights were set beyond mere carnal conquests, had drunk herself into a stupor. Afterwards she suspected that John, her research chemist escort, had interfered with her drink as he'd certainly interfered with her body. Kate, the virtuous, intellectual icicle, found herself pregnant.

"Don't ever come home to us if you get into trouble," her mother had warned her when Kate was sixteen, mindful more of the neighbours' censure than her own daughter's possible despair. But it would never have crossed Kate's mind to seek help at home where the wages of sin had been so meticulously apportioned. And anyway the chance of that kind of trouble seemed remote enough at sixteen. At nearly twenty-one, however, there it was and not likely to be overlooked.

Kate had spent two days considering her situation, forcing down the panic and anger. Then she cancelled her application for a post-graduate year at London's Institute of Education and enrolled instead for a crash course in shorthand and typing at a secretarial college in Reading. That September she'd gone back to her own college to find Celia, who was distractedly packing her books for her move to Reading University. Kate didn't allow her instant smile of welcome to deflect her from her immediate purpose in calling.

"I'm pregnant," she began baldly.

Kate earned herself a tongue-lashing she may have deserved but could hardly bear.

"You bloody stupid little fool!" Celia raved when she found her breath. "What will you do now?"

"I'm already doing it – a typing course."

"On a grant?"

"With my family background? Barmaiding and waitressing at nights and weekends."

"Christ! But can't your parents help?"

"They don't know yet, but they wouldn't."

"You futile little fool! You of all people! What a criminal waste!"

"So," Kate continued as calmly as she could, "I thought you'd need help with moving and your writing and everything. It's a six months' course. At the end of it I'll be able to take dictation and type up your manuscripts. I'll do anything else – cook, clean, wash, iron – if you'll let me stay with you." Celia struggled for words.

"You're mad! Do you know what a pittance I'll be paid? I couldn't afford you even if I wanted you."

"I'll work for nothing."

"But I'll have the extra expense of getting a flat or something, you lunatic! I couldn't keep you in my room. Use your few wits!"

"I'll go out and earn as well to help out, and when I can't I'll get typing to do at home. I'll pay you to have me."

"You'd need to. And when the baby comes, what then? Sleepless nights – "

"I'll keep it quiet."

"Then you're going to keep it? You might as well cut your throat! Or does the thought of a life sentence stimulate you?"

"Not its fault I'm lumbered."

Celia stamped round the room.

"And then, just when you've got me used to being waited on and typed for, you'll bugger off with some half-wit prepared to make an honest woman of you and give your child a name."

"No. I've forsworn men."

"You great booby! You can say that now – "

"Definitely no men. I'll make an honest woman of myself, if you'll help me. And I can help you. You've always said what a time-consuming bore it is setting up your manuscripts. I'll do that for you. You can off-set me against tax or something. I'll make it work. And if it doesn't you can still chuck me out and move back into residence. I could devil for you. Anything."

"Where are you training? Near home?"

"In Reading. My Post Office account will cover my digs for another month."

"You've got it all worked out, haven't you, you bloody child. But do you really expect me to agree?"

"I hoped at least you'd give me a hearing and then think about it. You know *Republicanism in the Reign of Charles II* would've come out months earlier if you'd had someone else to do the boring work. You know that."

"Oh Christ, Kate! I'd have to bum round flat-hunting. I'd have to – "

"I've heard of one that might suit. Not far from the main university buildings and to be let furnished. A chap who comes into the pub – he's been seconded for a year to Seewanee. He'd prefer an academic. I said I'd pass it on."

Cheek upon cheek, but Kate had prepared her campaign carefully to block any reasonable protests. Afterwards she'd wondered at herself – like an ignorant child, tenaciously certain that if it pesters enough it'll get the sweet. Only Celia's positive unwillingness or emotional dislike of Kate's proposition could have defeated her. Kate wasn't certain how deep that might be. But her campaign had been successful and so was their professional relationship. Until that car crash.

In fact, Kate considered uneasily, she'd made unashamed use of Celia, for all her representations of the offer as a mutual benefit. The years had tended to disguise that aspect. If Celia had told her to run away and find her own salvation, as Kate had suggested Peter ought to, well, she'd have dug herself out of that hole somehow. But it wouldn't have been easy and the quality of her life would certainly have been brutish and nasty. Despite her sudden death – and to a certain extent because of it – Kate had a lot to thank Celia for.

4

"Kate? Kate Henderson! Wait for me!" Kate turned to see Barbara Jones toiling up Carriage Hill, her bulging brief-case bumping awkwardly against her bird-thin legs. Barbara always seemed to carry half the Reference Library about with her, as if, should she let the brief-case out of her sight, all the knowledge in her head would disappear with it.

With a sigh Kate resigned herself to being accompanied for the rest of the way to Morgan's Mount while Barbara tried out her latest essay for ideas and opinions. She waited as Barbara, her pointed face peaked with preoccupation and concern, staggered nearer.

"Have you got *The Normal Child*?" Barbara called, while twenty paces still separated them.

"Eh?"

"I've been trying to get hold of a copy all weekend." They continued walking up the hill. "I knew Liz had her fiancé visiting so I didn't like to call on her, and when I went to Elinor's digs she was having a fearful row with someone. And I didn't know where you lived so I couldn't get in touch." Thank God, thought Kate. Just ten minutes of Barbara thinking aloud was exhausting enough, without being button-holed in her own home with no hope of retreat.

"You're in luck now, anyway. I've got him in my locker – him and some of his abnormalities. But what's this about Elinor?"

"Isn't it intriguing? But it's true. When her landlady answered the door you could hear her voice – absolutely roaring at someone. Or she might have been on the 'phone. Anyway, it obviously wasn't a good time to call and so, you know, I went. Without discovering anything. But I've got this essay to do for Miss Welborne for Friday and it doesn't leave much time." To write, re-write; check, double-check; and discuss it with anyone who stood still for long enough, Kate supposed wryly, as the breathless prattle at last stopped.

"Is it for a discussion seminar, then?"

"No, tutorial – which is even worse, being on your own. Though Miss Welborne's terribly kind and helpful."

"Well, then. She isn't likely to eat you." Kate's voice sounded impatient in her own ears and she tried to make amends. "Have you read her *Fetish and Fantasy in the Pre-School Child*?"

"No? Miss Welborne wrote it? I ought to look at that – but she didn't put it on my list."

"She wouldn't, but it's interesting to read with *The Normal Child* – "

" *– and Some of His Abnormalities.* Honestly, the titles alone make you wonder whether you shouldn't be serving in a shop instead. But Dad's a teacher, you see." The apparent non-sequitur seemed at least to Barbara to account for everything and Kate felt suddenly sorry for her. Parents' emotional blackmail had a good deal to answer for and its use and abuse was hard to counter even when it occasionally ran against their own interests.

"It must be marvellous to have his confidence," Barbara sighed as Peter's steel-grey VW Golf slid past them on the drive. "He doesn't even need to think about what he does, it just always comes out right. He's so gifted, isn't he?" Kate could have smacked her ears.

"What can you be discussing so early on a Monday morning?" Peter joined them. "Has the Prin. eloped with the Registrar?"

"Oh, Peter! You ought to write a book about us – you've got such a marvellous imagination! Much better than fact."

"I could make you all do what I wanted, then, couldn't I? And settle a few scores. So, am I to believe the Prin. still sits in his ivory tower, unaware even of our Registrar's attractions?"

"We were talking about my essay – for Friday, you know.

Kate was recommending Miss Welborne's *Fetish and Fantasy*. Have you read it, Peter?"

"Yes, you ought to read that," Peter agreed thoughtfully. "Good thinking, Kate. Then there's her *Incest and Insects in Suburban Gardens*. You should keep that by your bed." Kate started to grin in spite of herself but Peter kept a straight face.

"Heavens! But is that relevant to Nursery and Primary – "

"It's about Kate's years the locusts have eaten." So much for not flaunting the stigmata of age, thought Kate crossly. "Really, it's a shame to take the money, little Babs! You should develop a more healthy scepticism. I shall make you my mascot and wear you as a memorial to my lost days of innocence. But seriously, you ought to try *Coming of Age in – in Clacton*. That won the Andrex Medal, you know."

"Oh, but that's – in *Clacton*?" Barbara appeared thoroughly confused, but still prepared to credit Peter with honourable intentions. Can she really be so naïve, Kate wondered.

"Ah, you're remembering Margaret Mead's old classic, *Coming of Age in Samoa*." Peter's voice grew heavy with tutorial emphasis. "Though Miss Welborne's *Clacton* is identical in everything but punctuation, her clarity is quite indifferent. It is this that singles her out as one of today's more glaucomatous theorists. Gone are the naïve days of erudition, of facts, research, lucidity. Now tautology and – and obscurantism rule, and Miss Welborne leads the field."

"He's pulling your leg, Barbara, for heaven's sake!" Kate laughed at Peter. He was bloody wicked – a rogue intellect.

"Well, I thought there was something funny somewhere," she replied good-humouredly. "But he seemed to know what he was talking about."

"You've just explained that modern phenomenon, the Rise of the Expert, little Babs. Often self-appointed, self-opinionated and self-styled. And it's perhaps all that Morgan's Mount is based on – that they seem to know what they're talking about, though you feel there's something funny somewhere."

They'd reached the main building and Barbara peeled off towards the cloakrooms.

"I'll see you in the Common Room," she called after Kate,

as if her own continued existence could only be guaranteed by appointments made ahead to cheat emptiness.

"God knows what she'll put in her essay now that you've got at her," Kate told Peter. "Why is she so convinced she hasn't a mind of her own?"

"Perhaps that middle-class god, Agreeable Uniformity, presided at her birth. His voice can often be heard in 'What the Neighbours Say'."

"Why middle-class? I imagine even Hell's Angels or – or pretty well any community aims for some sort of agreeable uniformity."

"Hm. Uniformity is not necessarily unity, bright Kate, and the upper classes aim for agreeable eccentricity. By the way, have you seen Elinor this weekend?"

"Elinor! What's she got to do with agreeable eccentricity?"

"Nothing, dear Kate. The question was entirely unrelated. It's just that I'm not her favourite man at the moment, and I wondered if she'd said anything to you."

"I haven't seen her since Friday." Kate busied herself in her locker, suddenly unwilling to discuss Elinor with Peter and watch the dawning of that appreciative gleam as he hinted at shared but secret knowledge.

"And you won't involve yourself in us fellow-humans unless we positively force ourselves on you," Peter murmured waspishly, looking round the Common Room. "You leave us so much in doubt as to how you'd react to pretty well anything, Olympian Kate. However, as she lives so near you I wondered if you'd seen her. That's all."

"Does she? How do you know where I live? I've never run into her."

"Oh, a mere stone's throw from you, I understand." He wandered away to a group by the windows.

Kate watched him curiously as he said something that made the others laugh; stooping his sleek blond head to light his cigarette, his left hand tucked in his trouser pocket, carelessly deft. He looked like an ad for one of the classier brands of smokes. But there wouldn't be time to finish that fag before the first lecture.

Shifting groups gave Kate cover while she continued to

speculate. Peter never did finish his cigarette, as if the ritual of lighting up was merely an affectation, not a need. An opportunity to flip a long, slim brown cigarette out of its case and thumb his streamlined, electronic lighter. "Thanks, I prefer my own," he'd say if he was offered one of a lesser breed. That added a few more inches to his platform too.

The bell put an end to Kate's stalking and, as she expected, Peter casually doubled up the remaining length of his cigarette as he passed a convenient ashtray on his left. Kate noticed that he'd taken a knock on his left thumb over the weekend. The nail was quite black and looked shocking in conjunction with his carefully maintained hands. Like an obscenity scrawled on a new headstone.

Kate felt half uneasy, half amused by her unwilling interest in Peter, but she couldn't deny a repelled fascination. As if he were a snake or one of those rather beautiful lizards, she told herself as she followed his group down to the lecture hall, and then wondered why reptiles should have come immediately to her mind.

★ ★ ★

First thing on a Monday morning was the Principal's weekly lecture, on the education of handicapped children. It was one way of getting them all at least starting the week together. She glanced round the hall for Barbara and saw her settled uneasily with Elinor, almost immediately in front of Peter and the group he'd walked down with. Judging by the look of avid expectation on her face and withdrawn mulishness on Elinor's, Barbara had decided to dispense with instant access to *The Normal Child* in order to pump Elinor about the row she'd overheard.

Kate was afraid that as well as being a vicarious thinker, Barbara was a vicarious liver – of even more irritating proportions than Kate herself since she required spoon-feeding. A sort of Ancient Mariner in reverse. And you couldn't be sure of her loyalty either, if you did take her into your confidence, since she was an indiscriminate admirer and quite childishly indiscreet.

Kate sidled through the rows of chairs will she reached Barbara.

"*The Normal Child,*" she dropped the paperback in Barbara's lap and sat down beside her. "It's my own copy, so let me have it back when you've finished. I've put my name in it."

"Gosh, thanks." Kate watched her cram the book into her brief-case.

"What'll you do when you can't fit any more in there? Carry two cases about?" Elinor gave a bark of laughter as silence fell and the Principal arrived, beaten by a short head by Liz looking flustered.

"Ooh! She cut it fine, didn't she?" Barbara twittered in sympathetic horror. "He looks thunderous!"

After the lecture Kate escaped into the gardens. The sun was sharp and bright as she walked between the ordered rose-beds of the upper level and headed for the stone bench by the goldfish pool. The gardens now offered a last weary show of roses before the winter set in and cold winds blasted the exposed slopes of Morgan's Mount. Already their colours weren't true, lost in anonymous misty pastel, and the flowers only half opening. Soon there'd be nothing.

Kate had a paper on Vittorino da Feltre to read to a discussion seminar at eleven; part of Dr. O'Hare's course on the History of Education. She couldn't really see where Renaissance educational ideas – or the rest of Bunny's course for that matter – applied in the current technological scene. No doubt all would be revealed in time. But Kate had decided to take this option, as well as the Comparative Education course, in the hopes of widening the basis of her qualification. There might be a niche found for her, perhaps in some back-room or administrative capacity, if her age put prospective employers off the idea of loosing her onto a classroom. Meanwhile she wanted to read her paper through for the last time before submitting it to a no doubt amazingly bored audience. Kate was surprised at her own lack of confidence as the moment for her public appearance approached. It was, she supposed, partly through not having a personal point of reference among her (own) peers.

But Kate had only reread the opening paragraph before she became aware of a spiky susurration approaching across the grass; a crinoline sound of taffeta flounces inappropriate to its source. Without looking round, she knew who it was. The scrape of strained tights across massive thighs was a sound peculiar to Elinor, who sensibly never wore trousers.

"Kate, I need a transfusion of calm common sense. Or are you busy?" Elinor sat heavily on the bench without waiting for a reply.

"So? Who's drained you of your natural unflappability? And how can I supply such a virtue when just about to read my first paper?"

"Oh, you'll be all right. Don't be so affected. It's just that sometimes a little of Barbara goes a hell of a long way. She's such a desperate baby."

"Mm. Late developer."

"Don't you believe it! I didn't mean desperate in that sense. She's got a mental grip like a mechanical grab when she wants something – and don't tell me you haven't been involved in helping her without even being asked to. She's a very adult brain-picker."

"Is that how you see her?" Kate was interested. "I thought she was just insecure and naïve."

"There needn't be any 'just' about that. You can turn even disabilities to your own advantage if you package yourself properly. She's as much of a manipulator as Peter is, though at least Peter isn't a freeloader."

"How did you ditch her?" asked Kate, intrigued by Elinor's assessment of Barbara's character.

"You realised I was cornered, did you? At the time I thought you were an innocent reward from the gods for keeping my temper. I suppose I was being obvious again. It's becoming my most obvious characteristic. She couldn't wait to grab Liz and ask if the Prin. had given her a blast for being late this morning. Hardly worth the effort, would you say? But then – she's got a small mind. What you think of as naïvety. Actually Liz and Adrian had an appointment with the Prin. before Adrian went back this morning. They wanted to ask him about getting married in the university chapel."

"Really? You're not having me on?"

But one look at Elinor's sturdy features convinced Kate that she hadn't suddenly developed a facility for leg-pulling.

"But is the chapel licensed, or whatever, for weddings?"

"Apparently." Elinor scuffed moodily at the gravel round the base of the bench.

"It's a nice idea. It could set quite a fashion."

"Fashion? Where's the queue? Are you proposing to stagger off some emotional precipice onto a nuptial water-bed in the hopes you'll keep afloat for life?"

"Who're you kidding?" Kate laughed suddenly.

"What I thought," Elinor grunted. "Not but what Liz and Adrian seem well enough suited. Liz wants the Prin. to give her away too – her father died yonks ago – if he can persuade them to let her be married in the chapel."

"Well, that news should keep Barbara off your back for a bit. What's the problem?"

"It'll make Jessica mad as fire."

"Why?"

"Because Liz got engaged before she did, for one – the first of all us Fourth years. And now, unless Jessica gets a heck of a wiggle on, Liz is going to beat her to the altar too. And right here. I don't think I can bear the sight of Jessica stepping up her – her enticement level in competition."

Kate gazed hopelessly down at Elinor's stodgily set expression and wondered what on earth she could find to say to her.

"Look, I'm sorry to dash but there isn't time – " the distant tolling of the cathedral clock sounded right on cue. "I know for once they can't start without me, but I ought to be there," Kate grinned deprecatingly. "I'm free all afternoon. What about you?"

"Essay," Elinor muttered grumpily, as she lumbered off the bench.

"Well, so've I, but so what. I'll meet you in the Union bar for a wet lunch, if you like, and we'll take it from there. If you don't show up I'll know you've thought better of it. Come on. We'll all be dead in a hundred years."

"But I'd like to outlive Peter Colebrook," Elinor laughed shortly. "See you at the Union, then."

★ ★ ★

"I'm sorry I'm late, Dr. O'Hare," Kate panted as she slipped into her usual place.

"A simple miscalculation, no doubt, Miss Henderson, redeemed by your excellent speed through the gardens." Kate felt her cheeks flush their unbecoming clash with her hair. He must have been watching for her. "Would you prefer to remain seated?"

"On the grounds that 'He who is down need fear no fall'?" Kate winced at her sickly display of unconfidence. "Thank you. But I'll stand to receive the bad eggs at the end."

"You anticipate some – some spontaneous discussion?"

"Er – some comments, anyway, Dr. O'Hare. It seems to me that although Vittorino had several ideas that we tend to think of as modern – subsidised education, coeducation, all that – his belief in the 'universal man', with fully extended and cultured intellect and trained abilities, is at variance with the modern concept of the specialist, the expert." (Pompous twerp, Kate told herself.) "Mr. Colebrook made a point something to that effect this morning." Kate glanced at Peter and wondered how long before her nerves settled enough to read her bloody paper. Peter graciously inclined his smooth head – and winked. "And also," hysteria threatened at the back of Kate's throat, "how far in the context of universal education and the demands of modern society, it can be realistic to aim to educate 'universal' people."

"Indeed? Then I look forward to hearing your opinions, and any subsequent comments from the group. Please begin, if you are ready."

Kate reached the end of her paper, reading slowly and deliberately like the Speaking Clock, in order to calm herself and spin out the time. She had already delicately hinted at the direction she expected the discussion to take, so there was no difficulty in getting that started. At least she needn't be left with the impression that she'd bored them all to stone like an academic Medusa. Now she sat quietly and tried to look intelligent, while she remembered how Margaret O'Hare had said that her husband described Celia as a true Renaissance mind. A complete person.

Peter waded straight in on the subject of experts – arguing from the opposite stand he'd taken that morning – which prompted Robert Denham to query sarcastically whether jacks-of-all-trades were any improvement. Dr. O'Hare called them to order and directed the group to consider the fact that, though a few poor scholars might have been subsidised – at Vittorino's own expense – his 'complete man' was the product of an élitist education who took his place in an élitist society, whereas –

Again Peter was ready to make himself heard and this time Dr. O'Hare seemed willing to let him hang himself. Peter confidently asserted that natural selection favoured brains and ability, however much part that old comedy duo, Heredity and Environment, had to play. An intellectual élite was therefore natural and should be catered for. Even bred for. Only such an élite should or could be trusted with the balance of social and even international power. Power? By that he meant top-level decisions affecting ultimately civilisation itself. Heads nodded in agreement.

Kate noticed idly that Peter's left thumb was now wrapped round with sticking-plaster. He must have bothered to get some from the medical room during the coffee-break.

"But that's like resurrecting the Druids, or implementing 'Brave New World'," Liz scoffed. "And eugenics? You can't be serious, Peter! The herrenvolk have been discredited." Heads nodded again.

"So was Copernicus discredited. It didn't make him wrong."

"Who controls the controllers?"

"How far would free thought be possible?"

". . . a sort of universal Index . . ."

". . . Inquisition . . ."

Nod. Nod. Nod. An agreeable disunity, thought Kate, and all old hat. But she'd done her bit. Let someone else produce something startlingly new.

When the bell went for the lunch-break, Dr. O'Hare

solemnly thanked her for the 'thoughtful' paper. There's damning with faint praise, but Kate accepted it with a grin. After a moment she followed him downstairs.

She left Peter in the thick of a more passionate argument, now that Dr. O'Hare had gone, and there were also a few more ready to declare themselves as Peter's allies. Among them was Barbara, who 'just felt' that what Peter said was right, though she couldn't put it into words; and Jessica, in an unusually intellectual mood, who thought Kate's paper was superficial and needed more in depth research. Perhaps that was to be her line now, Kate reflected, since the vamping of Peter had fallen so flat.

She hurried on her way down Carriage Hill to the Union building on the university campus. Though Elinor was expected to attend Dr. O'Hare's History of Education lectures, it wasn't one of her options and she didn't come to the seminars. So she'd been free since eleven, and Kate rather expected her to have talked herself out of their meeting. Elinor prided herself on being self-contained and dependent on nobody, and it amazed Kate all the more that she should have approached her as she did.

Peter too had given the impression of being prepared to confide in her that morning; which was odd enough in itself, though it might show that he was ready to overlook her disapproval of his behaviour on Friday. Big of him. But why should he have been fishing for her address? Kate wondered uneasily.

5

It was nearly twelve-thirty by the time Kate reached the cafeteria in the Union building. The bar had already opened and was crowded. Kate didn't very often use the Union, preferring any of the accessible city pubs where she felt more anonymous.

She spotted Elinor at one of the tiny bar-tables, sitting with two glasses in front of her.

"I don't know what you drink, but lager's harmless enough. Okay?"

"Fine, thanks. Quite full already." Kate sipped and gazed round.

"Some of 'em live here, I swear. They vanish into the woodwork like cockroaches when the shutters come down and pop out again when it's opening time. It can be hell on earth at night. Like everything else, it was never designed to hold so many."

"Do you often come here? Er – what is this lager, Elinor?"

"God knows. Their own, probably. Ghastly, isn't it? Like washing-up goo. Can you drink beer? They've got Newcastle Brown. We'll have that next, if you like."

"I like. Do you know that wine-bar in Foundry Street? Peter swears by it."

"Is that your style?" Elinor asked glumly, as if her worst suspicions were confirmed. "Couldn't afford it as an undergrad. and wouldn't afford it now - except as an occasional emetic. Too much Beardsley-style decor and Châteauplonk-style wine, unless you mortgage your soul to get a decent bottle. And the clientele – all wildly impressed with itself and trying to impress each other. It's immoral to pay that sort of money for food and drink, I don't care what anyone says. Still, you're not really a student, are you, so I suppose it's different for you."

It's difficult for me, Kate corrected with irritation for her private record, but Elinor's was a fairly understandable assumption and she let it pass. Her age alone should put her beyond that kind of unintentional pin-prick. Yet in a sense it was her age that made her feel unconfident among the others. Kate might not want to share whatever it was they had in common, but there was no denying her occasional feeling of disadvantage.

"Let's try the beer. Newcastle Brown all right for you? I should be able to manage it out of my pension." Elinor glanced up quickly and gave an unwilling grin.

"Whatever you're having."

Kate returned with the drinks and took a gulp of hers to wash away the soapy taste of the lager.

"Actually I wouldn't be able to do this Dip.Ed. course but for a legacy linked strictly to it. I asked about the wine-bar because I went there once with Peter and I wondered whether it was the in place for Morgan's Mount, that's all." In which she was being pretty machiavellian, Kate thought. She'd been racking her brains thinking how to introduce Peter into the conversation without cueing him through a trap-door in a puff of smoke, so that if Elinor preferred she needn't take up the reference.

"Oh, Peter," Elinor shrugged. "That poseur. To hear him talk you'd think he was one of the founder members two years ago. He must be the only one of us who can afford to use it. No doubt it suits his image."

"But was he here two years ago? I didn't know that."

"Yes. Him, me, Gordon Watson and Linda Mayer were all students at the university. You'd think Peter was ex-Oxbridge, wouldn't you? But he's just a little ex-provincial like the rest of us."

"Linda? Is she the tall, Latin-looking one?"

"Startling, isn't she?" Elinor grinned. "Peter was quite bearable then. Didn't insist on calling me 'Little Nell'. You don't want anything to eat here, do you? Food's worse than the lager. I've got some Greek wine and brandy I brought back from my holiday – come back to my digs and help me broach them? Perhaps our essays will write themselves under the influence."

Kate would have preferred not to accept that kind of hospitality, with its built-in assumption that it would be returned some time, and she would have liked something to eat first to neutralise bottles of wine and brandy. But it would have been stuffy to refuse and she could hardly expect Elinor to wait patiently while she wolfed a despised sandwich. So Kate merely finished her drink and got up to go.

"It's Helen, isn't it?" A youthful pair of jeans, topped by a small fluffy beard and middle-aged eyes, barred their way to the door. Elinor paused while a smile ruffled the beard and crows' feet crinkled ingratiatingly. Kate saw that the golden fur was receding from his forehead leaving a tidemark of small freckles. Another mature student, she guessed.

"Wrong Helen, Paris. You need an oculist." Elinor side-stepped and continued on her way. Thoroughly embarrassed, Kate aimed a bright smile at the pale fluff and hurried after Elinor.

"Who was that?" She caught her up outside the door.

"One of the university teaching staff, would you believe? Typical of him to use the students' bar. He's so conscientiously youthful and with-it he's forgotten his original brief. They're either trendy pseuds like him or Rip Van Winkles like Bunny, still waiting to wake up. Yes, I know that's not fair."

"I was only going to say he seems friendly enough."

"Obviously. He wanted to meet you."

"Me?"

"Mm. One of our lunch-time Lotharios. He certainly wasn't after me. He must have spent a good while trying to remember even half way to my name. He was my tutor for a term – see what a place I hold in his memory! But I wasn't good grading-couch material. Merely *virgo laborans per ardua ad diploma* – and understandably *intacta* at that."

"It's some time since I did Spanish," murmured Kate. But thankfully Elinor was rummaging in her bag and missed the sarcasm.

★   ★   ★

They left the university campus and crossed the Centre; where the statue of Queen Victoria, overtaken by modern developments, stood pointing its sceptre imperiously at the public conveniences from the middle of the one-way traffic gyration. Soon they were in a residential suburb unfamiliar to Kate, but Elinor walked on through neat estates and led her into Kaleyard Lane.

"Nearly there. We're below and behind the cathedral now. You can hear the bells from my room. This area was the monks' cabbage patch. At least they had the wits to keep the old names when they built these estates. I don't know that Cabbage Patch Lane has any more of a ring to it than Acacia Avenue, but it's got nearly a thousand more years of history. Are you interested in local history? Here we are."

Elinor led the way into a semi-detached house, as identical to its neighbours as Kate's own house in its terrace row.

"I'll just see if Peggy's in." She left Kate in the hall while she looked in at a couple of doors and then disappeared through to the back of the house. "She's in the garden," Elinor called. "Come and meet her." Kate followed her out into the garden. "Kate Henderson, Peggy. One of our more responsible students. Kate, meet Peggy." Kate smiled and nodded at a woman younger than herself who eyed her curiously as she got stiffly to her feet from the border she'd been tidying.

"Hallo, Kate. You've both arrived just in time. I'd nearly set solid. Make your friend at home, love." Peggy turned to Elinor. "I'll have to start cleaning up soon to fetch Craig. See you again, I hope." She smiled cheerfully at Kate and hefted a bucket of weeds to the heap at the end of the garden.

"Come on. We're dismissed." Elinor ushered Kate back into the house and led her upstairs. "I always let her know I'm in, and if I've got someone with me Peggy knows not to flutter round. Here's my room. Nice, isn't it? Gets the afternoon sun. I've been here since I was a Second year. Peggy's first student, actually. Her husband was killed in a building-site accident when Craig was only a baby. She's a good sort, Peggy."

While she talked Elinor busied herself in a cupboard finding glasses and bottles.

"Metaxa. That's the brandy. The white wine's retsina. We

used to drink a lot of that. I don't know anything about the red-mavrodaphne. It sounds attractive. What'll you begin with?" Kate's heart sank. But at least there wasn't any ouzo.

"Heck! Do you see us ploughing through all three bottles? I'd like some of the white, please, but I may stick there. I've got to get home, don't forget."

"It's only Monday," Elinor reminded helpfully, as if Kate had the entire week to find her way back. She poured out two glasses of retsina and sat down.

"This is very civilised," Kate thanked her, sipping the wine which always made her think of paint-stripper. Or piano varnish. But mavrodaphne was like syrup of figs, so Hobson's choice. "Whereabouts in Greece were you?"

"Mykonos. Do you know it?" Kate shook her head. "Not much there. No vast archaeological site or anything, though Delos is only a boat-ride away. Great if you want to do nothing at all but relax in the sun and enjoy yourself. Have you ever been to Greece?"

"Crete only. It was heavenly but too long ago." Kate looked away as sunlit memories of Celia came shimmering back. "Are you a Historian, Elinor? For some reason I wondered if you'd done Classics, but your books – "

Kate had never seen Elinor at the History Methodology seminars, but the handicapped teaching specialists were a race apart on Morgan's Mount.

"It nearly was Classics, actually, till I started the degree course. I'm glad now I changed my mind and opted for History."

Kate wondered if Elinor had had any contact with Celia – it would only have been during her first year as an undergraduate. She continued to sip her wine, trying to hurry it past her taste-buds, while she gazed thoughtfully out into the autumn sunshine and waited for Elinor to initiate the next subject.

"You're my second visitor this week. Peter came round here on Friday evening, after that disgusting episode with Miss Welborne," Elinor said at last. So, the row Barbara had overheard *had* been with Peter; and with the slightest encouragement it seemed that he had been prepared to chat about it that morning. Kate wondered why she should be involved in it either by Peter or by Elinor, as was now inevitable. Elinor poured more wine into Kate's glass without asking and refilled her own. "God knows why he chose then of all times to call. Some feeble excuse about a book on remedial teaching. He's no more interested in remedial teaching than – than one of the Borgias. He might've known I'd be in a mood to tear him apart. And as if that wasn't enough, Barbara turned up in the middle of it all – not that I knew at the time. Peggy told me after Peter finally left. God, he needled me! It was almost as if he meant to. I asked Peggy to say I wasn't at home for the rest of the weekend, and just as well because Barbara called a couple more times. She was nearly wetting herself with curiosity this morning till Liz caught her attention." Elinor laughed sourly.

"You didn't give Peter a dose of thumbscrews, did you, by any chance?" Kate grinned.

"Wish I had. He told Barbara he'd cut his hand clearing up a broken champagne bottle. Typical! Pity it wasn't broken over his head." Odd, thought Kate; but like Peter to opt for a stylish wound.

She decided to give Elinor a lead. It was obvious from her unusual chattiness that she was trying to find her way into a difficult subject; and just as obvious that she'd never make it without assistance.

"It wasn't entirely Peter's treatment of Miss Welborne that bothered you, though, was it?" Kate suggested. "What you wanted to talk to me about?"

"No." Elinor swigged off her wine and emptied the bottle into their glasses. "No, you're right. It was – it has been all term – Jessica's behaviour that made me murderous. Suicidal, actually. Do you know what I'm talking about or must I spell it out?"

"I – rather suspect it's not Jessica's behaviour towards the men, is it? So much as your – your own attraction to Jessica. I'm sorry. You must find her very – er – uncomfortable."

"Uncomfortable!" Elinor exploded. "You feel this frightful torture, day and night, and to anyone else it's just a bit of a snigger. I don't know how to bear it. Yet she turns my stomach half the time. She's silly and shallow and her *stupid* attitude to men makes my blood boil. As if we need their approval. But I still can't detach myself – my emotions. And then to see her so put down on Friday and *still* defend him! I could've throttled her, I promise you. And what I could have done to *him* doesn't bear saying – but it would've made the Ashante women look like a Brownie pack."

"You singled me out this morning to tell me this," Kate said after a pause, made thoroughly uncomfortable by Elinor's hopelessness. "Why? There must be someone you're, well, closer to who'd understand and sympathise more – more constructively than I can. I can only listen."

"But that's all I want you to do, Kate." Elinor opened the bottle of Metaxa and slopped brandy into each of their glasses. "I suppose you because you're older and detached – outside everything. You're not involved in our rat-race. I need someone simply to know about me, someone who isn't involved, or I'll burst. I don't need an improving lecture – I know all the things I should be doing, ignoring Jessica, sublimating my feelings, channelling them into my work and career. But if I didn't have this pain I'd have nothing. God knows I don't need telling how hopeless and – and unattractive the situation is. It's grotesque." Elinor gulped a mouthful of the spirit and waved her glass at Kate. "For Chrissake drink, or I'll feel all lopsided. You're not judgemental like I am but you will be if I get drunk on my own."

Kate raised her glass. Before it even touched her lips the raw-smelling fumes caught her breath. Metaxa wasn't one of the things she remembered from Crete. She took a cautious sip and felt her eyes smart as the brandy seared down her throat. This was not Remy Martin. Kate clunked her glass down on the table.

"Dear heaven! How did you get used to this?" she demanded. "It's like sword-swallowing!"

"It took me a fortnight of dedicated practice," Elinor grinned. "Lethal, isn't it? Drink up. Another thirteen days and you'll be as immune as me. I've never seen you discomposed before!"

"Decomposed, if I have any more," Kate grumbled. "It's

enough to induce the bends. Can't I just sit quietly and sniff the fumes now and then?"

"No. You've got to jump. It's lovely once you're in. What am I to do, Kate?"

"You said I was to listen, merely. Now you're asking my advice. I haven't any," Kate replied brutally. She took a courageous sip of the Metaxa. "Find someone else to – er – take your mind off."

"But I haven't anything to spare for anyone else, even if I wanted. I *know* there can't be anyone for me but Jessica. The first time I saw her I just went crunch. It's like being bewitched by a – a dream of completion. Of perfection."

Oh Lord!

"Er – is Jessica the first time? Or – or – "

"Oh, I've always been gay, if that's what you're asking. Don't be so coy. There's no need. I've had a few affairs and I flirted a bit with Gay Soc. in my first year – and that nearly turned me off for good. A bunch of dizzy little daisies or bull dikes like me. But teachers can't afford to let it be known they're gay, and teachers of handicapped kids even less so, good God! For all they'd have a hell of a job staffing any of the caring professions if they threw out all the gays. So anyway, I thought everything was reasonably under control – until I saw Jessica. And I have to fall like a ton of rubble for someone who's straight. It's hell, Kate. Absolute hell! And almost the worst of it is that Peter knows about Jessica, or knows enough to prod anyway. I never made a secret of belonging to Gay Soc. I know you two are friendly, so perhaps he doesn't with you, but he likes jumping on your corns if he knows you've got them. And you can never be certain with him, but if he decides to flex his claws and give me away they might withhold the diploma. Even if they let me stay on to the end of the course."

"There's nothing Peter could tell anyone without sounding ridiculous. You don't actually make it obvious – quite the reverse." But Elinor shrugged, unconvinced.

"You knew. Did he say something to you?"

"We aren't on those terms," Kate said patiently. "It was just an idea I had."

57

Kate privately thought that Peter would enjoy himself more watching Elinor's discomfort. Just the threat of publicising her homosexuality would give him power enough, if that was what he wanted out of life. But she couldn't see any way that Elinor might escape from her dilemma; she'd hardly retire from the course – would she?

"You know the only possible thing is to grin and bear it, Elinor," Kate said finally. "For God's sake don't start imagining you're not fit for your job. You'll be perfect for it. Just hang on and – and let it wear off. Or hope something'll cause it suddenly to shut off. Even better." Age at least conferred on one the privilege of offering sound advice with an appearance of tested conviction. Inevitably its acceptance depended on whether it matched Elinor's intentions, and with her remained the responsibility and the inconvenience. But for that reassurance and Elinor's vulnerability, Kate would have refused to comment.

"But I know it won't shut off," Elinor groaned in despair. "Dammit, you don't seem to understand. I *love* that silly bitch! Haven't you ever loved anyone? I suppose you're too cold. Even a week's a long time for me and I've felt this – this desperation for a month now, with no sign of it easing off."

"Well, don't be tempted into telling her. She'll have a field day," said Kate bluntly. She had no liking for Jessica and the level of the brandy, sunk to half way down the bottle, encouraged Kate to be less than usually detached now that she'd allowed herself to become involved at all. And cold? That was the second insensitive remark Elinor had made, thought Kate crossly. They all behaved as if they had the answers to life, but when it came to the crunch they acted like resentful children. If you didn't fall over your feet to force-feed them with understanding and support they blamed you for being uncaring. Kate felt even her tentative sympathy dissipating in the face of Elinor's determined suffering.

"God, don't I know it! But the awful thing is that I've got to the point where I don't care what she does or what she thinks about it as long as she knows how I feel."

"She's more likely than Peter to bring it to the Principal's attention, you chump. She may see your – attraction as a socking blow to her femininity and feel called upon to repudiate it as publicly as possible. Just in case."

"In case what?"

"In case anyone suspects her of being that way inclined too, of course."

"Do you think she might be?" Hope flickered in Elinor's slightly unfocussed eyes. "Is that why she goes for the men? To – to try and repress her lesbianism?"

"No," Kate answered baldly. "Don't con yourself."

"I think you're very good for me, Kate," Elinor said owlishly. "I think I'll be glad you know. It helps. 'A friend in need is a – '"

" – blinding nuisance," Kate finished. "Come on, Elinor. You've got loads of courage and determination. For God's sake don't use me as a crutch."

Kate had tried to speak bracingly, but though she heard a distinct echo of her old hockey mistress there seemed to be a lack of definition about her actual words. They sounded only approximately right and she couldn't be certain they'd carried correctly to Elinor. They hadn't carried even as far, it transpired.

"What did you say? 'A friend in need is a blinding nuisance'?" Elinor started to giggle and her chest became an alarming agitation under her jumper. Kate watched fascinated but called herself to order.

"Time you had a nice lie down." She rose unsteadily and lurched round the table. "Come on. Bed. At least you'll be safe there. I must get back now. Thanks for the drinks." Jeez! She couldn't even begin to lift her and the attempt felt indecently intimate.

Tears squeezed out of Elinor's screwed-shut eyes and hopped down her cheeks.

"Bloody funny!" She gasped. "You *are* bloody funny, Katie!" Katie? Yuk. "Used to think you were so stern. Wodjoo doing, pulling me about? Hey, nice Katie!"

"Come to bed, you moron," Kate panted, wishing she'd chosen her words more sensibly.

"Hey, yes!"

"Hey, no!" Hey nonny-no and up she rises. "Bed, because you're bottled. Ought to get your head down."

They hauled and lumbered together across the room in a lunatic *pas de deux* that made Kate want to giggle; while in the sober part of her mind she wanted it all never to have happened.

"Not as drunk as tinkle peep I am."

"This people think you're drunk as me. Okay. Now just fall back. I'll take your shoes off." Kate stooped unwarily to heave Elinor's legs onto the bed and the room suddenly concertinaed round her. She stood up more cautiously.

"Twirly-whirlies," Elinor complained as she lay back.

"Don't shut your eyes for a bit, then. You okay, now?" Kate asked thickly, trying to cope with her own drunken stumblings. A wordless mumble came from among the pillows and Kate pulled the duvet round the stranded-whale hump on the bed. Elinor's breathing raced, then steadied and she slept.

★   ★   ★

The room smelt like a still. Kate latched open the window quarter-light and shambled across to the door. She wondered uneasily how she'd manage the stairs. She was half-way down, grimly clinging to the banisters, when a door opened and Peggy looked out into the hall. Kate stopped and boggled at her helplessly.

"Are you all right?"

"Fine. Elinor – in bed." Talking made it worse.

"I – see. Have you far to go?"

"Centre. Bus."

"You'll never make it. Let me ask someone to take you home." Peggy came out into the hall and shut the door behind her, cutting down the sound of rifle fire and thundering hooves. Kate continued her stately minuet down the stairs.

"Thank you. But no one knows where," she slurred politely.

"Well, *you* know where you live, don't you? And you could tell them," Peggy smiled encouragingly. "Or you could stay here until you felt more – um - ready to go."

"Ready now. Fine. Thank you very sorry," Kate gabbled as she aimed herself at the front door in a quickening trot to keep pace with the unbalancing weight of her head. She managed to whip open the door with hardly a check and her impetus carried her down the path to the pavement.

After that Kate's impressions were largely a blur, but she knew what she had to do and clung to her intentions as if she were drowning. She resisted the urge to lie down on the pavement – a pavement strangely mobile as it tried to move away at her approach – and wait till the world had stopped rolling and undulating past her. She paused only once, to heave quietly and neatly into the bottom of someone's privet hedge, and after that her gait became less of a waddle and more precariously dignified. What else is a privet for, she reasoned, past caring whether she'd been noticed.

By the time Kate reached the Centre her head was clear enough to realise that a cup of tea was an immediate necessity if she was to survive the jolting of the bus. Still determinedly dignified and stately, she went into the bus station cafeteria. Sure that her breath must resemble a flame-gun, Kate turned her head aside and on an indrawn gasp asked the wispy popsie behind the counter for a cup of tea. She drank it as hot as she could bear, hoping to cauterise the mildew growth that seemed to line her mouth.

The tea was a mixed blessing. Kate had to make a dash for the station lavatories, but she emerged steadier if weaker and there were no further emergencies on the bus ride home.

It was growing dark as she tottered up the flagged path to her front door. There was a cat, black and white, sitting on the doorstep. Kate paused only to scoop it up – for no better reason than that it seemed disinclined to move out of her way – before diving for the nearest armchair where she fell heavily asleep.

6

Kate woke to pitch darkness and a raging thirst. As memory returned she staggered stiffly into the kitchen and had a long drink of water. She checked the doors and went up to bed, feeling the beginning of a nagging headache over her eyes. She took two aspirins with another long drink in the bathroom before trundling to her bed, shedding clothes as she went.

But in proof of Sod's Law Kate felt wide awake as soon as she was under the covers. She tried her usual trick of lying still and pretending she wasn't there, but it fooled no one this time. She debated fetching herself a book and reading herself to sleep, but in the end she simply lay and thought about Celia; at first with tenderness and love and then with passionate intensity.

Had she ever reached her, Kate wondered, when she marshalled all her visual and sensual memories like this? When she summoned up not only Celia's image but her touch, her voice, the sound of her at the piano, the warm, soft smell of her hair even. Was there anything to reach? Or was she perhaps straining too hard, too brutishly, for a presence more delicate than should answer her impetuous unhappiness? Kate deliberately emptied her mind and into the vacuum projected the finest of webs to be found on a summer's morning, her private epitome of delicacy. Only the jewelled shimmer of dew suspended along its perfection made it visible.

Perhaps it's true that the dead only exist through the memories of the living; memories that hang like starry beads on their dead invisibility, Kate thought uncomfortably. She preferred to imagine a more positive survival for Celia than as a sort of celestial clothes-line hung with unnaturally whiter-than-white washing.

The memory that came into Kate's mind, apt but unbidden, was of a night some weeks after the baby was born. It was the midnight feed – she'd practically force-fed the poor little scrap so that there should be no crying in the night to wake Celia. Kate smiled at the memory. She could have fed four. She'd felt like a cow and looked forward to the day when the sweet, dense smell of milk no longer hung about her clothes. Celia had encouraged her not to resent becoming a walking milk-bar. 'It keeps over the weekend and the cat can't get at it,' she'd laughed. 'Or you could revive the once fashionable duties of a wet-nurse. Remember Philip IV of Spain.'

Anyway, Kate had been along to leave the wet nappy in its covered bucket. On her way back past Celia's room she heard a cry, as if Celia had called out in a dream. Without a second thought Kate opened the door and looked in. The bedside lamp was lit. Celia lay back on the pillows; one hand at her breast, the other hidden under the sheet across her hips. While Kate stood in the doorway, gawping like a yokel, Celia opened her eyes and saw her.

Kate shut the door quickly and fled for her own room, her cheeks burning to the tips of her ears. She checked the baby, still newly-hatched looking with its crest of dark down peeping above the laboriously knitted shawl, and bundled herself into bed. Now what the hell, she wondered. What if Celia felt she could no longer cope with Kate about the flat? Perpetually reminding her of her embarrassment. Good God, it wasn't a scene you chose to play to a capacity audience. For all the easiness of their friendship that had developed since Celia's move to Reading, Kate had no idea how that night's episode would affect their relationship. She dreaded the worst. Most of all she dreaded their next meeting across the breakfast table.

But Kate didn't have to wait that long. There came a gentle knocking and her bedroom door opened a few inches.

"Kate?"

"Yes?"

"Kate, I need to talk to you. Please?" Kate clambered out of bed and struggled on her dressing-gown. She followed Celia to the sitting-room.

"We won't disturb her, will we? Talking so late?"

"Not even the crack of doom. She's dead to the world," Kate tried to answer lightly. She watched while Celia poured out two glasses of brandy and wished she could take the initiative. If she could just say, 'I'm terribly sorry I woke you but you were having a nightmare', or something; but Kate knew Celia wasn't in the mood for a gloss. The brandy proved that. It was going to be all cards on the table. God!

"Neither of us will be comfortable tonight until we've neutralised our embarrassment," Celia smiled as she handed Kate her drink. "This should help." She switched on the electric fire and sat back. "You know what you walked in on, don't you?" Kate nodded unhappily and gulped half her tot of spirit. "You're such a child in some ways I couldn't be sure. Now you see how staunchly I'm refusing to be affected," Celia grinned wryly. "So what about you, Kate? You look wildly disapproving. Because of what you saw? Or because I'm putting you on the spot."

Kate watched her bare toe trace the pattern on the carpet. True, she was naïve. Childish. Rushed into an adult rôle as mother, without preparation or desire; and now her self-centred, childish nose rubbed into Celia's private - er - personal affairs she'd never even given a passing thought to.

"Not disapproving," Kate mumbled at last. "Not my business. But," she looked up from her wandering toe, "I was afraid you - you'd want me to go. At worst. At best your embarrassment or - or annoyance might change everything."

"Kate. Get one thing fixed in your head. I'd never want you to go. You're far too necessary to me - as you promised you'd be, if you remember. It'll be up to you to decide. As for being embarrassed, well, of course I was. But that's gone now that I know it wasn't your own reactions that were bothering you. Annoyed I certainly am not. It won't make any difference to me. Can you say the same for yourself?"

"Of course, if you can - "

"Pretend it never happened?"

"No need, if it makes no difference."

Kate finished her brandy.

"It's time I grew up. I've never even considered you needing – that sort of thing." Kate spoke casually but a new fear came to nag at the edges of her imagination.

"All sense and no sensibility? Is that how you think of me? What about love, Kate? Have you never thought of me falling in love?" There! The fear nibbled nearer. "Or have you hoped I never would?"

"Of course I haven't!" Kate protested, just too quickly.

"Well, then, Red Kate. I do need – that sort of thing, as you so delicately put it, and I have fallen in love. But in default of such consummations as may be wished, you found me as you did tonight."

Kate suddenly felt unearthly sick.

"Head down – right down." Irresistible pressure on the back of her neck pushed Kate's head between her knees. The bloody acanthus-leaf pattern swam up to meet her. Kate closed her eyes. "Stay like that. I'll pour you another brandy."

"No!" Kate moaned. "I drank the last too fast."

"Medicinal, this. I know what I'm doing, my dear. At last I know what to do. Yes, your face is now more suitably pink. You may sit up, you green girl, and drink this one with respect and gratitude. Then back to bed. And don't forget what I said," Celia added as they finally separated for the night. "I'll never want you to leave."

*   *   *

But Kate lay awake until she heard the baby begin to stir for its six o'clock feed. Like Pavlov's dogs, the pair of them; at four-hourly intervals the baby's superhuman timer nudged her into requiring milk, and her first awareness prompted the milk-flow in Kate. She leapt out of bed clutching a clean towel to her tingling breasts.

But tending the baby didn't bring its usual sense of pleased accomplishment. The same demons warred in Kate's head as had kept her awake staring into the darkness. For though Kate might choose to believe Celia when she promised never to send her away, the fact that she'd fallen in love hideously complicated their relationship. If Celia married, the logical conclusion surely, she'd hardly be welcomed into the matrimonial home with a tame char and its baby in tow. And Kate wasn't even certain she could live on with Celia in the flat knowing she'd fallen in love. Never mind with whom, or which of the names Celia casually mentioned had this power to turn the blade in Kate's heart.

For Kate too was in love; and had been for months, she realised in confusion. Deeply in love. Why else should she have turned to her former tutor when her life seemed in ruins? The thought of leaving Celia suddenly became exquisitely unbearable, yet to stay with her was to invite disaster. And she the mother of a child! There could never have been a more mistimed, mismanaged commitment; to have become a conviction at its very point of rejection. Still-born. The fool it was that lived.

Kate gazed hopelessly down at the replete, glowing little woollen-wrapped bundle in her arms and wondered what on earth she was going to do. Impulsively she buried her face in the shawl and breathed the scent of warm, clean baby, as fiercely binding as steel shackles; and considered her other equally unknowing, equally implacable bond.

Kate didn't hear the door open.

"Kate? I knocked but you didn't answer. I only wanted to say I've done the breakfast this morning. I woke early. How is Her Ladyship?" Celia put a mug of tea down on the bedside table. "I'll hold her while you drink your tea – or were you just going to put her down?"

"Oh God! Am I late? No, I'll get her to sleep. I'm coming right away. Thanks. Sorry," Kate gabbled.

"No hurry. It's early still. Just I decided to skip the library this morning and work on today's tutorials at home for a change. If you can bear that. Come as you are."

Kate covered and settled the baby, drank the tea and followed Celia to the tiny kitchen. She poured herself another mug of tea, wondering if she could bear any breakfast at all and wishing Celia hadn't decided to stay at home. She needed time alone.

"You don't look as though you've slept much, Kate. Second thoughts?"

"Not exactly."

"Not as easy to overlook as you gave me to understand?"

"Not that."

"My dear, you're being strangely negative on this clear spring morning. The baby kept you awake, then?"

"Negative." Kate determinedly crammed her mouth with toast.

"The coward's way out!" Celia laughed at her bulging cheeks. "Can it be that your curiosity to know who I've fallen for is niggling you into asking a personal question for once in your life? What ghastly sentence construction. Been reading too many rotten essays. It's what any normal person would've asked last night. Being kept awake serves you right."

"It'd only be a name to me anyway," Kate said thickly.

"Is that all it would mean, Kate? Just a name?"

"Does he know? Does he love you?" Goaded, Kate tried to wash down the recalcitrant toast with a mouthful of tea.

"I shall never – tell any man I love him. Try a smaller mouthful next time."

"But what's the point of that? You said you needed – that sort of thing. Isn't it – ? Wouldn't it be – ? You're not making sense. What *do* you want?"

"I want you, Kate. It's you I love. From when you were a self-opinionated student."

* * *

It was all a long time ago, Kate sighed wearily. Yet Elinor, twenty years later and with the support of a supposedly more tolerant social climate, could describe her own love as 'grotesque'. But then, Jessica wasn't Celia. Elinor hadn't that much luck. Celia could touch anything and make it fine.

'Self-opinionated', Kate remembered with a wry grin into the dark. But perhaps it was now she herself who had the arrogance of one who knew all the answers. Kate hadn't invited the younger girl's sad confidences and it was plain that Elinor hadn't approached her because of any inconvenient conclusions as to her nature. In the circumstances she could afford to be more generous in her attitude than she had been. It was an uncomfortable thought.

Kate turned over in another attempt to find sleep. Something landed lightly on the foot of the bed and progressed stealthily along her covered body. She froze in bewildered horror. Then suddenly galvanised into action she switched on the bedside lamp. The black and white cat stared reproachfully up at her from the centre of the floor where Kate's sudden movement had driven it.

"Hey! Oh – Lord!" Recollection dawned. Kate chirruped to reassure the stray she'd quite forgotten. At least, she supposed it was a stray. Apparently she succeeded in pacifying it, for it suddenly kicked up a hind leg and vigorously washed the inside of its thigh.

Kate got out of bed, thankful to be given a positive alternative to sleeplessness, and picked the cat up cautiously. He – she? – she seemed perfectly amenable. Kate didn't recognise her – it – but judging by its leanness it'd been a stray for some time. Mrs. Harrison might know more about it. She'd better ask her, or advertise or something.

But for now it must at least have some milk. Kate pattered down the stairs with the cat in her arms, feeling the bones through the fur and, more angrily, one or two scabs. No, she was damned if she'd ask around. It had come to her, hadn't it?

Kate watched while it lapped up a saucerful of milk. It looked about half grown. Kate had never taken over a half-grown cat. Could be more traumatic for both parties. On an inspiration she opened a tin of pilchards and watched half of them vanish to an amazing accompaniment of lip-smacking and juice-slurping. What about fleas – worms? It otherwise looked fit enough. No limping or obvious open sores.

Kate continued to watch while it meticulously cleaned its paws and face and then settled down to a more complicated toilet. Really, it was a very attractive little thing; white mittens, white bib, but otherwise black with longish fur. Matted in places. Soon cure that. She'd call it – what? Magpie? Too obvious, and not an easy name to squawk round the street trying to get it in at night. Hoopoe would be better for that, but hardly the name for a proper cat. Domino, then? Too masculine. Domina. The mistress of the house. If she stayed.

How do you tell if they've been spayed, Kate wondered. Wait and see? Or house-trained? Ditto.

So Domina should stay mistress only of the kitchen until certain checks had been made. Like for fleas. Meanwhile, the newly christened cat showed no inclination to go out. Kate covered the floor by the back door with newspapers and left her still busily teasing and coaxing her coat into decent order. Kate shut the kitchen door and went back to bed. This time sleep came easily.

★   ★   ★

The next morning showed the kitchen still immaculate, to Kate's relief, and she put down the rest of the pilchards and some more milk. She left the outside door ajar while she got ready for her day, pondering the various claims, ties and responsibilities she'd so casually let herself in for. Where was Domina to call a part of the house her own? Kate remembered the ancient picnic hamper whose lid had come adrift years before. It never seemed worth getting it mended or useless enough to throw away. Now she raked it out of the landing cupboard together with a stained and faded cushion, and went to show Domina her good fortune.

Kate found her in the yard, neatly filling in an excavation in one of the flag-sized squares left for bulbs among the paving. She'd have to take a chance and wedge the back door ajar for the day. Perhaps Willy Frost, her local handyman, would agree to come round and fit a cat-flap that evening.

★   ★   ★

Her morning's errands done, Kate just had time to leave her bag of shopping in the cloakroom before the Comparative Education lecture. Marginally more interesting than watching paint dry, she thought, wondering how Dr. Jarman amused herself in her free time. She looked bored to death by her own lecture. Quite different from Ruth Stanton's infectious enthusiasm.

There had been a letter from Vivvy that morning, but what with Domina and the shopping for supper Kate hadn't time to read it. It had crossed with the one posted on Friday evening.

At the end of the lecture Kate retreated to the goldfish pond to read it in peace.

But she seemed fated never to find peace at the pond. Kate had just slit open the envelope when Peter's voice came cheerfully down the garden.

"There you are, elusive Kate! Hope I'm not intruding but I wanted to catch you first." He looked curiously at the envelope in her hand as he sat down beside her. Kate held it address side down to open it, and now she slid it among her lecture notes.

"Oh? What's important?" Kate asked him casually.

"I wanted to sound you out about a party – just to celebrate the end of our first month, you know, not a fireworks party. I suddenly thought I'd like to host a bright gathering – say, Friday night? – and perhaps you'd help me with the guest list."

"Surely that's up to you?"

"One wouldn't like to overlook anyone important," he replied airily. "But perhaps I ought to invite everyone. What do you think?"

"Wouldn't you be limited for space?"

"Not really, it's a big enough flat. But perhaps you're right. Perhaps I ought to make the gesture and ask everyone, even if I can't stand some of them and vice versa. Try and rise above it, eh?"

Kate wondered how he'd managed to invent her participation in his plans quite so smoothly, and why. She didn't think it was worth the effort to insist on her own refusal to take a hand, but merely asked where he lived and what time he planned for.

"Oh, I'll come and pick you up, of course."

"Good heavens, no! You can't be ferrying people on the night of your own party. Besides, I prefer to be under my own steam."

"So independent!" Peter gave his address in St. Dunstan's Square, an estate agent's dream area not far from Morgan's Mount. "I'll put up a notice about it now and catch them all properly at lunch. Oh, by the way, I was looking in Barbara's copy of *The Normal Child* and found it was yours. What does R stand for? K. R. Henderson?"

"Rose," Kate answered shortly.

"Really? What shy secrets lurk in our hidden names! I've never thought of you as a 'Rosie' for all its aptness."

"Why should you? It's a surname – my mother's maiden name – that's all."

"Unusual. Anyway," Peter got to his feet, "let me know if you change your mind about a lift on Friday. At least let me drive you home. I'll leave you now to your goldfish. This seems quite a favourite haunt of yours. At this time of year too! Hardy Kate!" He waved a carefree hand and walked away.

And not before time, thought Kate grimly. She couldn't imagine what his reasons might be, but she was convinced he'd fished in that book to find her address. Nor would he find a 'phone number listed under her name, always supposing he realised she was a native and not a student lodger in digs. And what did he mean – if anything – by secrets lurking in second names? Perhaps it was all just idle chat. But Peter never chatted idly, Kate reminded herself. He probed and waited for clues.

She turned back to Vivvy's letter. Vivienne had been Celia's second name. She had stood godparent to the baby and was quite ridiculously pleased when Kate asked if she might name her Vivienne. Everything had been so bright in those days. Now, though much of the old happiness remained, the shining brightness was gone, except in Vivvy of course. Kate smiled at the superlatives that scattered through her daughter's letter and the lively little line-drawings that were always included.

★ ★ ★

After the coffee-break Kate had a History Methodology seminar with Professor Humphries. At least his feet and sense of humour were firmly rooted in the earth. After lunch on Tuesday Kate met him again for her weekly tutorial, in many ways the high-spot of her week. He was humane, clever and humorous and reminded her of Celia in many of his attitudes.

Kate was on her way out to lunch after the seminar when Elinor pounced.

"Kate – look – I don't know what to say! I've been trying to get to you all morning. Peggy said you looked bloody when you left yesterday but you wouldn't let her help and she didn't like to push. At least you seem okay now, though my head's going like a brass gong. I'm terribly sorry, truly, and all out of self-indulgent emotion on my part. I daren't offer to stand you a drink but at least let's find a butty somewhere."

"Please – it's all right. I'm sorry Peggy was worried. Let's try The Happy Man and see if it lives up to its name. It's about the nearest and you could change your mind about that drink – medicinal, you know."

"Hm! What's got into Peter with this party idea? It'll cost him heaps if we all roll up. Why didn't you stay to hear about it?"

"He ambushed me earlier. What about you? Are you intending to go?"

"Look a bit off, wouldn't it, after the row on Friday. You're going, I suppose?"

"If I'm not mistaken he's intending to give everyone the impression that it's been all my idea. I don't know why. I don't intend to stay long, though." Elinor slanted an interested look from under her thick eyebrows.

"I thought he was your *fidus Achates*, yet you sound a mite impatient."

"I just have the impression he's planning some mischief – and you'd be closer with Iago, you know. Jeff and Gordon reckon he's involved in something queer in the town." Kate led Elinor into the pub.

"Language, ducky! I've never been in here before – hey! Talk of the devil!"

Elinor nodded across the room where Jeff and Gordon were sitting with a third man Kate didn't recognise.

"He's not one of ours, is he?" she asked.

"N-no. But I'm sure I've seen him before. You don't want to go and fall on their necks, do you?"

"Funnily enough, no. Choose yourself some fodder. I'll pay for that and you can get the drinks. Bitter for me, please."

"Hell, you're so disgustingly forgiving, Kate, you make me bilious. Ham and lettuce roll, then."

"How smashed were you?" Elinor asked when they were

sitting down to their lunch. "Can you remember much of our – our conversation?"

"Pretty well all of it, I think. Why?"

"I was afraid you'd say that," Elinor groaned. "If I were to insist it was all said simply to test your sense of humour, would you try and forget it?"

"Sure, if you want. You may rest assured that I found the whole subject inexpressibly – hilarious."

"You did?" Elinor flushed darkly and her brows drew down.

"Of course I didn't, you great bullock! What do you bloody think I am? And stop trying to pick a quarrel with me or – or I'll sick Barbara onto you."

"Come and help me drink the mavrodaphne," Elinor begged.

"Will I hell as like! But I'll call in after Peter's blasted wake, if you want, with smuggled goodies tied up in a spotted hanky. What's your fancy, sweet or savoury?"

"Jessica."

"You daft baggage!"

7

After her tutorial at the end of the afternoon, Kate snatched up her jacket and shopping bag and hurried from the nearly empty building up the drive. It was already growing dark, but with any luck she should catch a bus home fairly promptly, Kate calculated, as she trotted down Carriage Hill. She glanced in through the window of the leather shop as she passed, again promising herself a new pair of sheepskin mitts before winter really gripped. There had been a pair, smoky-brown — yes, still there. And then Kate stopped dead.

Superimposed over the mitts was the image of the scene on Carriage Hill and the entrance to the narrow side street opposite the shop. Momentarily visible through a gap in the traffic was the ghost of a steel-grey car, a battery of badges across the radiator grille, nosing out of Plague Yard. Peter? The shadow slid out like a silver shark across the shoal of traffic. It turned and cruised down Kate's side of the hill, passing just behind her, but she couldn't make out the driver and she didn't turn her head. If it was Peter she didn't want to meet him just then, to be delayed by a skirmish as to whether or not he should drive her home as he seemed so determined to do.

Kate continued on her way hoping that Peter, if it was Peter, hadn't pulled in to wait for her. But there was no sign of the VW, though she checked both lanes of traffic and the kerbside parking. Kate was almost running by the time she reached the Centre.

And then she saw it. Just a glimpse of quiet grey parked discreetly in the yard of the Midland Bank, round the corner from her direct line of approach. She'd have missed it but for her determination not be ambushed. It needn't be Peter, of course. There were plenty of grey cars about. She was growing paranoid. Good God, she'd be imagining men under her bed next. But as she hurried on, Kate heard an engine start up behind her. She took off in an undignified gallop.

Kate headed for her previous escape route, a dive straight through the supermarket. First she checked in the plate-glass windows. Yes, bloody hell! There was no mistaking that badge-bar. The grey wolf was still in slow pursuit. She pushed her way through the aisles.

The back exit led to narrow, one-way streets from which Kate could approach the bus station more indirectly. To catch her now Peter would have to follow on foot – which, if he succeeded, would make him appear uncharacteristically impetuous and put him to the trouble of inventing a believable excuse; or lie in wait somewhere near the bus station on the off-chance she'd be making for there. Kate hoped he was still waiting at the front of the store and in danger of a parking fine.

But, knowing Peter, he was probably perfectly aware he had her on the run and was thoroughly enjoying himself. Kate decided on a belt and braces alternative, avoided the bus station altogether and ran for the first stop away from the Centre. The bus approached as she reached the stop, so she was spared an agonised lurk while she waited for it.

* * *

Domina greeted her mistress' arrival home with a trill of pleasure – she hoped, but suspected it was really hunger – and fell upon the helping of cheapest, own-brand supermarket cat food. Kate opened the back door and switched on the yard light. While Domina retired discreetly to her earth square, Kate started to prepare and set out the supper. She pondered the fate of next spring's bulbs, which would stand a better chance if Domina had alternative scratch-sites. When she was fully grown and had her proper strength and fitness she would no doubt roam the wasteland behind the terrace. There was a door in the wall that led into the wasteland of bramble clumps, rose-bay willow herb and domestic rubbish, and Kate always kept that locked. When Domina was bigger she'd be able to get over the wall via one of the flower tubs or the small lean-to shed. But meanwhile Kate had better lift some of the flags on the sunniest side of the yard. They were only set in sand and the job shouldn't be too arduous.

Five minutes later a ring at the front door announced the arrival of Willy Frost, taciturn and skilful and booted as usual in army surplus, which he meticulously shed on the doormat. Kate wished he wouldn't, for all she appreciated his thoughtfulness. His socks smelt of silage – or something.

"Will it be a long job?" Kate asked, as Willy got out his tools.

"Ng."

"Marvellous! Will you eat first or do you want to get on?" But Willy was already rootling for a T-square and keyhole saw. Kate moved slightly more to windward and watched him for a moment as he plucked a stub of pencil from behind one ear and drew a rectangle into the bottom of the door.

"Tha'?"

"Perfect," Kate enthused, and poured out one of the cans of beer to set it beside his carrier. She turned back to preparing the vegetables.

In a gratifyingly short time Willy gave a grunt and began packing his tools away. Kate went over to look. She was always impressed by neat, deft work and her thanks now were genuine. The flap fitted snugly in its cut-out, swinging on two-way hinges. Two small brass bolts, screwed one to each side, locked it shut when required. It was a necessary arrangement but it represented a breach nevertheless. Kate wanted to see Domina try it immediately, but it was obvious she'd stay glued to her cushion till Willy had gone.

"And nicely timed," Kate added. "Supper's just ready."

The pork chops, peas and chips, followed by apple pie and accompanied by cans of beer, were soon gone. Willy extracted a dog-end of whiskery cigarette from behind his cigarette ear. When he'd got it alight, in a small shower of flaming tobacco shreds, Kate knew he was ready to leave.

"How much do I owe you, Willy?"

"Ng. Cost nothing. All come-by bits from jobs." He padded to the door.

"But your time, Willy!" Kate protested, hurrying after him.

"Well spent. Well ate 'n drunk." Willy bared his gappy teeth at her as he stepped into his boots and vanished into the darkness. She'd drop him off some cigarettes, Kate promised herself, and sped back to familiarise Domina with the cat-flap.

She washed up and cleared away the supper things and settled down at the kitchen table to get on with her essay. At her tutorial that afternoon Professor Humphries had criticised her for thinking too much about what she intended to teach and not enough about what her hypothetical pupils were learning. 'Remember, you're not simply teaching History. You're teaching through History.' So, all right. This time –

Domina hopped neatly up on a chair and stepped onto the table to push her blunt little head against Kate's hand.

"You're a calculating cat," Kate observed, stroking her from head to tail so that Domina's back paws almost lifted off the table-top at each stroke. She was standing all over Kate's papers, her front paws gently stamping up and down. Kate propped her feet against the table stretcher and lifted Domina down into her lap where she settled, filling the kitchen with her purring like the roar of a small dynamo. Strangely comforted, Kate continued with her essay for the following Tuesday, freshly inspired to tackle Professor Humphries' criticisms.

★ ★ ★

The rest of the week continued peacefully for Kate, though she kept a conscious look out for Peter's car on her way to or from Morgan's Mount and she avoided the bus station. It was a bore, and the sensation of being under secret and inexplicable observation made her thoroughly uncomfortable. Kate suspected Peter of being as calculating as Domina, though with none of her endearing habits. He remained, at least superficially, as friendly and as charming as he'd always been, but Kate couldn't ignore her intuition although she could find no explanation for the interest she seemed to inspire. She even went so far as to approach the Department secretary, asking her not to give away her address should anyone try to find it out. 'Thet would be meost unprofessional,' she'd been told huffily.

Even the sight of Peter's new attentions to Jessica, as if making up for his earlier behaviour, didn't provide reassurance. It made Robert Denham the butt of Peter's cool malice, while Elinor's expression grew more ominously dour as the week went by. However, Kate recognised that all this was good news for Alice Jepson, who tried to redirect Robert's attention and defuse his angry mortification; and for Jeff and Gordon, for the pressure was off them.

Jessica herself, Kate saw with irritation, was quite impossibly cock-a-hoop. She developed a proprietorial archness with an equally unlovely overlay of fluttery submission. Kate wondered how Peter could bear it.

And so it went on till Wednesday, when the whole morning was taken up with 'The Learning Process'; first the lecture and then seminars. That morning covered an aspect of the course which particularly interested Kate, motivation in the classroom, and the seminar was based on a paper by Peter. But Kate was disappointed to find his approach so restricted – privately awarding him nil for constructive analysis and maximum marks for gratuitous provocation – and after a while listened with only half an ear while she in turn watched Mr. Grundy. She wondered what he thought of her year's 'bright lot' and suspected from his occasional ironical glances that he was a lazer in glow-worm's clothing.

Kate sat back to await the firing of the big guns she heard being loaded and primed as Peter came to the end of his paper.

"Thank you, Mr. Colebrook. Very interesting as far as you go." Mr. Grundy raised his baton, in Kate's flash of imagination, ready to cue and control the various sections of the orchestra. So, it was to be a concerto, not a cannonade. "It's a pity you limited your observations to the private sector. No doubt I should have made your areas of reference clearer." He tapped his baton, gently admonishing.

"But I'm only interested in the private sector," Peter murmured languidly. "Anything else seems unnecessary in my present circumstances." Kate shifted uneasily. The implied insult was so overstated it surely couldn't be ignored.

"Indeed? Are you perhaps assured of a post in your area of interest?"

"Virtually. At Lethbridge, if I choose to take it up." Kate felt herself blushing at Peter's casual arrogance.

"You are to be congratulated, Mr. Colebrook. May I ask if anyone else is so happily situated?" Mr. Grundy gazed mildly around at the blank faces. No one uttered, but Kate felt the shock and resentment of the group like a physical blow.

She suddenly realised what Peter was doing. He wasn't specifically provoking Mr. Grundy as he'd baited Miss Welborne; he was spoiling for any sort of confrontation. He'd set himself up as the punch-bag. But why? Pure mischief? Kate looked across at Jessica, wondering if she'd already heard Peter's career news. She plainly hadn't. Her expression was such a mixture of pique and conscientious admiration that Kate nearly giggled out loud. What was she expecting for herself then? Benenden?

"Yet there is time for the rest of you." Mr. Grundy's gentle reassurance gathered their attention. "But meanwhile Mr. Colebrook's truncated paper presents us with certain interesting hypotheses." Tap-tap, thought Kate. "Miss Purbeck? Would you care to comment?"

He was obviously hoping to draw in Elinor's handicapped against Peter's privileged in a vibrant counter-point; but in the event the discussion merely became hooked on the corny private-versus-State education argument, perhaps as Peter expected. Kate was disappointed again. Back to the concert hall. If Peter was the soloist, what was his instrument, Kate wondered. A siren-voice solo?

* * *

The discussion continued down the stairs to the Common Room, where it quickly became a rancorous argument respecting neither personalities nor neutrals, though Peter remained urbane.

"You haven't yet declared yourself, quiet Kate. I shall call you Griffin, because you're like the listening bank that stores everything in its vaults but gives very little interest. Which side are you on, sensible Kate?" Peter tried to beguile her.

"Why do you particularly want to teach in a public school?" she asked instead.

"Because I want to teach my subject, not spend my time among the forlorn hope beating off muggers and disturbed adolescents. Let the police or the Welfare see to them. Surely that's reasonable?"

"But good heavens!" Liz expostulated. "It's silly to talk of all state schools as if they were borstals. You can't – "

"You're only thinking of your needs. What about the special needs of the children? The handicapped, for instance, or the socially handicapped?"

"Little Nell, you can take care of one lot, and Robert and his lefty friends can have the other – with my heartfelt sympathies for his own handicaps. But you'd neither of you be teachers as I understand the term. Merely – "

"It's your immaturity I'm sorry for," Robert snarled surprisingly, as if a lamb had suddenly turned temperamental. "You set yourself up to be watched and admired the whole time, like a child afraid of the dark. Might you vanish if you're not constantly in the spotlight?" For a moment Kate thought Robert had finally destroyed Peter's amused cool. His head whipped back, almost as if he'd taken a blow on the chin – or like a snake ready to strike, Kate thought with a tweak of panic. But he righted himself in an instant.

"And are you afraid of the light because there's so little of you worth seeing? You're merely a transparent fool, Robert."

"Oh, come on, Peter!" Jessica had been standing by, first on one leg and then on the other, long bored by the argument and piqued by Peter's distracted attention. "It's all too stifling and Jessica's frantically thirsty." Kate contrived a look of amused nausea at Elinor and turned to her locker as Peter and Jessica walked past.

They'd got just outside the door when Peter's voice could be heard quite clearly.

"Just a minute. I meant to ask Kate to come with us."

"Oh, Peter! What a wet blanket! What on earth for?"

"I feel sorry for her."

A pure rage seized Kate so violently that she had to hold onto a chair back to stop herself racing into the hall to smash their two heads together. She had been meant to hear that. Peter had intercepted her glance at Elinor, she supposed, and felt his vanity niggled. But so too had the entire Common Room heard. She pulled herself together and looked around, directly meeting Linda Mayer's interested scrutiny.

"Wow! Some wet blanket!" She grinned at Kate. "Till you just drilled me with that look I might have agreed. They're bugs, Miss Henderson. Don't let them get to you."

"Thanks," said Kate tightly. "I step on bugs. And I'm Kate, you know."

"Yeah, I know." Linda turned away.

Blow upon blow. Kate felt doubly rebuffed. She supposed she'd let the acid spill over onto Linda's friendly approach, off-beat though it was. She wondered if the fall of Kate the Immune was being viewed with a certain amount of secret glee. Serves me right for being so aloof, she told herself. They probably think I feel superior.

★   ★   ★

Her own annoyance apart, Kate was increasingly intrigued by Peter's behaviour. He seemed to be going out of his way to win the Shit of the Year award. Was it simply that he cared for no one? Yet at the beginning of term she'd thought he made quite noticeable efforts to be agreeable – though now it appeared that pity had been the reason for his friendliness towards herself.

But his behaviour made nonsense of reasonable discussions during the course. You couldn't be sure how he'd set out to provoke; and those who championed the opposite view did so at least as much to challenge him for personal reasons. Or like Jessica they supported him out of a sickly sycophancy and without too many ideas in their heads. If Barbara had been at the morning's session, Kate believed, she'd have contributed her witless mite on Peter's side – 'I just *feel* he's right'. Only Liz seemed to make a decently unbiased contribution.

Kate had a Comparative Education seminar after lunch and to her irritation she found herself landed with a paper on current French educational systems. That just about crowned her day and she was glad to get home, via her circuitous flittings, to Domina.

But Domina was not easily to be won over when Kate had jostled a worming-pill down her throat. After a decent interval she stalked to her basket, twitching her tail in resentment, curled up and eyed her mistress malevolently for a few moments before falling asleep with her tail wrapped round her head: the final rebuff in what had been a thoroughly demoralising day.

8

Kate's easy timetable on Thursday allowed her to pick up a bottle of Martini on the way home and to make a start on lifting the extra flagstones for Domina. The bottle was for Peter's party the next evening, the arrangements being that the guests would supply at least some of the drink while Peter organised the food – 'knowing someone in the trade'. Kate supposed he meant the manager at the wine-bar in Foundry Street.

The following evening – party night – Kate tried to psyche herself into a sociable mood as she changed into something festive. Most of her wardrobe was 'useful', 'discreet' or dual purpose. Nothing at all of the kind that her daughter should want to burgle – to Vivvy's chagrin whenever she got behind with her ironing or mending, Kate reflected wryly. 'I'm not suggesting you suddenly blossom out in tempestuous frills and flounces, just something less severe.' Kate grinned at herself in the mirror. Vivvy's concern for her mother's appearance was touching, but as self-motivated as Domina's rarely given affection.

Kate left her mini in the car-park at the Department and walked on to Peter's flat in St. Dunstan's Square. She was surprised to glimpse the sturdy figure of Elinor disappearing round the corner ahead. Kate couldn't be certain in the light from occasional street lamps but she hurried to catch up anyway.

"Hell, where's the fire?" asked a husky voice from behind. Kate spun round. She'd been so intent on pursuing the half-recognised figure ahead that she'd been unaware of her own pursuit. "I thought it must be you," said Linda Mayer. She always sounded as if she'd been weaned on gin.

"These lights make your hair look like a geranium. Is it natural?"

"Not naturally geranium."

"I nearly bust a gusset catching you up, and now we're early. There's time for a couple of quickies before we go and admire Peter. Just down here there's a place. Come on." Linda turned down a cobbled alley.

"Er – " Kate stood still, unhappily waving her bottle of Martini.

"Shove it up your jumper or something, if you're bothered how it'll look."

"It's not that – " How could she explain that she'd feel awkward arriving at a party already huffing alcohol over the welcoming host?

"Christ! You can't go to these things dry! Come on! What've you got there, anyway?"

"Martini. I wasn't quite sure – "

"Mine's supermarket plonk. Taiwan Bordeaux or something. No expense spent," Linda grinned cheerfully. "Come on."

Kate followed Linda to the bar, admiring her nonchalance as she elbowed her way through the crowd. She hoped just one quickie would be enough to put Linda in the elusive party mood.

"Have you been to Peter's flat before?" Kate asked for want of something to say as they waited to be served.

"Only before he moved in. It's not his flat. It belongs to Terry, a friend of mine whose father bought it to let to students when Terry was a student. It didn't work out for some reason and Peter more or less took it over. As he took Terry over. But as far as I know Terry still lives here."

While Kate digested this unexpected information Linda looked impatiently along the bar, where the bar-tender was trying to cope with the crowd.

"What's Peter up to?" she asked Kate surprisingly.

"Is he up to anything?"

"Sure as eggs. I know him. Nothing dropped in your ear?"

"We're not on such confiding terms. And contrary to popular belief, cradle-snatching isn't my hobby."

"I wonder what is? I only thought he might have said something. I realised yesterday you weren't emotionally involved. It made you much more interesting."

"What am I supposed to say to all that? Crash down on my knees and sob my thanks?" What on earth can she be like after a couple of drinks, Kate wondered, as Linda eyed her speculatively.

"I was certainly wrong." Linda turned suddenly and called down the bar in her improbably suggestive voice, "Hey! Who do you have to fuck to get a drink round here?"

Their drinks came promptly after that and Kate removed herself from the ribald offers to lean thankfully against the wall by the cool doorway while she gulped her beer. Linda seemed unperturbed by the raucous flutter she'd caused – the place was like a cageful of randy parrots, Kate thought disgustedly.

Linda joined her and glanced pointedly at Kate's empty glass.

"Hate being late," Kate gasped through excessive carbonisation. "Also hideously embarrassed."

"Your generation would be. But it pays off sometimes as you saw."

"I sustained a – a slight culture-shock, that's all," Kate protested, nettled. Kate had never had much to do with Linda, observing her striking, dark and rather disdainful beauty and overhearing her pungent comments from a distance. She now wished that peaceful arrangement had never been altered.

"You shouldn't be so prim." Linda emptied her glass and put it with Kate's on a handy window-sill. "Is that why you never got married?"

"The question didn't arise," Kate answered shortly, and hurried out of the pub with Linda in pursuit.

* * *

Jessica opened the door of the ground-floor flat to them. She was dressed in the sort of glittery outfit that Kate had seen on Vivvy's *Top of the Pops* programmes. There was even a hint of sparkle in her hair.

"Oh. It's you two," she said ungraciously. "Peter's through at the bar. We thought you weren't coming."

"I'm afraid we are a bit late – " Kate was beginning apologetically, but Linda cut in.

"Christmas decorations already?" She stared mockingly at Jessica's clothes. "Oh, and I left my baubles behind!" Jessica returned her look with dislike and led them through into a large room where Peter was emptying bottles into a punch-bowl.

"At last!" he called across gaily and came to meet them, talking in a carrying hoot. "Linda! My party would've been a poor thing without your decorative presence! And here's Kate too, our collective conscience, looking flatteringly smart! What kept you both?"

"Called in at The Dunstan's Pincers," Linda replied laconically. Kate thrust her bottle of Martini at Peter and he accepted it with the excessive congratulatory delight you direct at people who've done something simple but unexpectedly cleverly. She nearly snatched it back.

"Kate! How marvellously sensible! And Linda! Perfect for my vat of sluggo! Jessica, pet, show them where to leave their coats – but no dallying, mind! This party's about to die on its feet."

"If it's in the smallest bedroom, I know my way." Linda forestalled Jessica and Kate saw Peter give her a swift look. Linda walked down the hall and pushed open a door at the end. She dropped her duffle carelessly on the bed piled high with coats, but Kate hung hers on a hook on the back of the door. She intended to leave early and anyway had no wish to have it used as part of the furnishings for some amorous interlude.

As they returned along the hall, Kate reflected that Peter might have good reason for feeling the party was dying on its feet. The murmur that sounded from the room was of people good-naturedly willing to humour their host but uncertain how to manage themselves; how to reconcile their discomfort in the face of Peter's apparent affluence and sophistication with their own desire to enjoy a simple booze-up. And not as many had come as Kate was expecting. Robert was there, firmly anchored to Alice Jepson. But for her, Kate was sure, he wouldn't have shown up. Kate saw Liz, and Barbara huddled in a corner – but not Elinor. Jeff and Gordon were missing too, and most of the others she knew only by sight.

"Nice and quick," Peter approved, when Kate and Linda returned. "First, you must have a drink – Kate? Linda?" He urged them towards the drinks table, his eyes glinting and almost predatory. His party might be dying but the host himself seemed pleased and excited about something. Kate glanced at Jessica darting from group to group like a shimmering dragonfly.

"Martini for me, please," she answered. "Just as it comes."

"Whisky, thanks," Linda said casually as she gazed round the room. "Neat. Quite a few seem to have fallen by the wayside."

"A few, but not enough to hurt." Peter handed each their drinks and put an arm round their waists. Kate flinched automatically but felt herself held.

"Right, ladies and gents." Peter raised his voice. "Before we get down to the serious business of enjoying ourselves – " polite laughter " – I've got a couple of announcements." The gentle droning of voices stopped, and those who were standing turned to face Peter and his flanking acolytes. Kate felt ridiculously conspicuous and wondered how she might extricate herself smoothly. She caught Jessica's startled look as she took in the group by the bar. "First, in case you haven't all heard, Liz has got permission to be married in the chapel. Congratulations, Liz. End of June, isn't it?" Liz nodded and smilingly accepted the good wishes of those around her. She really does look happy, thought Kate. Good for Liz.

"Marvellous," Peter went on. "Now, you've seen the array of food – we'll get round to that later – and there's plenty to drink. The mixture in the bowl is lethal, I warn you. Christened 'Sluggo'. One glass and you're sand-bagged." Warmer laughter. Peter's arm gripped Kate more tightly and he gave her a gentle shake. It was noticed at least by Jessica. Kate could clearly feel the slight trembling of Peter's body against her own, a vibration of excitement – or anticipation, she thought irritably, and her annoyance began to simmer. Jessica sidled closer.

"And finally a toast to our absent friends. Jeff and Gordon

work on Friday nights – we won't ask what at – and Elinor, well, she's crossed in love and not in the mood for parties, poor dear. (Jessica, my pet, you simply don't know what fascinated amusement you've caused me all term.) So, cry havoc and help yourselves to drinks. Then if you'll all arrange yourselves in a circle, we'll start with a game."

Jessica had stood looking at first resentful and then bewildered by what Peter had said to her. When Kate took the opportunity to release herself and find a seat with the others, Jessica moved quickly to take her place. God, she must really feel insecure if she thinks I'm any competition, Kate thought, bored by her antics. Why is everyone determined to tie me to that shop-soiled little snake?

"Congratulations from me too, Liz," Kate murmured as she sank down onto a cushion by her.

"Isn't it wonderful? But is Peter setting up a harem or something? Jessica's nose can never be the same again."

"I've never felt so spare," Kate snapped. "I think he's drunk."

"You could've moved away."

"I was gripped as, presumably, was Linda. And I've never been very hot on wrestling in public."

"So you'll take what any jerk hands out?" Linda had curled up on the floor beside Kate. "It's women like you who've encouraged men to think we're all push-overs. Your face, Kate!" Linda giggled suddenly. "Liz, if you think that expression of 'Who's shat in the State coach' represented Kate being turned on, you'd better go back to square one with Adrian. And Peter's never drunk. Just excited. Now, Robert's zonked out of his tiny mind. See? Eyes swivelling independently already."

"What a pair you are," Liz reproved. "But what did Peter mean about Jeff and Gordon?"

"Just a needle planted where it might damage the patient," Linda retorted. "They don't like it known, but on Friday and Saturday nights they do a voluntary stint as duty officers at that old people's home in Souters Lane. I only discovered it when Gran was admitted there last month, though Gordon's worked at that place since his undergraduate days."

"But where does Elinor come into it? What's this nonsense about her being in love? With Jeff? Gordon? I don't believe it. And Jessica wants a few answers too, look."

"Peter won't like her trying to keep him on a leash," Linda murmured with satisfaction. "Stupid little bitch!" she added with startling venom.

But it seemed that Linda was wrong. Peter suddenly smiled his attractive smile and took Jessica in his arms for a long, explicit kiss. The room fell silent but for a few muted cheers and giggles, while the tableau held for just long enough to make Kate feel like a prize voyeur.

"Come in, number seven. Your time's up," muttered Linda, an interested spectator. "Kate, you're not looking. Surely you don't want to disappoint Peter?"

"Stop teasing, Linda," Liz said peaceably. "You know, it must be like kissing a mirror. All cold and flat, and you only see and feel your own emotions."

"That's very perceptive of you, Liz," Linda remarked. "Not like Adrian?"

"Not at all," Liz smiled complacently.

Peter finally released a radiant Jessica who draped herself over his arm as they walked to the chair left decently free for the host. Peter sat in it, crossing one nattily tailored leg over the other, while Jessica stood looking nonplussed. She so plainly wasn't expected to sit in his lap. Peter smiled amiably round.

"Jessica would like to dance. Someone take her out and find a disco or a club or something. Robert, what about you? I'll keep my eye on Alice. Robert'll be glad to take you off, my pet."

"But – of course I don't want to leave the party, Peter! Can't we dance here?" She was really quite pathetic, Kate decided. Not a femme fatale at all.

"Kate!" Peter suddenly seemed to catch sight of her. "You shouldn't be on the floor! Whatever next! Jessica, my love, you can't stand there but there isn't room for another chair. Take Kate's cushion, and Kate can have this chair. I'll sit on the arm." Jessica swayed like a pendulum between Kate and Peter, hurt and unable to decide whether Peter was serious.

But he was, Kate saw, and once again dragging her in to add zest to his game with Jessica. Good God, in Jessica's place she'd –

"What price public wrestling now?" Linda nudged her. "What're you made of? Sugar and spice?"

What indeed. Fire and ice and more unprintable emotions. Kate wanted nothing more than to surge to her feet with a roar and smash that coolly smiling face into pulp. Instead she answered Peter calmly.

"Thanks, but I'm fine here and the company's my own choice. And you're as big a bitch as he is," she added fiercely to Linda.

"So separatist," Peter complained, apparently unmoved by Kate's dig. "Always in splendid isolation. Jessica, there's Tony offering you his chair. Don't disappoint him. Well, if we're all sitting comfortably at last, let's begin. What I propose is a grown-up game of absolute honesty. That should thaw the ice. Those unaccustomed to honesty will find it a bracing experience. Anyone without the courage for a little fun, hands up. So, you're all committed," Peter said with satisfaction when no hands were raised. "And to prove how easy I'll let you start on me. Any questions for me? I promise to answer with complete honesty."

A vague chattering broke out, but more as a release from tension, Kate thought, than discussion or approval of Peter's plan. A few seemed even more uncertain whether the evening would provide them with their kind of entertainment.

"Where's Terry Sinclair?" Linda asked after a moment. Terry? The friend she'd mentioned in the bar, whose father owned the flat, Kate remembered.

"Terry?" Peter seemed to echo, and Kate saw that he looked disproportionately startled.

"Well, I know he still lives here. I really only came to see him," Linda explained casually.

"If he'd known that I'm sure he'd have taken the evening off, but he works. At The Duke's Wine-Bar. Didn't you know? When did you last see him?"

"Ages ago. It's been a couple of years."

"What touching loyalty!" Peter grinned and seemed to

relax. Had there been some sort of traumatic triangle, Kate wondered. "But if you want to see him, that's where you'll find him. He'll be glad of a friendly face, no doubt. He's been getting himself into hot water, recently. Now I'll ask someone. Alice, what on earth do you see in Robert?"

"Basic decency you wouldn't know how to spell," Alice retorted with commendable honesty and Linda gave a chuckle. "Why have you treated Jessica like a peep-show tonight?" But that's just what he's done, Kate realised, surprised by Alice's perception. Linda and herself had been part of the show too.

"Oh, but – " Jessica began to protest, no doubt preferring to believe that Peter's carelessly hurtful treatment had been unintentional. Or charismatic.

"But is that how you see us, Alice dear? I've merely complied with whatever Jessica needed to satisfy her vanity. Isn't it a well-known feminine trait?"

"Narcissus was a man," Linda reminded quietly and everyone gave a relieved laugh.

"Touché!" Peter laughed with the rest.

But the lightened atmosphere was suddenly shattered by a roar from Robert.

"An' look worrappen' to him!" He sounded as if he was bawling down a cardboard tube. "Drowned by 's own vanity." Robert suddenly drained his glass and stood up, swaying and blinking. "Lesh go, Ally."

"Sh! No. Sit down." Alice tugged at his hand. "It'd be rude to go now."

"Want to be rude. Wanna bite 'sh balls off."

"See if you can't sober him up, Alice, or you'll be left with a heap of dirty laundry. One more word, Denham, and I'll have you pitched out of that window straight into the parking lot. This isn't a four-ale bar." Peter's voice cut like a barbed lash and Robert suddenly collapsed into his chair. It was clear that even if Alice had wanted to go, Robert was incapable.

"Another question?" Peter broke the discordant silence. "Come on, there must be! What's Kate's secret vice, for instance?" He grinned wolfishly as Liz protested. "You think Kate shouldn't be asked because she's so much older than the rest of us? Or because of her respectable image? But that only makes her more able to look after herself and more interesting to – er – deflower, if I may use the term poetically. Well, Kate?"

"Which guilty secret do you want first?" Kate asked evenly as she got up to refill her glass. "Liz? Linda?" Only Linda reached up her glass and Kate walked to the bar. Be damned if she was going to cower on the floor.

"A retreat!" Peter crowed. "An expertly covered retreat! What can she be guilty of? Ask her. Statues do come to life, it's well known."

"I've got a question for Jessica," Liz interposed angrily. "It's tit for tat, Peter. Jessica, what on earth do you see in him?"

"Not fair, Liz." Kate returned with the drinks. "She's had enough."

"If you mean I'm drunk, I'm certainly not!" Jessica flared up. "That's just what a prissy old maid like you *would* say! You think you're safe to be so insulting because you're old, like Peter said, and – "

"Jessica, my sweet," Peter guillotined her tirade. "The game is to answer honestly, but I'm not aware that Kate's actually asked you a question."

"She resents our – our friendship and she was hinting – "

"She wasn't, my pretty nitwit, and she doesn't. She isn't interested in me, you know, charm I never so wisely, and I want to know why. My vanity." Peter smiled engagingly at Kate.

"That's just her cleverness, smarming – "

"Dear Jessica, do give yourself time to think. Really, I don't know why Elinor bothers," Peter drawled.

"Elinor?" Jessica was momentarily side-tracked from her suicidal lashing at Kate. "What's Elinor got to do with anything?" Damn, thought Kate, still standing like a hypnotised rabbit in the glare of Jessica's unexpected attack. "She'd look better anchored off the docks on the end of a cable. But Liz sits there, so superior about getting married, and Kate pretends she's above it all but she's mad for a man. You can always tell."

"Shift your ass, Kate," Linda rasped. "You're blocking my view. I almost can't see the scorch-marks on that little tramp's legs from dropping her pants so fast. How can – "

"Leave her," Kate found her voice at last. "It's not worth it."

She turned to hand Linda her whisky and watched the liquid tremble in the glass.

"Will you answer my question?" Peter persisted.

"And then I must go." Kate made a play of glancing at her watch but rage blurred the dial.

"You need your beauty sleep?" Jessica sniggered and exposed tiny white teeth. Kate wished she'd drop suddenly dead.

"Kate, is there a man in your life?" Peter demanded with the air of a hunter reaching out to spring the trap.

"No."

"Why not?"

"Because she couldn't catch a man." Jessica was indecently triumphant. "Isn't she the classic soured spinster? She never had children and now she wants to work out her frustrated mother instinct on school kids. It's unhealthy!"

"Jessica, you're quite priceless, but – " Peter began suavely, but Linda had had enough.

"For God's sake stop drivelling, you stupid little tart! You don't know how you're exposing yourself! You make me ashamed for my sex."

"Hear, hear," said Alice quietly.

But Kate had been deciding what to say. Refusing to say anything further could lead to the kind of speculation she definitely didn't want. Furthermore, Jessica's final accusation revolted her to the core. She gave a small sigh and faced her taunter.

"I don't know why you should feel threatened by me, but you're wrong on all counts. I do have a child, a daughter." Yes, I wondered if that'd make you sit up, you arse-hole, thought Kate savagely as she noted the surprised look on Peter's face. "She's just started at college. She's illegitimate and I've never pretended otherwise. It's known by the staff at the Department. You could've known it too, Peter, if you'd ever discovered where I lived. It's not a secret. And you'd better lay off the amateur psychology, Jessica. It's really not your forte, any more than amateur sleuthing is yours, Peter. You're just a ten-a-penny Peeping Tom and shabby with it."

Kate took her glass back to the bar without waiting to see reactions to her verbal undressing. Then she left. She had nothing to thank Peter for – it was her own Martini she'd been drinking.

★ ★ ★

Kate gave herself a moment to recover her calm before she left the flat, but she was still trembling as she hurried out of St. Dunstan's Square. The sound of Linda's husky call, like dried leaves scuffling over the pavement, did nothing to ease her discomfort. The last thing she wanted was a post-mortem.

"Are you going my way? Abbey Green?" Linda panted.

"No, I promised to look in on Elinor."

"I'll walk with you as far as the Centre then. Okay?"

"My car's parked at the Department."

"Cheeky! Give us a lift to Abbey Green, then?"

"Why didn't you stay?" Kate walked on.

"It suddenly grew less inviting. Jessica started a new tack – should you be allowed to teach with your background. So I clocked her one and called it a day."

"You shouldn't have done that on my account!" Kate was appalled and at the same time unaccountably humbled by what seemed like Linda's unsolicited support.

"It wasn't entirely. God knows what Elinor sees in her, but it's a disease you catch from the most unlikely people, isn't it? Like clap." Kate gave an involuntary laugh.

"I don't think Elinor would appreciate your very, very lovely word-picture." She negotiated the mini down Carriage Hill. "Did Elinor tell you?"

"If you're good-looking people assume you only bother to gaze at your own reflection and never notice what's going on round you. I do what you do, Kate Henderson. Keep my eyes open. You need to be observant to be a worthwhile teacher. Left here. Though it's not easy to interpret what you see and

I've been wrong once or twice recently. Peter's cleverer than I realised. Third along, by the street lamp. What was he trying to do, do you think? Apart from dropping Elinor in the shit and trying to get something on you."

"Setting us all by the ears?"

"But why? What's he got out of it? Even your thumbnail autobiography must have fallen to the ground like a lead balloon once he realised it was all ancient history."

"Less of the 'ancient'," Kate grunted, pulling on the handbrake. "I'm fed up with being treated like a pensioner. Soggy in the head and menopausal at that."

"I'd say you were pretty well on the ball. For your age." Teeth glinted. "But I wish Terry'd been there. I was expecting him and he might know what Peter's at these days." Linda jack-knifed her length to get out of the passenger seat. "Thanks for the lift."

There was no reply to Kate's knocking at Elinor's digs, although a light was burning downstairs, and she drove home very relieved. Domina met her in the kitchen, sleepily stretching out one back leg after the other as she stepped out of her basket. Kate picked her up and tickled her ears, but she was quite content to be put back onto her cushion where she curled up once more like a woolly ammonite.

Kate went into the living-room and poured herself a stiff whisky, the first time for months she'd felt its need. Stupid sods, she reassured herself. Yet she'd thrown them Vivvy, an offering to the pursuing wolves, rather than let them come within sniffing distance of Celia. Where had Peter picked up a clue to their relationship? Had he only been fishing? Vivvy, who'd dined out for years on her life history – to Kate's occasional embarrassment – was invulnerable, but Celia deserved better. *She* couldn't answer back.

9

The chief source of speculation after Guy Fawkes weekend was not Kate's past, however, but Peter's inexplicable disappearance. His car was parked at the Department on that Monday morning, the keys still in the ignition, but by lunch-break it was clear that he was nowhere in the building. When, after several days there was still no sign of Peter and his car hadn't been moved, the Principal notified the police. They towed the car away and searched the flat – flat and car keys being on the same bunch – but they found no trace of him and the flat was as it had been left on the night of the party. But nastier. Presumably Peter's family was approached, but nothing was known of his family among the students.

A second mystery was that Terry Sinclair had also disappeared. He hadn't shown up for work at The Duke's Wine-Bar since about the night of Peter's party, as far as his employer could remember, and he hadn't been seen since. Whether or not the two disappearances were connected no one knew, and nor could anyone see why they should be, except for the fact that the two men had shared the flat. Kate didn't care to question Linda about the traumatic triangle idea she'd had at the party, and Linda for her part didn't seem concerned by either man's disappearance.

Were it not for his car, Peter might simply be imagined to have left to take up his offer at Lethbridge – if they were prepared to have him without qualifications – intending to let the Department know in his own good time. It was presumed that the Principal must be in touch with Lethbridge, but there was no announcement of anything resulting from that contact.

It was not a very likely lead but there seemed to be no more probable alternatives and for some it explained his insistence on throwing the party as a hero's farewell. Kate privately believed that, having stirred up trouble for himself in the town, Peter had discreetly retired. And no great loss. Jeff and Gordon might have known more through their friend, but Kate was inhibited from asking by their unexpectedly distant attitude.

The Principal made vague enquiries about the party held on the fourth of November but nothing much was learned. The others had more or less all left together around midnight, the gaiety having fallen rather flat after Linda's exit, though Peter had remained as fit and cheerful as ever. Jessica, sent home by taxi shortly after the rest, agreed that Peter was in good spirits and they'd planned to meet the following day, Bonfire Saturday.

Jessica wasn't happy, however, and she grew more sulky and withdrawn as the days went by without a word from Peter at Lethbridge, where she insisted he must be. Peter had promised to take her to the British Lions bonfire party and he hadn't come for her. She at first felt let down and annoyed and after that perhaps even very lonely, since there was no longer any of that earlier competition to squire her about. She had no time for the women, except to dramatise her dislike of Kate and Linda, and when she shrugged off Barbara's twittering offers of support she was left alone. Elinor watched Jessica more and more thoughtfully but didn't approach her directly – or not as far as Kate knew.

For her own part, Kate was aware of a change in the quality of her relationships after the party. Liz became even more protective, Linda more friendly, Elinor more dependent. However, she was surprised to find Jeff and Gordon apparently more wary of her, though they hadn't even been at the gathering. Barbara too, more exaggeratedly, treated her with caution and behaved as if Kate might suddenly dart out and bite her. But Kate had most grievously offended against 'What the Neighbours Say' and she recognised Barbara's symptoms.

Kate herself allowed no difference to show in her attitude, and particularly she tried not to appear unnaturally natural.

She had a Comparative Education paper to prepare and so concentrated on that, content for the moment to establish a new equilibrium.

* * *

That was the position till one Friday lunch-break three weeks after Peter's party when Kate was with Ruth Stanton by the goldfish pool. A spell of wet, misty weather, during which Domina had trailed muddy paws incessantly through the kitchen, had been followed by a run of piercing frosts. On the Thursday there had been a brief thaw with what Kate grew to think of as 'floor-cloth weather'. But late that night the sky was like a pin-cushion of stars and the temperature fell back down around freezing. Friday at the poolside was bright and sparkling with the sun shining a false promise. Kate gravitated to the peace and the distant prospect over the city to be found at the stone bench, and Ruth joined her there while she waited to give her architectural lecture at two-thirty.

"It's quite solid, the ice," Kate told her as she sat down. "What happens to the goldfish? I've often wondered."

"My dear Kate, I've no ideas at all about the metabolism of garden goldfish. Perhaps they hibernate. There may be clefts under the rockery where the frost doesn't reach. You can't know the ice is solid to the bottom, anyway."

"But even so, it must block off their oxygen supply."

"Hm. It's broken up among those reeds. Perhaps there is enough disturbance with the wind or something to stop it freezing over completely. Kate, I find this subject entirely boring."

But Kate, gazing at the reeds that fringed the far side of the pond, felt a sensation like a mule kick in the pit of her stomach. She looked away and back again. It was still there. She gave a groan and half rose to her feet.

"Kate? I didn't mean – my dear, are you all right?"

"What can you see among those far reeds, Ruth? Say, four o'clock from that pinkish stone." Kate couldn't now drag her eyes away.

"Nothing exciting. No – wait. I see where you mean. A glove, is it? A gardening glove."

"No, Ruth. It's too – filled out, sort of."
"Wait there."
Ruth walked round the pond, peering, and trod cautiously over the frosted rockery. She crouched, leaned forward and touched.

"Kate!" Ruth raised horrified eyes. "I think you'd better find Professor Edwards. Don't make a noise about it, but ask him to ring the police and then come here." Ruth's voice was unsteady. Kate felt her own knees give as she tried to walk calmly over the crisp grass. Peter had been found.

* * *

The Principal walked back with her to where Ruth sat on the stone bench looking sick. He examined what they pointed out to him; the tip of a hand, its curled fingers probing through the ice at the base of the reeds.

"I must go back and wait for the police," his voice shook. "Miss Stanton, I should be most grateful if you felt able to continue with your lecture as usual. And you, Miss Henderson, would you normally attend Miss Stanton's lecture?" Kate nodded. "Then please do so today. I need not ask you to – be discreet about this discovery. I imagine you might both be required to see the police officers after the lecture. Will you make yourselves available? Perhaps if you came straight to my study you would be more comfortable."

Kate and Ruth made their way in silence to the hall.

"God knows how I'm going to manage this," Ruth said at the door. Kate could only give her a wavering smile as she walked like a zombie to a seat at the back. The blackout blinds were pulled down ready for the slides. Ruth asked for the lights to be put out immediately instead of beginning with her usual introduction.

Kate believed little out of the ordinary would have been noticed. Ruth instilled more interest in her subject even on an off-day than some of the others could manage at their peak, and Kate could only admire the even voice and lucid-sounding delivery, though she comprehended very little herself. Her brain seemed to rattle in her head like a billiard-ball, cued first this way then that as each fresh thought struck it.

She stayed behind at the end, as she usually did now, to help Ruth pack her slides away and carry the projector back to the equipment store. There was no sign of activity round the pond as they walked back from the hall. Kate tried to pull her wits together as the Principal answered Ruth's knock.

There were two men with Professor Edwards and he introduced them as Detective-Chief Inspector McPherson and Detective-Sergeant Breckon. Plain-clothes policemen, Kate registered, and saw her own name and Ruth's noted down by the Sergeant.

"Which of you ladies first saw the – the indications of something abnormal?" the Detective-Chief Inspector asked. His voice was soothing and he looked friendly and interested; like a terrier, Kate decided. Rather like Ruth's Hermann. She smiled dimly at him while Ruth answered.

"I see. An unpleasant experience for the both of you. Then, unless you need to hurry off, Miss Stanton, I'll talk to Miss Henderson first, if I may. Is there somewhere you might sit with Miss Stanton, sir?" he asked the Principal without giving Ruth time to reply.

"A cup of tea in my sitting-room, perhaps?" The Principal smiled encouragingly at them both. "Just press that bell-push when you're ready, will you?"

"Well, now, Miss Henderson," the Detective-Chief Inspector moved a chair forward for Kate when Ruth and the Principal had left. "Just a few facts. First, your full name and address – " the Sergeant wrote busily as Kate dictated. "Second-generation expatriate, Miss Henderson?"

"Both my parents were born in England."

"Mine likewise," he beamed at Kate. "I was born in Hexham. Do you know that part?" Kate shook her head, wishing she could say she knew Hexham very well and they could talk about that instead. "Ah, well. We cannot all be so fortunate. Now, just tell me how this discovery came about."

So Kate told him, slightly self-consciously, about the goldfish conversation and her recognition of the object among the reeds.

"Yes. I see. That's very clear," came the soft voice after a thoughtful pause. "Isn't it, John?" the Detective-Chief

Inspector added more sharply, recalling his Sergeant's attention from Kate's hair at which he seemed to have taken exception. Let him thank his lucky stars he doesn't have to live with it, Kate stared back defiantly. She turned back to the Detective-Chief Inspector in time to catch the tail-end of a grin. "Now, about your colleague, Mr. Peter Colebrook – he's been missing for several weeks, I understand. You knew him pretty well?"

"We all knew him pretty well," Kate replied stiffly. She resented the grin. "He was one of our leading lights."

"I see. Well, that's all we need for the moment, Miss Henderson. You'll be asked to sign your statement when my Sergeant translates it from his version of shorthand, but we'll let you know." He pressed the bell-push. "You'll maybe find a cup of tea for yourself?"

* * *

Kate followed the Principal to his sitting-room and thankfully accepted the tea. Reaction had set in and she was grateful for his presence. He no longer seemed so distant.

"Professor Edwards, the pond was frozen solid. I could stand on the ice. Will they have to – to leave him there?" Kate blurted, unable to blot out the thought of those sad remains awaiting a thaw.

"My dear Miss Henderson, you're having waking nightmares! They have removed him. In effect they have almost emptied the pond. He – the body – had been lashed to the basket affair the water-plants grow in. The police officers merely raised the entire block, ice, plants and all. There was no brutish handling, you may rest assured, for they summoned a Land Rover with lifting gear. I am afraid Mr. Watt is not going to think much of the tyre marks across his lawns or the – er – evacuation of his pond."

The Principal talked on until Kate had recovered her equilibrium. And he was so right, she thought. These were all details she'd wonder about in the dead of night. But – what? Lashed to the basket of plants? Entangled in the roots, she supposed.

Kate braced herself for another question.

"You were there? What happened to Peter?" She thought he

gazed at her almost pityingly and imagined she must look as sick as she felt. He went over to the window, where the near darkness of the late afternoon brought its own touch of dread, drew the curtains and switched on the light.

"It was my duty to be there. Not only has the tragedy occurred in what I think of as my domain, but more importantly it may have involved one of my own students. As you too have assumed. My dear Miss Henderson," he returned to sit opposite Kate and she saw how drawn he looked. She wished she'd had more tact. "My dear Miss Henderson," he repeated heavily, "I was inexpressibly shocked. One cannot tell, you see, who the unfortunate man was. He was naked and virtually – in short – headless. That is all one could see." He wiped a hand down his face as if reassuring himself of his own identity.

Murder? Kate was more incredulous than shocked, now that her own private horrors were under control. She could hardly believe that Peter, so strong in his self-confidence, his powers of attraction, his cleverness – all the qualities Kate had felt reserve about but which gave Peter the edge over anyone else she knew – that Peter with all his advantages could suffer such a miserable defeat. Headless and naked in a goldfish pond?

Yet hadn't he in that week edged and niggled many of them to the verge at least of physical violence, herself included? Elinor, Robert, even Jessica – or especially Jessica – maybe Alice, Linda and who knew how many others outside the Department had cause at least for anger. But murder? It was the fact of his murder that seemed more dismaying than its method. Kate felt ashamed of her inability to share the Principal's horror at what he'd seen.

"Murder!"

"Yes. Oh, yes. There can be no doubt about that. But you must try not to anticipate the worst, Miss Henderson. We do not yet know that it was Peter Colebrook. I shall have to make a formal announcement of this discovery on Monday, and perhaps by then we may at least know the – the dead man's identity. But I cannot expect it to remain unpublicised till then. News of this macabre quality travels unhealthily fast.

And I must warn you, in case you have not already considered the point, that you may find yourself uncomfortably situated, Miss Henderson. Curiosity, speculation – and so forth," the Principal explained as Kate looked vacant. "You did find him, after all. But please do not allow yourself to be troubled. Refer anyone to me. It will not be a pleasant time for any of us, I am afraid." Rather late in the day, Kate remembered the avidity of newspapermen. Such a sensational discovery would be their meat and drink and a breakfast-time delectation for a million households.

Ruth returned to the sitting-room escorted by Detective-Chief Inspector McPherson. She looked strained.

"We've finished here now, sir, though I'm afraid we may be back for further enquiries. We'll inform you, of course, as soon as we know any details. I'll be leaving some of my men to search the grounds and my Sergeant will interview your head gardener. Meanwhile, Miss Stanton, Miss Henderson, will you be at your homes over the weekend? Yes? Just to know we can be in touch if necessary." As he left the room his smile reduced the possibility of a visit from the CID to the level of a carefree social call. But even the Principal's authority in his own domain had been superseded.

"May I recommend that you say nothing of your part in this affair to anyone?" the Principal advised. "I shall certainly tell no one. It may help to minimise your – inconvenience over the weekend. The Detective-Chief Inspector agrees with me that no good purpose can immediately be served by publishing your names. Meanwhile you have friends you can call on for company? Family?" He looked dubiously at Kate. They both reassured him, bleakly. Kate felt a sharp pang of loneliness for Vivvy and wished on the one hand that she was at home, and on the other was relieved that she wasn't.

"Are you going to be all right?" Kate asked Ruth as they walked downstairs.

"Oh, God, Kate! Only if I can talk it out. How do you feel? Could you bear me to take up your invitation to spend an evening at – at your place? I'll drive you there now, anyway."

"Please," Kate answered with relief. "It'll be the pottiest of pot-luck, but of course you must come."

"Thank heavens! I'd better give Hermie a trot first – may he come too? He'll be no trouble."

"What's he like about cats?" Kate asked tentatively, as she shut herself into Ruth's car and fumbled for the belt.

"Indifferent. His litter was brought up with a couple of family cats. You've got one, have you? Hermie won't mind."

Not quite my point, thought Kate limply, picturing Domina's petulance, or worse still her rancorous removal to a more considerate address.

★ ★ ★

Kate peered cautiously down the hall as she opened the front door. There was no sign of Domina and Kate knew she'd taken cover until she'd sussed out the stranger. She took Ruth into the living-room only to find, when she switched on the light, that Domina was already there crouched on a chair inside the door. Now what? Ruth was hard on Kate's heels, with Hermann sniffing the interesting strangeness around him.

"I'll light the fire," Kate said, and leapt like a bolting kangaroo across the room. She stood rooted to the hearth-rug watching Ruth's conventionally slower approach with Hermann behind her.

"No hurry," Ruth told her placidly, "though I do like an open fire." She sank down on one of the fireside chairs. Still mesmerised, Kate watched Domina lean down and take a swipe at Hermann as he trotted past.

He must have felt the breeze of the near miss for he stopped and looked round, more aggrieved than annoyed, Kate thought, mentally standing on one leg with suspense. But Hermann sat down to gaze peaceably at Domina. She stared back offensively, her fur slightly ruffled. Kate willed her to stay put.

"Kate?" Ruth prompted.

"Er – they've met." Why hadn't she the nous to catch Dommy up as she passed? Ruth turned to follow Kate's look.

"Hermann, here!" Hermann merely gave his tail a couple of thumps on the carpet and didn't move.

But whatever it was, Ruth's voice or Hermann's obvious

innocence, Domina's explosive potential was defused. She suddenly yawned, rudely and pinkly in his face – solely for the purpose of showing off her needle-like teeth, Kate believed – turned her back and apparently fell into a bored sleep. Hermann whimpered and beat the carpet invitingly, but Domina merely twitched the tip of her tail. Hermann wandered disconsolately to the hearth-rug where he threw himself down. Kate breathed again. She knelt to give him a relieved pat and set a match to the fire.

"It's a sort of recycled steak and kidney pie, more or less, for later," Kate told Ruth as she drew the curtains. "Have a drink now? Something recuperative rather than preprandial, perhaps. Whisky?"

"The hot button, Kate, you discerning woman! And neat, please. This is wonderful, you know, in spite of the grisly lead-in. I've always loved this room. It's ironic, isn't it, that you must've been somewhere in the house when I used to visit Celia and we never met. And now it's Celia who's missing. Who's the lady?" Ruth asked after a pause. "She's new," and she nodded at the framed portrait over the mantelpiece. It was a head and shoulders study of Vivvy on her eighteenth birthday. Kate was particularly pleased with it.

"My daughter, Vivvy," she answered calmly, as she'd answered over all the years. Kate gave Ruth her drink and sat down. Ruth's expression remained pleasantly enquiring, though one eyebrow quirked in surprise. Live and let live. "She's just started at college. Celia gave me a home when I was pregnant and nearly at my wits' end. Vivvy adored her."

"The girl with you at Celia's funeral? Celia never mentioned her."

"Only on my account, though neither of us swept Vivvy under the carpet. They were good friends, Celia and Vivvy."

Domina slid off her chair like a slow cascade of black silk, and flowed with scarcely perceptible movement over the carpet. She loved the fire and even Hermann's presence on the rug didn't stop her making for her favourite place on Kate's lap. When Domina had settled, head down along Kate's trousered legs, her purring finally penetrated Hermann's dreams. But he only lifted his head to look at her, flattening his ears placatingly and thumping his tail, before he flopped again with a sigh that seemed to inflate his entire body.

"Look," Ruth spoke at last. "If it doesn't seem too prying I would like to know more about – you know – your daughter and how you came to live with Celia. But for the moment what you've told me adds a worrying dimension to one of Goronwy's fears. He thinks, you see, that you may have been carrying a torch for that student who disappeared – and who may or may not now be found. I suppose you know what they did find?"

"Who? Goronwy?"

"Professor Edwards to you. He seems to think you and this Colebrook boy were pretty close at one time. Knowing what I thought I knew about you, I felt he was barking up the wrong tree. But now – " Kate sighed violently.

"I would've thought that he at least had more discernment. It seems to have been the in-gossip at the Department all term and I'm just cringing to find the staff thought no differently from my blasted colleagues. Dammit, Ruth, Peter was nearly twenty years younger than me! He only loved himself and he was a nasty piece of work into the bargain. Believe me, I was not beguiled. I don't know why he tried to reel me in – make me an accessory, but he did. Literally, like a button-hole or a tasteful pair of socks. It made some of them think there was something going on between us." Kate stroked Domina's back and set her off purring again.

"Odd," Ruth murmured thoughtfully. "To take the trouble, I mean, if you were indifferent – not that you aren't worth the trouble. Goronwy also thinks that latterly he was involved with someone else. I suppose he finally took the hint, did he? How did you feel about that?"

"Bloody," Kate replied abruptly. "But only because he used me to stir her up and then to fend her off. I don't think he felt anything for her, either, but it amused him to – present himself as Adonis snarled over by a couple of bitches. In the end I hated him because of what he was playing with and the humiliation he inflicted on me."

"Hate? Humiliation? Those are strong words, Kate. Because of this other woman?"

"No. He built me up – set me up to be stripped in public. I realised afterwards he'd planned the exercise. A stupid party he threw just before he disappeared. A truth game. He stirred speculation so skilfully, and partly through the jealousy of this ineffably stupid woman, I told them about Vivvy to defend myself. He seemed to be hinting about Celia, though God knows how he can have discovered anything. But he was very clever, you know. Talk to Miss Welborne. I'm – academically sorry he's dead, I suppose, but surprised more. I thought he was a winner. But I don't feel anything personally except the dregs of the old anger against him."

"If it comes to the question, Kate, you may find it difficult not to – to give the impression that it's the anger of a woman scorned. You realise that?"

"Not possible," said Kate indifferently, but Ruth still looked concerned.

"You haven't convinced me. Academically speaking."

"I don't know that I need to convince anyone. Those who know me know the truth and those who don't, don't matter. And if it isn't Peter's body the question doesn't arise anyway."

10

In the event Kate was untroubled by visits from the police over the weekend. She and Ruth agreed to take Professor Edwards' advice and not even hint that they'd made the discovery of the body. No doubt it would become known in time, but by then their part wouldn't hold the same interest.

And meanwhile it seemed that everyone concerned was keeping quiet about the affair. None of the weekend nationals carried the story of a headless corpse in the lily-pond, and nor was there any hint of it in Monday's dailies. The local paper came on sale on Tuesdays.

So the Principal's announcement, at the start of his Monday lecture hour, came as a stunning shock to the other students. Though he stressed that a firm identification was not yet possible, Kate saw the general assumption that the corpse had to be Peter's. He gave no details other than that the body of a man had been found in the ornamental pond over the weekend.

"Since I cannot expect any of you to be receptive at this moment," he'd ended, "I am cancelling the rest of this period. However, I must ask those of you who attended Mr. Colebrook's party to gather in the Common Room. Detective-Chief Inspector McPherson, the officer in charge of the investigations, will find you there in due course. Please answer his questions as helpfully as you can."

Kate returned with the others to the main building, grateful that Professor Edwards hadn't given away her involvement. She found herself a chair in the Common Room, wondering if the police would need to see her again, and tried to shut out the sound of Jessica's raised voice.

For Jessica had emerged from her cocoon of gloomy

indifference and seemed now to be making the most of her escalation into hysterics. After all, thought Kate sourly, Peter's death reinstated her at the centre of the stage.

"He must've come up here to – to think. To get over his hurt at the way you all abused his hospitality. You all treated him disgustingly that night," she rounded on the crowded room, her strident voice lashing at them while they stared morosely back at her. "He was walking in the fresh air and tripped and fell in the dark. Depressed and preoccupied he would've been. Physically and emotionally exhausted. You all killed him!"

"Why would he have brought his car?" Liz asked reasonably. "It's hardly any distance from his flat. If he wanted a walk, why didn't he walk here?"

"Because he was physically exhausted, of course," Linda grunted, as she tried to work her way over to where Kate was sitting.

"And if he was going to use his car anyway, he could've run you home," Alice pointed out. "But he called you a taxi – "

"We don't know it happened on the night of the party, though," Liz objected. Kate wondered at the calm that seemed to have settled on them all after their immediate reactions to the Principal's announcement. Perhaps Jessica's words had forced an introspective detachment. Or it was simply easier to bear the news that way.

"He wouldn't have left his place in all that mess, surely? It must've happened that night. And anyway, he couldn't have drowned in such a didi pond by accident unless he was paralytic. He wasn't drunk when we left," Alice declared unwisely.

"Of course he wasn't drunk! And why do you say it wasn't an accident? It was you and Robert, wasn't it? *You* were blind drunk, Robert! It was disgusting! You pushed him!"

"Having first persuaded him to drive me here?" Robert asked, red in the face.

"You waited for him and – "

"Oh, don't be so ridiculous! How could he have known Peter'd come here?" Alice demanded hotly.

109

"Have you wondered why, if it was an accident that happened on the night of the party as Jessica first suggested – until the chance to sharpen her claws became too attractive – why the body wasn't found floating weeks ago?" Linda's croaking voice shut off the noise in the room. "It's what I've been wondering," she continued in the thoughtful silence. "And while we're talking about disgusting behaviour, Peter's takes some explaining, Jessica. Why did he go out of his way to be such a prick that night? And you behaved like a cheap trollop."

"*You* to talk of disgusting behaviour! You *hit* me!"

"While Peter watched with interest. And you were trying your not very fine Italian hand at character assassination."

"Kate Henderson! It was *she* who ruined the whole evening! She knows more about it than she's saying! Ask her where she went when she ran out on the rest of us!"

"I know where she went," Linda replied with contempt. "I was with her. And you'd better watch what you're saying or you'll find yourself in trouble."

"I'm not afraid of *you*, Linda Mayer, or any of you! You were all jealous of Peter. He outshone you all. You planned this between you, pretending to be his friends and then – "

"Linda meant in trouble with the police," Kate interrupted. "Wild accusations will only – "

"*You* did it! You wanted to hurt him! I saw how you looked – murderous!" Oh, go and stew, thought Kate wearily. "You were jealous of me – "

"For Chrissake!" Robert exploded. "You're off your loaf! We all heard Peter tell you he got nowhere with Kate. If he had, do you think he'd have looked twice at you? Why should she be jealous of you?" That's torn it, Kate decided, as Robert's good intentions merely poured oil on dying embers. "And if she was, she'd have tipped *you* into the pool, not Peter. Make sense!"

"You don't know anything about it! You were so drunk you couldn't even walk across the room! *You* were jealous of Peter!"

"You can't have it both ways," Alice snapped. "If Robert was that drunk he couldn't have hurt Peter. And if he wasn't, kindly bloody well shut up saying he was. Why are *you* so keen to call this murder anyway? We only know he's dead. What do you know we don't? *You* were the last with Peter. We've only got your word for it that you left so soon after the others. Really, you're *so* bloody stupid, aren't you?" So much for introspective detachment, thought Kate, remembering that it had been Alice herself and not Jessica who'd first hinted that it couldn't have been an accident.

In the fierce, no-holds-barred recriminations that followed no one heard the door open. Only a brief lull, while Alice and Jessica refilled their lungs, permitted a man's voice to be heard.

"Ah! Here you all are. Thank you for being so prompt." Detective-Chief Inspector McPherson made his way to the centre of the room. Detective-Sergeant Breckon remained by the lockers, where he rested his notebook as he wrote. "Can you all find yourselves somewhere to sit?"

To Kate it seemed a chilling replay of the scene in Peter's sitting-room, as all those standing quickly formed a rough circle round the room either on the remaining chairs or on the floor. There was complete silence.

"That makes it much easier," the Detective-Chief Inspector approved. He introduced himself and his Sergeant, genially chatty, yet Kate thought they all felt like mice hypnotised by a snake. "Now, you'll have been told why we're here. I understand you were all present at a party given by one of your fellow-students, Peter Colebrook, on November fourth. Is anyone not here who attended that party?" No one answered but all stared stolidly back at the Detective-Chief Inspector. "Good, then. Your Principal has given me a list of your names and some information regarding the order in which you all left that night. I'd just like to recap. It'll not take us long." He smiled comfortably round the room. A friendly snake, thought Kate. Look, no fangs. But if anything could neutralise the taint of sudden death and project an appearance of normality it was this gently interested approach.

He started with Kate.

"So." He looked briefly at his notes. "Miss Henderson left first – quite early on, about nine o'clock, would it be? Miss

Henderson?" The D-C.I. looked vaguely round the room, his eyes sliding casually over Kate.

"Yes." She raised her hand to catch his attention.

"Ah. Miss Henderson. Why did you leave so much before the others?"

"But I followed very shortly after. I'm Linda Mayer."

"Indeed so." The D-C.I. regarded his notes while the Sergeant stared at Linda in frozen disbelief. "About ten minutes later, I see. Would that be right?" Linda nodded. "But that still doesn't answer my question, Miss Henderson."

"I left early – I didn't see the time – because the party had taken a – an embarrassing turn and I felt uncomfortable." For God's sake put it down to me being of a certain age – or uncertain age – Kate prayed, sensing the uneasiness in the room.

"Peter let her see she hadn't deceived him with her lies," Jessica broke in, scarlet with feverish anticipation of Kate's further humiliation. "He made her admit her – her immorality! He showed her up!" Bugger Jessica. In the dumbstruck silence that followed Kate heard the Sergeant utter the sound usually spelt 'tsk-tsk'.

"Dear me," murmured the D-C.I. at last. "Can you be referring to Miss Henderson's daughter?" Kate stiffened, bothered that the police should already be in possession of that tit-bit of information, but Linda gave an appreciative laugh.

"Yes! Yes!" Jessica began eagerly, and then realised that her punch-line was about to fall flat. "But she practically boasted about it," she rallied.

"I see. And you are Miss – ?"

"Jessica Nicholls. I was Peter's fiancée."

"Indeed? I was not aware – "

"Nor was he," Linda snorted, and a light rustle of laughter stirred in the room like leaves in a breeze. "He treated her like dirt but she bounced right back, begging for more. It was loathsome. And before you ask, I left just after Kate – Miss Henderson – because I slapped that stupid little fool. And who could follow that?"

Kate noticed crossly that the Sergeant seemed to have

constituted himself a barometer of social etiquette, and now he stared at Linda in shocked reproof. The D-C.I. too seemed taken aback by Linda's sunny admission.

"Er – do you confirm this, Miss Nicholls?"

"She hit me and left," Jessica agreed sullenly.

"Can you tell me why?" He silenced Linda with a look.

"Everyone was horrible that night," Jessica replied tremulously. Kate urgently wanted to tear at the intricately permed mat of cherubic curls arranged in such careful disorder around Jessica's unreasoning head.

"Well, we'll leave that just now," the D-C.I. said tactfully after a moment. "Miss Henderson, where did you go when you left the party?"

"I came back here to pick up my car. I'd parked it in the grounds – "

"So she *was* here!" Jessica pounced dramatically. "I said she knew more about all this – "

"Miss Nicholls!" The official voice cracked across Jessica's. "I must warn you against that kind of talk." But see; it strikes, it bites. "You really could get into very serious trouble, as Miss Henderson told you."

Kate's attention sharpened. She glanced at the permanently locked door near where she sat. It connected with a small study annexe which, like the Common Room, opened into the hall. She looked back at Detective-Chief Inspector McPherson's rueful expression.

"An unworthy thought, Miss Henderson. And you were all talking so loudly," he added plaintively. Kate was pleased to see the Sergeant looking decently mortified as Linda's sardonic laugh rang out. There was an uneasy murmur and sound of shuffling as it dawned on them all that their accusations and counter-accusations had been overheard. Jessica merely looked excited and defiant.

"On my way back here," Kate continued firmly, "Miss Mayer caught me up and I gave her a lift to where she lives on Abbey Green. Then I went to call on Miss Purbeck in Kaleyard Lane. But it was only a vague arrangement and she – was otherwise engaged. So I drove on home."

"Miss Purbeck – is she a student here?"

"Yes. She was unable to come to the party. Quite a few didn't come."

"So. What time did you get home?"

"I can't be certain. My – my daughter's away at college. I don't know if anyone saw me arrive back."

"Perhaps you can help with times, Miss Mayer?"

"It was about nine-thirty when Kate dropped me off. Mum got me something to eat and we watched the box till we went to bed."

How strange, mused Kate, to think of Linda with a Mum who'll fix her a scratch supper when an evening out falls flat, and perhaps a Dad who'll sympathise with her disappointment, and a Gran who's been admitted to an old people's home. Linda seemed too rare for such an ordinary domestic background. When Kate listened again the Detective-Chief Inspector was questioning Liz.

"It would seem that you were the next person to leave, Miss Jackson. At about what time was that, can you recall?"

"Somewhere around eleven-fifteen. My fiancé was arriving by the ten-fifty-eight and we'd arranged to meet at Peter's flat. We left very soon after he got there. By the time he'd walked up from the station and I'd persuaded him he didn't want to stay on for the party it must've been about eleven-fifteen." Liz dictated Adrian's name and address – 'just for the record'. "But for that arrangement I'd have left with Kate. We all should've, including you, Jessica – "

"Those of us who could walk, anyway," Linda muttered.

"Peter's behaviour was, well, insane," Liz ended, the first time Kate had heard her so outspokenly critical of anyone. It was especially unexpected in the circumstances since with Liz's sense of fair play she'd have expected a much more nil nisi approach.

"If I hadn't been drunk I'd have knocked his block off," Robert angrily replied to Linda's implied criticism. "I'm Robert Denham and not very proud of my part that evening," he told the D-C.I. "As you'll no doubt have heard through that door, I disgraced myself and Miss Jepson who was with me. Peter behaved like one of the beastlier Roman emperors – Caligula or someone – and it's true we just let him. I'd sobered up enough to leave with Alice – Miss Jepson – not long after Liz and Adrian. About eleven-thirty. Peter was a beast and you ought to know that. But I'd rather explain myself to you in private," Robert ended grandly, even less inspired than Liz to speak well of the dead.

"Of course you may see me privately, if you wish," the D-C.I. said gently. "And Miss Jepson is – ?" Alice put up her hand. "Thank you. Do you confirm what Mr. Denham has said?"

"Certainly," Alice replied coolly. "Robert – had too much to drink but Peter was sober – and behaved like a pig. At about eleven-thirty we walked to Robert's digs first, in Pillory Street, and I saw him inside. Then I went on to my own place two houses away. You can confirm that." Alice dictated the addresses.

"Eminently checkable," the D-C.I. assured her calmly. "And then, apparently, the rest of you left in a body at about midnight, except for Miss Nicholls who waited for a taxi and departed perhaps five minutes later. Any corrections to that?" Heads were shaken silently. "And Mr. Colebrook seemed cheerful enough all that time? In spite of the fact that his party had, well, fallen rather flat. He made no mention of going away anywhere? Miss Nicholls?"

How soon were they all clear of St. Dunstan's Square, Kate wondered. Was there someone still there to see Jessica leave; who knew that Peter was left alone? For that matter any of them could have come back later after establishing some sort of alibi. The realisation made her uncomfortable.

"He wasn't planning to go away," Kate heard Jessica say. "He promised to take me out the next night. But the frightful trouble people caused all through his party must've depressed him. I mean, he'd worked terribly hard to make it a success. And once I'd gone everything was suddenly just too much for him." She put her hand to her eyes.

"Are you saying now that he drowned himself because his rotten Saturnalia didn't go with a swing?" Robert laughed in disbelief.

"And you say he was in happy spirits at midnight, Miss Nicholls, and looking forward to seeing you the next day. But you're all jumping the gun, you know. We cannot be certain yet that it was Mr. Colebrook's body recovered from the pool." The D-C.I. smiled cheerfully at their amazement. "Did your Principal not tell you that identification isn't certain at present?"

"Well, he did, but – not Peter? But it must be!" Jessica protested in dismay, for all the world like a disappointed child, thought Kate in wonder at her lack of poise. "Then who?"

"As to who, if not Mr. Colebrook – well, identification is always difficult where the head's been taken off." Kate felt the tension tighten like piano-wire and was shocked herself. It was an unnecessarily brutal announcement of murder, whose ever the body was. "There seem to be no immediately distinctive features at all on the cadaver," the D-C.I. continued chattily. "So you may be grieving prematurely, Miss Nicholls."

He had now successfully almost persuaded them that it couldn't be Peter's body, and he left them a moment to think that over. Suddenly he whipped his hand out of his pocket and held it high.

"Does anyone recognise this?" They all craned to look. Kate saw that the D-C.I swung a surgical finger-stall by its hook and clip elastic fastening.

"It looks like – Peter was wearing something like that," Barbara's high voice quavered across the silence. "He – he cut his thumb. I asked him about it." She looked ready to faint.

"Indeed so, Miss – ?"

"Jones. Barbara Jones."

"And was he wearing it that night at his party? Can you remember?" But Barbara shook her head. "Did anyone notice if he was?"

"I did," said Alice. "I watched him most of the evening." She glanced at Robert. "We must all have seen him wearing it the few days before."

"Good, good. So which hand, Miss Jepson?"

"His left. It was a lighter colour than that one, though. That can't be the same one."

"Several weeks' immersion in pond-water might account for the change of colour, would you think?" Detective-Chief

Inspector McPherson asked quietly and Alice paled. A sudden – and brutal – volte face on the policeman's part, Kate thought. "Who else knows anything about this cut to Mr. Colebrook's thumb?" No one replied. "Or of any hospital treatment? His arm in a sling? That sort of thing?" the D-C.I. pressed them but no one had anything further to add.

Kate tried to think. Somewhere at the back of her mind a memory tried to surface. She'd been vaguely conscious of Peter wearing a dressing during that last week – *was* it on his left thumb? An elusive shadow of doubt or true memory niggled but she couldn't focus it. Kate could only hear Elinor's voice talking about a champagne bottle, but her new concern for Elinor blotted out even that. She shook her head briefly, as if to shake off an irritation, and returned to the present.

" – so you may continue with today's schedules as planned," the D-C.I. was saying. "My Sergeant will be taking statements from you all about your various departures from and movements after the party, but meanwhile will you give him your names and addresses as you leave the room. Professor Edwards has kindly put a room at our disposal and if we need to see any of you separately we'll send for you there – Room 5. Mr. Denham, perhaps you'd care to come up with me now?" Looking extremely unwell, Robert rose groggily to his feet and Alice stood up with him.

"I'll wait here for you," she murmured, and got a sickly smile in reply.

"Nothing to fret yourselves about," the D-C.I. told them kindly. "But Mr. Denham wanted to see me and so – " he rounded his eyes, inviting a smile, "I make myself available."

"It's all a bit different when you're summoned," Robert mumbled.

"And I want to see you," Jessica said suddenly. Linda gave a noisy sigh. "I'll come with you now, shall I? While Robert's making up his mind."

"That's the spirit. Much better to get it all off your chest," the friendly voice approved ambiguously and Jessica looked uncertain. "Shall we leave it that I'll send for you when I need your help? In fact, you can help us now. The taxi that drove you home – which fleet did it come from, the All-White Cars or the Yellow Diamond? Or was it one of the smaller concerns?"

"I – it was light-coloured. I didn't notice. I was too upset."

"But Mr. Colebrook was in good spirits, you've said. I see." The Detective-Chief Inspector turned away abruptly.

"Will you take over now, Sergeant? I'll be in Room 5 if I'm needed. See you there in a few moments, Mr. Denham."

He went out, leaving a sense of bewilderment and strain at his unexpected return to a tough formality. Kate felt frightened. He knew what he was doing and he was trained to set about achieving his ends with single-minded efficiency. Even with ruthlessness if that became necessary. But they, herself and her colleagues, were like infants on their first day at school. She could guess at the sort of pathetic confidences that Robert intended to volunteer – whatever Jessica had in mind was derisory – but if it was Peter's corpse, heaven help them all. The Detective-Chief Inspector would have as little hesitation in shredding everyone to get at the truth as Peter had displayed for his own amusement.

Kate watched Jessica thrust through the crowd to leave her name and address with the Sergeant. She seemed to be questioning him, but for all her confiding smiles he merely shook his head, replied briefly and turned to the next person waiting. Jessica moved aside.

"Not impressed by the grieving fiancée," Linda observed with a laugh. "Do you think he ever smiles?"

"It would be out of place just now," Liz said quietly and focussed Kate's concern. Liz looked pale and distressed. After her uncharacteristic flare-up and the Detective-Chief Inspector's deliberately shocking description of the corpse, she'd sunk into an equally uncharacteristic state of confusion and bewilderment, turning from one speaker to another as if in hope that all might yet be resolved in decency. "It all seems so unbelievable," she went on, still pleading for some sort of reassurance. "The last thing I thought when Peter disappeared was that he'd been murdered. Oh, I know he'd been pretty unbearable, but this – ! It must've been a chance prowler – psychopathic – like that Nilson creature." Liz shuddered at her own suggestion of a multiple murderer still at large. Oh, God!

She's no more than a child, Kate thought in despair. Not much older than Vivvy after all. For all her slightly maternal and adult impression of equanimity, Liz hadn't the maturity to cope with the sneaking whiff of horror. Liz needed the world to be well.

"All too disorderly, Liz?" Linda asked with a curious look at her. Linda at least wasn't overset. Her cool unconcern seemed to argue a certain callousness, though she was sensitive enough to recognise the cause of Liz's distress. Or perhaps that callousness too was a sign of unnatural pressure, thought Kate, prepared at last to concede that as an onlooker she had seen only such parts of the game that had interested her. She'd been too ready to label and dismiss. And was Linda's callousness any more sinister than her own? "But why a chance prowler? Why did Peter drive here that night, do you think? He'd been up to something, I'm sure of it, and got caught out."

"You mean something criminal? I can't believe it! Why should he?"

"Or something that backfired on him, anyway. Don't forget Terry's missing too, and he'd certainly been in hot water. That's what Peter claimed, if you remember."

"But to cut off his head – it's sick! Why do that? Nobody deserves that!" cried Liz in a last appeal for normality to be resumed.

"To delay identification, I suppose."

As she listened to Linda and Liz, Kate wondered about her original assumption, inspired by what Gordon and Jeff had told her, that Peter had fallen foul of his dubious friends in the city. Obviously, though, he hadn't escaped them. Once again she debated asking the two men for more information, and again she decided against it. It wasn't her business, as she'd pointed out so firmly; and for that reason Kate didn't now add her minimal surmises to the speculative debate around her. Out of a further consideration for Linda's possible sympathies, Kate didn't suggest that her friend Terry's timely disappearance might be susceptible of a more sinister interpretation in the light of events.

11

For Kate the rest of that day seemed to bear no relation to reality. The History of Education seminar at eleven o'clock seemed quite irrelevant in the light of what she feared would be the aftermath of Peter's death. Kate wondered what Dr. O'Hare had really thought of Peter, and others of the staff who'd had much to do with him; whether they believed his disappearance, either through absconding or being rendered a 'cadaver', really represented a crippling loss to the future of the teaching profession.

But perhaps it was she after all, through defensiveness or her non-conforming emotional slant – or perhaps even through personal resentment – who was wrong in dismissing Peter as no great loss. He mightn't, after all, have been much liked but his abilities at least were enviable. He could afford to be arrogant.

Kate suddenly wondered what Celia would have thought of him. Would she have succumbed to his charm? Or would she have recognised him after all as that saddest of all waifs, an egocentric intellectual searching desperately for companionship? Was that what he was? No, Kate reassured herself. He was not. Peter had been up to something and Linda, who knew him, felt that too.

And perhaps others did as well. Kate was aware that among her colleagues there was little more than a general uneasiness, once the shock of the Principal's announcement had been assimilated; uneasiness that would retreat when the corpse's identity was finally established. It was the unease of not knowing for certain rather than the grief of missing Peter. But perhaps those who genuinely did had got over their missing during the weeks before the body was found. Though Kate was not inclined to mourn, she felt in her heart of hearts that someone should. But what if the identity never *could* be proved? It seemed obviously intended that it never should be. Yet what a place to put him, at the very site where Peter would be most readily missed, and where surely in the end he would have been found.

Kate's sense of dislocaton persisted over the next few days. Only Jessica maintained a show of mourning – on alternate days it seemed to Kate. (She now wore a ring set with small green stones of the same implacable shade as the municipal dustbin liners.) On other days she roused a flickering interest in her insistence that Peter was still alive and would return to confound them all.

"He'd better have a bloody good story ready," Linda advised. "Resurrection's been done already."

* * *

During that Monday afternoon and evening the weather reverted to a boringly permanent drizzle, which irritated Kate but left Domina undismayed.

"I thought cats weren't supposed to like the wet," Kate grumbled as she mopped up Domina's trail of footprints that evening. "Thank God you're not a centipede." In the past Kate had tried to towel off the worst of the wet on Domina's coat, but her resentment at such mollycoddling was unmistakable. Presumably she'd grown indifferent to the weather during her straying period. Now Kate merely called her through to the living-room and lit the fire. "Dry off there, you nit."

Kate had just sat down to her supper and a read of the paper when there was a ring at the front door. Unexpected callers were either neighbours, meter readers or double-glazing salesmen. At that hour it had to be a neighbour. Bum, thought Kate, shunting her shepherd's pie back into the oven to keep warm while she answered the door.

"Ah, Miss Henderson," said a soft voice. "I was just passing and thought I'd give you a call. May I come in, if it's quite convenient?" Kate gazed thoughtfully at him for a moment. Just passing indeed.

"Please come in, Detective-Chief Inspector McPherson. I was about to have my supper – which you're welcome to share unless it's forbidden to eat with witnesses. And in that event may I tell you that I'm ravenously hungry but couldn't possibly eat while you sat and watched. Nor can I possibly wait. Would you like to call back later? Or see me, more logically, at Morgan's Mount."

"No, no," protested the Detective-Chief Inspector hurriedly, stepping nimbly over the threshold. "Some supper would go fine – unpredictable hours – dyspepsia – ulcers – " Kate heard him burbling along the hall behind her. "But not if it's any trouble."

"It's shepherd's pie," she told him briskly, as she laid a second place at the kitchen table and brought out the food from the oven. She left him to help himself. "Is Detective-Sergeant Breckon outside and would he like something to eat?" The more the merrier.

"He's busy – interviewing. He may even go hungry to bed," said the D-C.I., helping himself enthusiastically. "But this isn't an official visit, you understand." Kate dug into her meal. She was extremely hungry, and also rather nervous, she realised. They ate in silence.

"That was very good." Detective-Chief Inspector McPherson looked lustfully at the remains of the pie. Kate laughed suddenly.

"Do you want to scrape the bowl?" She felt the indefinable power and pleasure of producing a meal, however simple, for someone hungry and appreciative. Like Domina.

"Now there's a well-loved phrase from my childhood," he beamed back at her and began scraping uninhibitedly.

"How are you about apple pie?"

"Devilish! You mean it?"

"Mm. With acknowledgements to next door's apple tree."

"Ah. The lady with the kittens?"

"You've met?"

"By report only. She can't remember hearing you come home on the night of November fourth. Her telly's at the back. And your other neighbour aggressively minds her own business."

"Which means she told your man to mind his," Kate grinned and passed him the jug of custard. "But she knows what goes on, all right, Miss Lawrence. She's better than a whole army of vigilantes – and a good neighbour."

"Hm. Do you know one William Frost?"

"Certainly. We all know Willy."

"He saw you come home that night. As far as my man could make out from his shorthand speech, you're the only one who dims the headlights when turning off the main road past his cottage, and doesn't light him up like an arc-lamp. Was he ever a P.O.W.? So when, about nine fifty-five on November fourth, a car drove into the village on dimmed lights he was interested – not having seen you set out. He saw you park in the bus pull-in opposite your house. 'And no crime. Only a little car.' He seemed to think we were trying to nick you for a parking violation. And he's sure of the date because it was his birthday and he nearly screwed himself up to ask you in for a dram. Or that's what my man understood him to mean. He got very hot and bothered. So I thought I'd call round and reassure you."

"Poor Willy," murmured Kate, but she was more concerned with the effect of the police enquiries on her neighbours – and, oh God, when the story broke in the papers – ! It didn't bear imagining. And what if they named her? Could they do that without her permission?

Kate got up to clear the dishes into the sink.

"Why such careful enquiries? You surely can't believe that any of us is involved in the – in that – "

"Murder? But why not?" Detective-Chief Inspector McPherson stood in the centre of the kitchen clutching the custard jug and looking vaguely around. Kate took it from him and shut it in the fridge. "Colebrook didn't apparently try to win friends and influence people – at least, I'm not so sure about the second. Even you must have felt the need to – er – chastise him somehow."

But Kate was only half listening. It was all rather hypothetical, and he'd made it clear that she herself couldn't be seriously under consideration after Willy's story. Yet he seemed in no hurry to leave.

"Coffee?" she asked at last, deciding he was friendly and fit to be treated to Celia's living-room.

"Please."

* * *

"Come through to the front. There's a fire lit." Kate picked up the tray of coffee things. Domina would please herself about staying with them. "I could have inflicted some serious damage the night of the party." She answered the D-C.I.'s earlier implication when they were settled by the fire. "But what you feel in the heat of rage is a thing apart. Translating that into cold-blooded action sometime later is quite another. Admittedly I didn't distress myself when he vanished, and can hardly pretend to much distress now he's been found."

"Yet there seems to have been a general assumption that the both of you were, well, friendly enough at one time. Even that you resented it when Colebrook turned his attentions elsewhere."

"I don't think you'll find many to bear out that last piece of – of self-gratification," Kate looked away from the D-C.I. into the fire. "As for the rest, it's true that we were often together, though usually in a group. But we were never 'close' in any sense. In fact he tried to – to collect me," Kate was careful not to protest too much. "But I was suspicious of his intentions. He wasn't a very – liking kind of person, you know."

"Fair enough. I'll come back to one of the points you've just made, but what kind of a person was he?"

There was a considering silence while Kate refilled the coffee-cups.

"He fascinated me," she admitted. "Like a conjuror showing you one empty hand when you're trying hard to see into the other. Perhaps we all saw different people in him and the others may not have my suspicious nature. But from what he generally showed us of himself, he was smooth, cool, sophisticated. Adult. Independent. He was better off than the rest of us too. We had the impression his family was bloated rich, if not belted earls, but he never spoke of his home. He was amusing, good company and very, very quick-witted. He could be quite snide but cleverly and amusingly so – earlier on, anyway. I think he had the sharpest brain of us all, but he sometimes made the mistake of believing we were always – gullible."

"Interesting. We get the impression that his attitude changed latterly – became more aggresssive. But before that was he generally popular? A lad for the ladies?"

Domina had slid away from the fireside like a spreading ink stain when Kate came in with Detective-Chief Inspector McPherson. Now she sat like a tea-cosy under the piano stool, her front paws tucked under her chest and her tail neatly curled to meet them, staring broodingly at the intruder. Kate picked her up and brought her back by the fire to sit on her lap.

"I think we all wondered about the change in him – which somehow brought out the worst in us too. It was as if he felt he had to underline his dominance. But he always seemed quite popular, perhaps more so with the women. They – we didn't resent his – his abilities and advantages, maybe. We were in the market for being mildly flattered, if you like. But he wasn't a ladies' man in your sense."

"And his relationship with you? You seem to have felt somehow threatened by it – did his aggressiveness extend to you?"

"Openly only right at the end, and even then it might've been seen as a bit of a giggle that went wrong at the party. Perhaps you've already heard enough about that. But he always treated me with – well, almost with deference, as if I was fragile. Well, look at me! It made my toes curl," Kate added hotly. "Or with the kind of familiarity that suggested we were two of a kind. Apart. It didn't make life easy. I don't know what he wanted – not me as a person, certainly. But he seemed to have some – some plan in his head. Yes, I know it sounds melodramatic. I think this is the point that struck you just now. Why should he have bothered? I'm trying not to sound like one of those pathetic women always convinced any man must be after them, but partly why he fascinated me was just because he seemed to be up to something and I couldn't see where I fitted in. In the end he made me feel quite nervous – well, anxious, anyway. He kept trying to find out where I lived, you see, not by asking straightforwardly but in devious ways. On at least one occasion I know he lay in wait for me, and after that I went to quite hectic lengths not to come directly home. Paranoid maybe, but it's the effect he had on me. He may have had the same effect on others."

"Did you ever confront him about this?"

"What on earth do you think I'd have sounded like? I'm only telling you because I assume you're reasonably detached and not likely to leap to embarrassing conclusions about middle-aged neuroses." Kate felt her face grow hot.

"You've no idea why?"

"None. I can understand him wanting to – to punish me at the party. In a way I suppose I asked for it. But I don't know why he should want to follow me home or why he behaved as he did to all of us in the end. The staff included."

Kate suddenly remembered what Jeff and Gordon had said about Peter's aggressiveness stemming from fear of his associates in the town, but she decided against volunteering anything for the moment, especially on someone else's behalf. She'd answer these supposedly informal questions and leave it at that. The D-C.I. seemed anyway to have sunk into a full-fed lethargy, his alert eyes hooded as he gazed into the leaping flames around the split apple logs. Courtesy of Willy Frost. The current coal strike had no power to bite while Willy supplied the logs.

Kate sat quietly and stroked Domina until the sound of her purring added to the sense of comfort in the room. This is what you miss in loneliness, she thought; not love so much, or even someone to look after. Companionship.

Detective-Chief Inspector McPherson threw off his thoughtful mood and got up to replace his coffee-cup on the tray. Kate thought he was ready to leave and she began to fold Domina up into a carrying shape. But the D-C.I. returned to stand by the fire and examine the drawing of Vivvy.

"Just discernible likeness between the both of you," he commented. "She has a better nose, would you say? Has she your colouring?"

"To our mutual delight, no," Kate laughed. "And as for the nose too, thank heavens." He peered closer.

"Not signed," he murmured. "An unknown artist?"

"Quite totally unknown." Kate sank back into her chair. The evening was not yet over, apparently.

"Your impressions of Colebrook agree in several respects with what we've already learnt," the D-C.I. sat down and picked up the poker. Who had they questioned, Kate wondered, watching him idly prod the logs and send a shower of sparks leaping up the chimney in a scented frenzy. "How would an artist have seen him? What were his most noticeable physical features?"

Kate found it surprisingly difficult to summon up an image of Peter in clear detail.

"So much of his appearance was clothes and grooming," she recalled. "I suppose he was fairly ordinary, physically, slightly built, not much taller than me." But he'd have seen these details for himself. "He had an attractive smile, good teeth, bright blue eyes and smooth corn-coloured hair. He always *looked* good." Kate stopped suddenly, aghast at the knowledge that remembered details above the neck were probably irrelevant. She continued carefully, "I think the features I found most attractive were his hands."

"His hands! Describe them, please." Kate glanced curiously at the D-C.I. and concentrated her memory.

"Well, they were beautifully kept for a start. Long and narrow, with tapering fingers and filbert nails. Really enviable. And his thumbs were almost as slim as his fingers, almost as if he had five fingers on each hand. They reminded me of portraits of Elizabeth I – you know, the way she displays her hands, hangs them out to dry, pretty well. Peter's were like that. Ladies' hands." But they wouldn't have resembled ladies' hands after weeks drowned in the pool, even in the cold. They would have bloated – rotted. And no fingerprints for possible identification. The goldfish –

"Any rings?"

"None. Perhaps surprisingly."

"A smoker, was he?"

"No nicotine stains, but he smoked occasionally."

"Left or right-handed?"

"Right."

Silence fell again in the room.

"To revert to this morning," the Detective-Chief Inspector said at last, "when I talked to you all in your Common Room. Now, you seemed disturbed by the mention of a cut on Colebrook's thumb. Why was that?" Kate felt the first cool touch of officialdom in the pleasant man across the hearth-rug. As she had surmised, he was a predator. He missed nothing.

"Oh – yes." The maddening half memory spiralled like free gossamer round Kate's brain. "I was puzzled. Someone told me he'd cut it on broken glass but there's something I can't pin down. I tried this morning but it seemed such an insignificant mystery by comparison."

"Hm. Look, I'm afraid my unofficial call has already put you to some trouble, but I'm grateful for your willingness to see me like this. Miss Henderson, may I ask you one more thing? Will you please write down your description of Colebrook's hands for me now? And then I'll go."

Without a word, Kate crossed to Celia's writing desk while Domina huffily retired again under the piano stool, and wrote as quickly and as lucidly as she could. The alternative, she supposed, was a visit to the mortuary. Celia's face as she'd last seen it rose horridly to her mind. As an afterthought Kate signed the sheet of paper and added the date before handing it to the Detective-Chief Inspector.

"Sleep well," he said as he left her. "And thank you for my supper." For which I've sung, Kate told herself wryly, though wisely she kept the comment to herself.

★   ★   ★

The following day, Tuesday, the local paper gave a lengthy, though not detailed, account of 'the shocking discovery on Morgan's Mount'; and there were shorter but more titillating paragraphs in the dailies which were shared round the Common Room. The dailies had arrived late on the scene, but Kate knew they'd soon fasten their scaly teeth into the more avidly readable details, leaving the weekly *Herald* far behind.

'The unclothed body of a young man,' the *Herald* began sedately – it prided itself on being a family newspaper and avoided words like 'naked' – 'was recovered from an ornamental pool at the Department of Education on Morgan's

Mount last Friday. A member of staff raised the alarm and the police were notified immediately. Detective-Chief Inspector McPherson, who is leading the investigations – readers may recall his successful conclusion of the baffling Horror Houseboat case last year – has confirmed that identification of the body is not yet possible. The corpse was headless. There are also other injuries.' Rather a gradiose description of a cut thumb, Kate thought, and read on with amazement that 'a bundle of clothing was discovered during a search of the grounds. The clothes are undergoing forensic examination and some evidence of the man's identity – '

"Did anyone know about these clothes?" Kate looked round from the *Herald*. But no one had heard of such a discovery until that morning.

"They're playing it pretty close to their chests, aren't they?" Robert commented uneasily. "We haven't been told anything."

"No reason to make us a present of everything they discover, I suppose," Liz had found her own safe path. "After all, we're outsiders really."

'No date for the inquest has yet been fixed but a preliminary examination suggests that the body may have been in the pool for up to a month or six weeks. It seems likely from the absence of any other fatal wound that the victim was killed by a blow to the head prior to decapitation.

'Readers are reminded of a short notice appearing in this paper (November 15th) reporting the disappearance of Peter Colebrook, a graduate of this university and a student-teacher at Morgan's Mount. His whereabouts have never been traced. Peter was last seen at a party he gave for his friends on November 4th. His mother, a widow and his only known near relative, died in Runcorn while Peter was still an undergraduate.

'Detective-Chief Inspector McPherson urges, through the medium of this paper, that anyone who saw or heard anything suspicious over Bonfire Weekend, either in St. Dunstan's Square where Peter lived with his friend, Terry Sinclair, also missing since that weekend, or in the area of Morgan's Mount, should get in touch with him at Police Headquarters or with any member of the police force.' There followed a description of Peter that had a slightly shamefaced air about it, as if it knew what a forlorn chance there was of anyone pin-pointed through something so general.

The *Herald* account was so obviously based on a police hand-out that its usually balanced prose was left teetering. Kate sympathised with the attempts of both parties to walk the high-wire of discretion and information. But the Department had been let off lightly as a result, she realised with relief.

★   ★   ★

But Kate's relief was short-lived, for the Wednesday dailies informed and shocked the Department students with new details that threatened Kate's breakfast. The *National Chronicle*, behind a thin veneer of detached investigation, positively wallowed in its slime. It described the 'decapitation' as 'frenzied hacking through the neck so that shreds of flesh were left hanging and splintered bone embedded in the wound'. The *Herald*'s passing reference to 'other injuries' was resolved into an almost visual account of savage castration. The *Chronicle* also revealed that 'the Maniac of Morgan's Mount' had tied the mutilated corpse to the submerged basket, as the Principal had described to Kate, and explained how a fraying rope had allowed a hand to drift to the surface.

The enterprising reporter, who seemed to have access to so much information, had also rooted out the Department gardener (see inset photo, – of Mr. Watt looking mutinous,) and learnt that after the Bonfire Weekend his shed was found broken open and a barrow and a slasher missing. The slasher had been in use several days previously to cut back the rhododendrons. It was understood that the police had removed both items for forensic tests. So regrettably there could be no photo. But there were pictures of the shed, the goldfish pond, the Department buildings, the grounds and the car-park. Yet Kate had seen no intruders nor fallen over hidden cameras.

But whose was the body? The *Chronicle* left itself an opening for further investigative reporting. Was it that of the missing student, Peter Colebrook? His car had been found abandoned in the car-park. His flatmate, Terry Sinclair, was also missing for several weeks but an interview with his family had not been possible, the account complained resentfully. The police had had no success in tracing either of the men, though Detective-Chief Inspector 'Sandy' McPherson claims to be in possession of several vital clues and is confident of an early arrest.'

"Pretty hideous, isn't it?" Robert asked, mistaking Kate's expression of impotent anger that any tragedy could be so further butchered to boost circulation. She handed him back his *Chronicle*. "I suppose everyone must be remembering what I said at the party." He looked sick and frightened.

"No one could imagine you were serious," said Kate, remembering. "I wanted to smash his head in myself."

"You didn't shout about it," he muttered.

Nausea of a more cloying variety was prompted by the *Pioneer*—'Always Ahead of the Times', it brayed. Though that shouldn't be too difficult, thought Kate with affection. The *Pioneer* went straight to what it saw in its tiny tabloid mind as the root of any matter. After a briefly screaming introduction to the murder and mutilation, it sought out the woman in the case. Under a front-page photo of Jessica, looking misty and remote despite her tight blouse and straining buttons and captioned 'I'd just know if he was dead', the *Pioneer* leered through its keyhole at the sex angle. Or sexual, or sexist, thought Kate resignedly when she read it; how would it know?

'"It was always a secret engagement, of course," Jessica Nicholls, petite, pretty girlfriend of the missing student, Peter Colebrook, murmured. "There would have been so much upsetting jealousy if we'd made it known. But it was a marvellous relationship. Peter was so charismatic: there could never be anyone else for me and I'm sure he'll come back one day."

'Jessica believes Peter may have seen something that fateful night and has gone into hiding for fear of his own life. "I know he'll get in touch with me. I'd know if he was dead," she insists.

'Only Jessica's modest blushes hint at the other men who'd be glad to see her free of her secret engagement. We must now consider whether this was a *crime passionel* of the most gruesome kind to achieve that freedom.'

"No need to ask who shot them this load of crap," snarled Linda, hurling the *Pioneer* to the floor. "Have you seen it, Kate?"

"No." Kate smoothed the crumpled pages flat. "Oh."

"Practically everything hinted at among her debauched colleagues but cannibalism. There isn't really any doubt that Peter's dead, is there? Just our Jessica being pale and interesting?"

"As far as I know," Kate scanned the flaring type. "But perhaps this has done the rest of us a good turn. They'll leave us uninteresting bums alone now and concentrate on her."

"Don't you believe it. Someone'll be round trying to dig up dirt on Peter as an alternative to the brilliant student-divine lover angle. You wait. Why, here's Miss Modest Blushes herself! Anything new on the E.S.P. front, Jessica? Or are you too busy getting your own profiled for Page Three?"

"You're hateful! How can you taunt someone who's – "

"How can you spread your silly story all over that rancid rag? What did they pay you? Or did you do it for love? You make me puke!"

12

The story continued to be front page news, no doubt to the despair of the Department staff who were trying to get some serious work out of their students. But after their questioning on Monday there was no sign of Detective-Chief Inspector McPherson or his Sergeant at Morgan's Mount, though Kate knew that several of her colleagues had been further interviewed at their homes. Linda, for instance, had been third degreed, as she put it, about the party and her earlier friendship with both Peter and Terry Sinclair.

"And he wanted to know about you," she told Kate. "Whether Peter could've palmed you a letter during the party or vice versa."

"What? Whatever for?"

"He turned coy when I asked. I told him you were so thick it was well known you couldn't read or write. He didn't, did he?"

"Oh, give me strength! Still, maddening that one can't follow their line of reasoning."

"Yeah. Must've been some fatuous red herring Jessica dreamt up for kicks."

On Thursday it seemed that Terry Sinclair might supplant Peter as star personality and deflect curiosity from the Department. The *Chronicle* ran an illustrated feature on The Duke's Wine-Bar which included an account of Terry's last few days of duty and a description of what he looked like and might be wearing. The description would have suited any fully-clothed and vaguely inoffensive young man. The Manager also spoke highly of Peter's appreciation of good food and wine. All useful free plugging, Kate realised, interested to see that photos of Terry seemed as hard to come by as photos of Peter. None had been published of either and presumably the police as well as the newsmen must be finding the lack a nuisance. Kate supposed they'd have to fall back on photo-fits and artists' impressions, neither very satisfactory.

However, a bombshell published by the *Daily News* on Friday gave further impetus to the sensation hunters, fixed attention back on Peter as being logically the corpse in the pond and struck a blow at the expertise of the *Chronicle* reporters. For the *News*, quoting an 'exclusive source', disclosed that the body had a few hypodermic punctures from mainlining heroin – though death was not the result of an overdose in the first instance – and added that the police were checking among newly registered addicts and local doctors for any leads. But even more riveting was its announcement that the murdered man had been 'a practising passive homosexual'.

These items of information were added to the local news bulletins. None of the details published by the media so far had been contradicted by police spokesmen and were presumably therefore all true. Odd, thought Kate, that they should have been released in such a piecemeal fashion. Perhaps it depended on the burrowing abilities of the reporters; abilities that had not yet tracked down either Ruth or herself.

"What price your 'marvellous relationship' now, Miss Golden Lay of the Year?" Linda scowled, waving the *News* at Jessica when she hurriedly came into the Common Room to collect some books from her locker. "He was nothing but a cleverly disguised poof. I could've told you he wasn't interested in women."

"That's disgusting slander!" Jessica stormed, red-faced and furious. She'd just been given a rough ride by the Principal, Kate learnt later from Liz who'd been waiting to see him, for allowing the *Pioneer* an interview. The secretary's duties had been complicated by a torrent of mail as a result, which Jessica had to open under the Principal's stern eyes. "It's the sort of lie Kate Henderson's clever at," she hurled at them as she swept out. "Who's their 'exclusive source', do you think?"

"The little darling! I don't know what I'd do without her to prop up my sagging morale," Linda sighed. "All the same, do you find it odd, Kate? The burgeoning addict bit might explain his behaviour, but the other thing?"

"Not like him to be passive, do you mean?" Elinor was interested. "Or the fact that he was gay at all? Would you expect him to be all camp?"

"I wouldn't have thought he had the interest, gay or heterosexual," said Liz. "I always thought he was too – oh, I don't know – too calculating for any sexual interests. Unless he got more than sex out of it, anyway. And wouldn't you describe a passive homosexual as in a rather one-down position?"

"I've no idea what sort of position – "Elinor began loftily, but Linda interrupted her.

"Because by definition it gives someone else active dominance, if only temporarily? Like being a woman. Yeah. I don't see Peter taking that. I wish we had a more knowledgeable opinion. But all the same, Liz, calculating or not, I can see Peter doing something aggressively sexual. Like rape. Even homosexual rape. Something really – inflicting. As a power thing, or revenge. That sort of kick." Liz looked sick.

"Mm," Elinor agreed. "He could be like that, Liz. He didn't forgive. Sometimes you'd think he hadn't noticed, but he always did and got back somehow. Quite tiny slights – or not even slights, oversights – he'd store them up."

"Yeah. It was one of the things that turned me off our first year. And he liked to know where your weaknesses were – just in case, I suppose. I told the copper that who came to see me. It made us all a bit wary of him but in the end he was bound to work up a real enemy. I thought at the time Peter had something to do with Terry chucking everything up like he did. They'd become thick as thieves about then – do you remember, Elinor? – and then suddenly Terry wasn't around any more. You know, it's amazing we didn't realise much earlier just how twisted Peter was. Yet he – he *felt* safe because he *wasn't* interested in women. You do come to know. But – a passive poof?"

Kate had listened with interest. Linda and Elinor had probably known Peter better than any of them. She now made a tentative contribution.

"Perhaps his image, his act, was to disguise the fact that he was?"

"But that would've been utterly exhausting. And what would be the point?"

"To avoid being known to be in a 'one-down' position?"

"Well, but someone must've known he was, unless he went cottaging with a sack over his head," Elinor objected. "And I can't think that would've turned too many on."

★   ★   ★

There were two notes in Kate's pigeon-hole that morning. One was from the Principal to say that Detective-Chief Inspector McPherson wished to interview her in Room 5 at two-thirty; the other was from Ruth. She informed Kate that her architectural lecture was cancelled that day but would Kate care for supper in her rooms, not in Hall? The strain of not being able to add one's mite was too indigestive. And weren't the papers simply awful? Like turning over a stone. Ring if unavailable.

Kate checked the Common Room notice-board and read the announcement cancelling the two-thirty lecture. There was also a formal request from the Principal for all the students to be at the lecture hall at two o'clock.

Inevitably there were grumbles from those who wouldn't normally have stayed on at Morgan's Mount on a Friday afternoon, but otherwise there was uneasy interest as to the reason for the summons.

The morning dragged, trailing the Growing Child through Mr. Grundy's lecture and a seminar. Kate wondered at the formality of her appointment in Room 5 and why the request had been relayed through the Principal. She didn't care to ask whether anyone else was to be interviewed and no one volunteered the information.

When they all eventually dribbled down to the lecture hall after lunch it was to find Detective-Chief Inspector McPherson and the Sergeant already there on the platform. A small suitcase lay closed on the table in front of them.

"First, I want to apologise for upsetting all your schedules," the Detective-Chief Inspector began appeasingly. "But we hope to short-cut on a vast number of interviews in this way. Now, you're all intelligent people, or you wouldn't be here, and naturally you must be wondering how things stand at present. So I can tell you that the details so far published by the media are substantially correct." A little flattery to keep them all happy, thought Kate grimly, and nothing at all given away.

"And so, appealing to your intelligence, we must ask for your help. It's the background we need filled in and you're the persons best able to do that. Now, you'll know about the clothes that were found last weekend in the grounds. Detective-Sergeant Breckon will hold them up for your identification. If you have a reason for disagreeing with someone's identification, please say so at once. Right, John."

Detective-Sergeant Breckon opened the suitcase and held up a discoloured grey suede jacket.

"Oh! But that's Peter's!" came Jessica's excited voice.

"How would you distinguish it, Miss – er – Nicholls?"

"Oo-h! Is there a – a smear of lipstick just on the edge of the collar? On the left?" Jessica's expression of coy dismay was stomach-turning. Silly little bitch! thought Kate. Doesn't she realise what this means? – but no one was in the mood to treat her indulgently just then. The sight of the jacket had dismayed most of those who recognised it.

"Indeed there is some lipstick," answered the Detective-Chief Inspector quietly. "Giaconda's 'Coral Frost' – 'The Hottest Thing Since Man Invented Fire', according to the advertisements. Our forensic lab is hot stuff too. "Is that your usual shade, Miss Nicholls?"

"I – I was wearing it at Peter's party. It was new. It – got on his collar when he saw me to the taxi."

"An unusually long-lasting variety, I take it. By the end of the evening, what with eating and drinking – "

"Oh, I'd just made myself up again."

"In order to go home? Of course. Thank you. Will you let me have the lipstick as soon as you can, please."

"She thought she was staying on, that's why," Linda observed conversationally to Elinor, who looked grimly down at her hands. "Unless she had plans for the taxi-driver."

"Do the rest of you recognise this as Colebrook's jacket?"

the Detective-Chief Inspector continued. There were nods and murmurs of agreement.

One by one the other clothes were produced for inspection; buckled shoes, a fawn shirt, underwear – which no one positively identified but which they all gazed at as solemnly as at the other items – trousers that had once looked smartly tailored, fawn socks with svelte clocking, a leather belt.

"Did Colebrook wear all these clothes on the night of November fourth?" A few believed that they could remember them all worn then; Alice, however, was quite positive. The Detective-Chief Inspector gave her an approving look.

"But he wasn't wearing the jacket at the party," Liz asserted.

"He put it on when he saw me off in the taxi." Jessica fluttered.

"Well, then. I think we've settled the ownership of these clothes. The next question: apart from Miss Mayer, which of you knew or had met Terry Sinclair whose family own the flat?"

It was news to most of them that the flat wasn't Peter's own and it caused murmured comment. Only Elinor and then, very hesitantly, Gordon Watson admitted knowing Terry Sinclair. Both agreed that he'd been a first year student with them but had then dropped out.

"So. When did you last see him, Miss Purbeck?" the Detective-Chief Inspector asked, when the Sergeant had noted down their names and addresses.

"Quite recently. I hadn't seen him since he threw up the History course, but a few days before Peter's party I saw him at The Happy Man with – " she stopped abruptly.

"Yes?"

"With Gordon," Elinor finished uncomfortably. Kate remembered the stranger sitting with Gordon and Jeff when she'd arrived there with Elinor. Yet Jeff hadn't admitted to knowing the other man. "I didn't recognise him, though I felt I knew him. When the papers first mentioned his name I remembered."

"You were not at the party on November fourth?" Elinor shook her head and blushed darkly.

"Can you confirm this meeting, Mr. Watson?"

Gordon and Jeff were sitting as usual with their eyes down and uninvolved. For a moment Kate thought Gordon hadn't even heard the question. Then,

"I would prefer to see you alone," came his abrupt reply. Detective-Sergeant Breckon looked sternly across in the startled silence.

"Of course, Mr. Watson. Perhaps you'd wait in the Common Room after this until I'm ready for you. Now, Sinclair worked at The Duke's Wine-Bar, as you must all know by now," the Detective-Chief Inspector continued smoothly. "Some of you may have seen him there. Did any of you frequent the wine-bar?"

"We didn't have the Kruger Rands," said Linda. "Only Peter could possibly have afforded those prices."

"He took me there once," Kate volunteered, remembering that she'd mentioned the visit to Elinor. "I didn't notice anyone in particular and if I heard any names they made no impression."

"Sounds like a really forgettable experience," Linda remarked. Elinor gave a bark of nervous laughter; the Sergeant looked scandalised.

"And no one else has anything to add? Miss Nicholls?" Jessica jerked out of a glum trance. "Did you perhaps meet Sinclair at the flat?"

"He wasn't there. Linda Mayer asked for him."

"At any time other than the night of the party?"

"That was the only time I was at Peter's – at the flat," Jessica answered in a small voice.

"What about Colebrook's friends outside the Department, then? Anyone know of any? Did he ever mention names?"

But no one had anything useful to add and the Serjeant began packing away the clothes into the suitcase.

"Well, then. That's all for now – unless any of you – ?" the Detective-Chief Inspector looked round encouragingly. "Yes, Miss Jepson?"

"It's only that – among those clothes – Peter wore a very distinctive watch, you see – "

"That's right," Liz agreed. "He used to say it did everything but make the early morning tea."

"Multi-purpose, was it?" asked the Detective-Chief Inspector abstractedly, glancing at the Sergeant who took out his notebook again.

"Yes, a mariner's watch," said Alice.

"Describe it, Miss Jepson."

"It was about the size of Robert's – show him, Rob." Robert grimly peeled back his cuff and held up his left arm for inspection.

"I see. Thank you, Mr. Denham. What kind of strap?"

"It looked like crocodile skin – hide – whatever. Quite wide. Black. The watch itself was gold-coloured."

"It wasn't your High Street mock croc. and rolled gold either," Elinor muttered in her booming undertone. "If it's missing, someone knew its value."

"Make?" the Detective-Chief Inspector prompted Alice.

"I – I couldn't say. Do you know, Liz?"

"But I thought 'Mariners' was the make. That's what he called it."

"As in 'seamen', Miss Jackson," Detective-Chief Inspector McPherson told her kindly. "With aids to navigation, I imagine. Anything else, Miss Jepson?"

"Well – he wore it on his right wrist."

"So he was left-handed?" the Detective-Chief Inspector asked sharply. But I've already told him he was right-handed, Kate remembered.

"No. Right-handed. It simply meant he flashed the watch about more."

"Anyone confirm that?" Several voices were raised in agreement. "Good. Anything else? The make of this watch, for instance? No? That's all, then. I'd like to see Miss Purbeck as well as Mr. Watson shortly, please. Will you both wait in the Common Room? And if any of you does think of any helpful details don't hesitate to tell us. Thank you."

The two police officers waited while the students filed out of the hall.

"That seems to settle it, doesn't it?" Liz asked with concern. "It must be Peter." Kate realised that all this time Liz had been

140

hoping against reason that that suspicion at least would be proved unfounded and so distance the horror.

"But if they're thinking Terry knocked him off they're wildly wrong," said Linda. "Terry wouldn't hurt a fly. He's always on the receiving end. The sort of wimp you feel maternal about in spite of yourself."

"You can't say what you'll do till you're up against it," Elinor pointed out. "I've felt like murdering Peter and I didn't live with him."

"Oh – you remember what Terry was like, Elinor. And feeling's one thing. You've got to have something a bit extra – or a bit missing – to make it murder."

"There's a difference between premeditated and spur-of-the-moment murder, though," Elinor pursued. "Anyone can get just so buggered up that they lash out."

"But this wasn't simply a lash out, was it? Look what was done to him," Liz objected. "They must truly have hated him."

"And it can't have been premeditated either," said Linda thoughtfully. "He must've arranged to meet someone at Morgan's Mount – after the party, it seems – and they clobbered him unexpectedly."

"Why do you think that?"

"Because his car's a dead giveaway, isn't it? It would've been moved if the thing was planned, not left there to draw attention. And then the shed burgled and all those things – used. They'd have brought their own – er – tools with them, wouldn't they?" Liz fell silent.

"Hm. Suppose so. A row got out of hand, then? And they tried to cover up?" Elinor asked. "But that's what I've been saying – it was spur of the moment."

"Maybe. But Terry wouldn't have needed to meet him like that. And he couldn't have done either the killing or the rest. He'd simply have sat by and cried, more likely."

"Then where is he now?" Liz enquired logically.

"Actually you could be right, from what I remember of him," Elinor admitted. "Terry was a bit of a weed. A born victim. But if you're looking for someone with a bit missing, he fits the bill – you know – like a child at his wits' end in screaming despair. The urge to smash."

"Why on earth do you think Gordon wants a private chat?" Liz wondered after a moment. She didn't know Terry after all. But neither Elinor nor Kate gave Jeff away. Kate would have liked to discuss Jeff's reticence with Elinor, but there wasn't the opportunity. Since Elinor had known Gordon from their undergraduate days she might be able to say whether he intended to admit Jeff's involvement or whether he'd rely on Elinor and herself continuing to cover for him. Kate couldn't immediately see why that association should be incriminating. Plenty of perfectly innocent people must have known Terry Sinclair. Why not Jeff?

Kate went upstairs to Room 5 without telling the others where she was going and, finding the door unlocked, sat inside to wait. It was well after two-thirty.

"Ah, Miss Henderson," Detective-Chief Inspector McPherson smiled pleasantly as he arrived with the Sergeant. "We have your original statements ready for you to sign. Just one or two points arising – " He took some papers out of his brief-case and read rapidly down the typed sheets. "Yes, here we are. You say the surface of the ice on the pond appeared 'broken up' among the reeds. Can you clarify that?"

"It looked, well, crinkled. As if the surface had frozen in mid-flurry, if you can imagine that. Miss Stanton suggested there was perhaps enough agitation among the reeds to prevent the ice freezing solid there."

"It was solid enough when they came to remove the cadaver. What were the weather conditions the day before?" Kate showed her surprise.

"On the Thursday? Frosty, I suppose. No – wait. It was misty and cloudy till evening, I remember. Then fairly late that night it was bright starlight and freezing again."

"Your memory parallels your observation, Miss Henderson."

"Comes of fussing over an ungrateful cat," Kate smiled easily, but she was aware of spikes in the policeman's voice and she couldn't understand why.

"You should get a cat-door fitted," he murmured absently as he turned the page.

"I have. You must've noticed it when you visited me. But I call her in and bolt it at night."

"Just testing, Miss Henderson," the Detective-Chief Inspector smiled suddenly.

"Testing me? Oh – you think I might've been aware of weather conditions because I was out that night sinking Peter's body in the pond before it froze over again? Where would I have kept it all that time? And why should I be a suspect now and no longer simply a witness?" Detective-Sergeant Breckon stared at her repressively and Kate felt suddenly cold. She hadn't expected her question to be taken entirely seriously.

"The body had been *in situ*, more or less, for several weeks," the Detective-Chief Inspector replied mildly. "But you see a good deal, perhaps even know a good deal, yet you're not telling us everything." Which was true enough, blast him, Kate thought bitterly, and blast Jeff. She stayed silent. "Now, your visit to the wine-bar. You went just the once?"

"It wasn't my kind of place. But in fact I did see Terry Sinclair once, when Elinor Purbeck and I went to The Happy Man as she's told you. I didn't know who he was then, but he reminded me of Peter."

"A much better effort, Miss Henderson," the Detective-Chief Inspector nodded approvingly. "When exactly was this meeting?" Kate kept her patience with an effort and wished she could control her colour as well.

"It wasn't a meeting. It was a – a sighting. And I didn't know who he was till Elinor spoke up this afternoon. But it was on a Monday, I think – no, a Tuesday. The Tuesday before Peter's party, so – " she counted backwards " – first of November." It'd been the day after the Grecian urnful at Elinor's, Kate remembered, and she tried to keep at bay the dark thought that constantly threatened to slide out into the light.

"We'll no doubt get Miss Purbeck's corroboration for that. However, you made quite an impression at the wine-bar, you know. The Manager gave us a most telling description of you. He spoke to the both of you, if you remember."

"I can guess his description," Kate snapped. "'Hennaed

hair and twice his age'." She caught the Sergeant's speculative look. "You'd have to be some kind of freak to dye it this colour, for God's sake," she told him infuriatedly. "As for the Manager, I wouldn't know him from a hole in the ground. People did talk – or Peter spoke to them. Women aren't introduced in those places – they merely hang about looking decorative or grateful. Is this wine-bar episode so important, then? Am I supposed to have been in cahoots with Terry Sinclair against Peter? What?" Kate was suddenly aware she'd been shouting.

"It doesn't seem to fit in with your picture of being unwillingly pursued," the Detective-Chief Inspector smiled placatingly at her. "The Manager remembers you as being the only woman Colebrook ever took there. Now, just think. Here's a man gives a lavish party that degenerates into fisticuffs. Yet he's still bright-eyed and bushy-tailed to the bitter end, when he dismisses his current girlfriend virtually with the other guests. So. One possibility is that he had something better lined up, yes? That perhaps he'd arranged to meet another lady at Morgan's Mount. You?"

"After what happened at the party?" Kate asked breathlessly. "And why there? Why not at the flat?"

"There may have been imperatives other than dalliance. Think about it."

"Given the way I was feeling, a meeting of any kind would've been unthinkable," Kate began heatedly, and realised what he'd meant by 'other imperatives'. "There was no such arrangement. As for the wine-bar visit, well, you can't keep on saying 'No'."

"So they tell me these days," the Detective-Chief Inspector murmured vaguely after a considering pause. "Now, this point about Colebrook's watch. Did he have a boat?"

"I don't know. But he told me once he was interested in a boat."

"A particular boat? Or boats in general?"

"I – got the impression he referred to a particular boat." Kate thought back to the last lift she'd accepted from Peter. It seemed centuries ago. "He gave me a lift into town one Thursday and said he was on his way to the docks where there was a boat he was interested in. Something like that."

"To the docks? Not to the marina?"

"I see what you mean. But at the time I thought he meant a small boat, with a view to hiring or buying."

"Well, that's cleared up a number of details," said the Detective-Chief Inspector cheerfully, "though it means another stint of signing for you later. And you know nothing of Colebrook's friends outside the Department?"

"Not – not precisely."

"Meaning?" He pounced like a terrier on a rat and gave Kate's conscience an uncomfortable shake. Now was the time to tell him what Jeff and Gordon had said?

"I assume those people at the wine-bar were some of his friends, but I don't know them or anything about them," Kate evaded. After all, Gordon himself was waiting downstairs and ready to spill all his beans. She stood up to go.

But Kate was not permitted to leave without one more uncomfortable thought to take with her.

"You said – off the record the other evening – that Colebrook seemed well off. And he must've been, mustn't he, so that's no secret. He couldn't have lived like that on a grant, could he? A new car, the rent for an expensive flat, good clothes?"

"Good heavens, no! We assumed his family was wealthy."

"You didn't know he was the only child of a grocer's widow?" Kate felt her mouth drop open. A Tesco heiress? "A hard-working honest woman, by all accounts, whose husband committed suicide when the boy was fourteen. No known reason. She worked to continue with the shop until she was put out of business by the opening of a new local supermarket. They say it finally killed her. You don't imagine she'd have got millions from the forced sale of a redundant little shop?"

"No, of course not! We knew nothing at all about his family – at least, I didn't till I read in the *Herald* that his mother died a few years back and that he had no other immediate relatives."

"Perhaps he was ashamed of his family, Miss Henderson. A poor scholar at Lethbridge College? He certainly worked hard to better himself – and hardly ever visited home. Maybe he succeeded too well. Thank you, then, Miss Henderson.

You've been most helpful," Detective-Chief Inspector McPherson added politely. Kate gave him a frosty look. "Will you send up Miss Purbeck, please?"

Brick after brick was being knocked out of Peter's sanctuary, and Kate was stunned to find so humble a relic in the exposed holy of holies. What had the edifice been built to protect, she wondered. Or avert?

13

On her way down to the Common Room Kate pondered the strangeness of her interview. Detective-Chief Inspector McPherson had let her see he didn't trust her – and nor should he. Hadn't he actively needled her, though? Yet what led him to imagine that she was withholding anything important to the case? Why on earth should he think that Peter, presumably through the letter Linda mentioned, had arranged to meet her at Morgan's Mount after the party? When there never had been such a letter. Apart from her few small reservations, Kate felt she'd given the Detective-Chief Inspector good measure. If he wanted verbal diarrhoea let him concentrate on Jessica.

"The long arms of the law are ready to enfold you," Kate told Elinor as she went into the Common Room.

"How come you?" Elinor demanded in surprise.

"They asked me in for a gossip."

"Will you wait for me?" Elinor stumped over to the door. "What're they like?"

"Their teeth are sharp as sharks', dear, and they grind exceeding small. Don't try and keep anything back. Which is what I did." Kate turned to Gordon after Elinor left. "And it's done me a lot of no good. I don't know what you two are playing at, but Jeff keeping quiet about knowing Terry Sinclair will land you both in lumber. And trying not to land you there ourselves will hurt both Elinor and me. So I hope you're going to explain things to them."

"It was a momentary weakness, that's all. I didn't want to broadcast everything. Sorry if you stuck your neck out, but thanks. I told Elinor to go ahead and say, if they saw her before me. But it's bloody complicated, Kate. I'm not sure how much you know and I'm not even certain I've got all the facts straight myself and God knows – but people like us aren't given the benefit of the doubt. I'm – I'm genuinely frightened, not just at the thought of telling them everything but so much is bound to become public now. They'll never let us finish the course. God knows what'll happen. He just wasn't worth all this – this uncertainty and misery. He was such a bastard, Kate. Such a bastard. Don't think we don't realise. We warned you what a load of muck would be stirred up if Peter didn't lay off, but you wouldn't listen. Hell, I don't know who to feel most sorry for, you or us."

Kate watched uncomfortably as Gordon put his head down on his arms. His outburst seemed hysterical and right out of character. And who was the bastard – Peter or Terry Sinclair? Sure they'd warned her, but was she now to be held responsible for Peter's death because she hadn't taken any action?

"I'm sure you're spooking yourself unnecessarily," Kate tried to speak reassuringly. "You both said you weren't involved in whatever mischief Peter had got himself into. Tell them everything you know about Terry, and about Peter too, if it's relevant. And get Jeff to do the same. As for what may come out, well, I don't know what sort of stand the Principal may feel forced to take, but I do know he tries very hard to protect his – his people. Really. And for heaven's sake don't worry about me! It was only a tiny rap over the knuckles I got for holding back."

Gordon lifted his head and looked at Kate for a moment, rather oddly, she thought.

"You feel I deserve something stronger for not taking you seriously? But truly, Peter and I weren't on those terms whatever you must think of me after that bloody party. You two – and you weren't even there! – and Barbara have treated me ever since as if you could hear me ticking."

"Nothing to do with that," Gordon mumbled, looking away. "Things became – very difficult just about then."

"Especially for Peter and Terry Sinclair. What do – ?"

The door burst open and Elinor erupted into the room.

"They want you now, Gordon. They didn't ask me about

The Happy Man, so it's up to you." Gordon left and Elinor flung herself dangerously down in a chair. "I didn't know enough about Terry to interest them. But you bloody well dropped me right in. Why didn't you tell me you'd called round that night? I must've looked pretty cock-eyed when they sprang it on me."

"It wasn't that important, not a firm agreement. You didn't hear, anyway, or you were out," said Kate pacifically.

"I was out. Peggy took Craig to her parents for the weekend. I told the detective I had someone with me and chose not to answer the door. I'd completely forgotten you'd said you might come round."

"Why in heaven's name did you say that? Elinor, were you somewhere round St. Dunstan's Square that night?"

"Actually I was. I couldn't stand it, Kate. I just had to know – whether she stayed on. You know – afterwards. I couldn't keep away," Elinor pleaded. "Though looking back on it all now, I think I must've been possessed."

"I thought I saw you on the way. You're a nut-case, do you know that? Anyone else could've seen you. So, if you were watching the place you were there when the party broke up. Did you see – ?"

"I didn't see anything!" Elinor made a sound like the bathwater running out. "It was damn parky so I sloped off for a drink – The Red Well at Rosemary Corner. I didn't want to be seen locally in case – you know – it got back to Peter. I meant to catch the bus back at closing time. But I overdid it. Partly to kill time and partly to shut out my thoughts, I suppose. I ended up pig-sick in the pub loos and then flaked out in the bus shelter. I came to about five o'clock the next morning. God, I thought I was dead I was so cold! I walked all the way home, went to bed and slept for hours."

"Is that the truth?" Kate asked grimly, remembering that, if asked, Peggy could confirm the hostile relationship between Elinor and Peter. "You didn't dong Peter and – and cut him up?" The preposterous thought was out in the light at last.

" 'Course not!"

"It's what they'll want to know if they find you've lied."

"Why shouldn't they believe me? I said I couldn't name

149

names – delicate business et cetera. He said in my own interests I ought to establish some proof, but I said other interests were more important to me. Seems fair enough, doesn't it? It's how it would happen if it had been true. All in character. And it's a chance I had to take." Elinor preened herself. "And I can place myself at home at one o'clock or so when you called – what the hell are you looking at me like that for?"

Kate struggled for words.

"Elinor, for God's sake! It was about nine-thirty when I came round! Haven't you heard *anything* about the party fiasco?" Kate's stomach lurched in sudden panic. "I left early."

"But you all left early, didn't you? I heard the party ended about midnight after some darn unparty-like behaviour and you shocked them all bandy. What I heard didn't encourage me to find out more about – about anything. But Linda said she was talking to you for a bit after you both left, so I reckoned you'd have got to my place about one. That bloody bluebottle didn't tell me you'd called even before the party was over – just he understood we had an arrangement to meet after it." Kate expired.

"Tell me exactly what you said."

"Well, after rapid calculation of times to allow for your walk from Peter's – "

"I drove."

"Well, Christ! I didn't even know you had a car! Anyway, I said me and my hypothetical had been in bed for hours by the time I heard you knocking at about one, and tried to look self-conscious."

Bloody twerp, thought Kate unemotionally, gazing at Elinor's stodgy, worried face. A shattering hiccup shook her. Serves you right. She'd as near dammit placed Kate at her digs long after Kate believed herself safely witnessed at home by Willy Frost. It was perhaps time to stop worrying about Elinor and start taking thought for her own position.

"Look, you'd better tell them the whole truth from the beginning – Jessica and all – before you land me in the soup as well," Kate said sharply, as Elinor convulsed intermittently. "Now. As soon as they've finished with Gordon. Give them a hearty bout of the mea culpas. They'll understand why you tried to cover up. And they won't broadcast it. But you don't know what'll come out if you try to keep quiet about it any longer. God! I've got to make a phone call – then I must get away to sanity. Or shall I wait?"

"Oh, hell! It'll keep me up to the mark if you do. I'm not looking forward to this, Kate."

Kate rang Ruth from the pay phone in the hall. She changed her mind about accepting the invitation for that evening, seeing herself nurse-maiding Elinor instead, and was making her excuses when Gordon came down the stairs looking wrung-out and miserable. He avoided Kate's eyes and said nothing, perhaps because Detective-Sergeant Breckon was with him. They walked out of the front door and Kate heard a car start up and drive off. Her farewells to Ruth grew increasingly distrait. Kate's unease wasn't lessened by the sight of Detective-Chief Inspector McPherson leaning over the banisters as she put the phone down and turned back towards the Common Room for Elinor.

"A word with you, Miss Henderson."

"I'll just tell Elinor – "

"She's still here? Call her into the hall, please." With a constricted throat Kate called twice for Elinor before she appeared.

"I've some business with Miss Henderson." The Detective-Chief Inspector came down the remaining stairs. Elinor took the heavy hint and left, giving Kate a pleading glance as she passed by. "Come up, will you."

* * *

Kate followed the Detective-Chief Inspector to Room 5 with the feeling that events were running away from her and out of her control. She couldn't imagine what Gordon might possibly have said to inspire the detective's portentous curtness, which also seemed too great a sledge-hammer for Elinor's inexpert lying if he'd found out about that already. Kate's instinct warned her, however, that she herself had somehow been found at fault.

"Let me present to you a hypothetical situation," the Detective-Chief Inspector began when they were sitting down. "Say, a film scenario, Miss Henderson." He looked impassively into her face, a look neither friendly nor hostile but as bleak – and penetrating – as a searchlight. "Let us imagine that A, we'll call her, has discovered something discreditable about B and C, two men who're living together. Discovered something not merely discreditable but involving the destruction of her whole way of life. Since whenever she made this discovery – it's an old story – she's managed to inveigle herself into the desired position close to B. It may have been through good planning or chance, but it gives her access also to C."

Kate listened to the cold voice, but as to someone speaking in Babylonian cuneiform. She vaguely understood the Detective-Chief Inspector to be referring to Jeff and Gordon, but her wits were clogged with apprehension at his manner which seemed so inexplicable and, as in childhood, appeared to be calling her to account for a misdemeanour she couldn't precisely remember having committed.

Detective-Chief Inspector McPherson was looking at Kate impatiently.

"Are you with me, Miss Henderson?"

"If – if you mean Jeff and Gordon, I can assure – "

"But I don't. Let us continue. The characters will emerge. A, you see, wants – perhaps is driven – to revenge herself on both B and C. Understandable, but not, unfortunately for her, legal except by due process of the law.. And the law would not give her the pound of flesh or the blood she's – hunting. Now, A's chance comes on November fourth, even possibly the day before but our attention is drawn to November fourth. That evening she is at a party. Not a very nice party but it gives her the opportunity she's waited for. There's even evidence that she initiated the very idea of this gathering. A leaves early. Very early. Removes herself entirely from the scene. Fortune favours her with the innocent company of D, who can swear to her departure from the area. To make doubly certain A calls on E – an unreliable witness and unreliable for A's purposes also, as it happens. That line of enquiry can be pursued further, I think, and should've been picked up earlier."

Kate at last realised where the Detective-Chief Inspector was leading, but not why. And because there could be no 'why' she found she'd lost her nervousness. Kate began to listen intently.

"Yes?" He noticed her new alertness. "The characters have emerged, Miss Henderson? So. A goes home and parks where her car can be seen more than usually clearly. A further quirk of fortune gives her a witness for the time she arrives home. By ten o'clock she is therefore established law-abidingly settled for the night. But at some later hour she returns to the violent city. Either in her own car or on foot – in at the front door, out at the back across the waste ground. Or perhaps she was picked up by prior arrangement. What do you think? Might A have needed an accomplice? Who were you ringing just now?" he shot at Kate.

Dumbly Kate felt in her trouser-suit pocket for Ruth's note and pushed it across the table.

"'Ruth'?" queried the Detective-Chief Inspector.

"Miss Stanton."

"Ah, yes. The lady who assisted at the resurrection of a body not safely hidden at all but arranged to be discovered. That startles you? But these assertions can be proved, and over-clever touches are notoriously broken reeds. Forensic science is a wonderful ally – of the law." The Detective-Chief Inspector looked again at the note. "Interesting," he murmured. "Well? What do you have to say? Does the scenario strike you as being true to life? We have no witnesses, so you can be quite honestly critical."

Kate hoped her voice would be steady when she spoke and was relieved to hear how calm she sounded.

"I think you'd need to write in more explanations, Detective-Chief Inspector McPherson. I can see why A may be thought to – to harbour revenge against B, but only *after* the party. You'd have to explain why she was – er – hunting earlier than that. Also why her revenge should encompass C, whom she'd never met as far as you've shown. And you'd have to indicate that A was emotionally and physically capable of this presumably double murder. If you award her an accomplice you merely redouble your difficulties, not halve them, in needing to show two people's motives and two people's capabilities."

"True, of course, and very coolly analysed. But you've already given us a hint this afternoon that the balanced, detached Miss Henderson was capable at least of rage. Hardly a fraction of what you must've felt towards Colebrook – even on the testimonies of those who know only half the story – but an indication, nevertheless."

"So that's why you stirred me up. Same reason as Peter's, to see what would shake out of the bag. It seems that self-control merely attracts the sappers. And you already have the rest of the story in mind, then? The explanation that would make A's motives and behaviour believable?"

"In outline as yet, but I think I have it, Miss Henderson." Kate fought not to let her amazement show.

"But there is no such explanation, Detective-Chief Inspector McPherson. Whatever it is you've come by, you cannot make it credible. May I hear what it is?" The Detective-Chief Inspector shook his head. "Then you can only have a hypothetical – and alphabetical – scenario that will never be a box-office hit."

"Maybe so," the Detective-Chief Inspector stood up. "But I have to try it out. That's my job. Do you deny that you've held anything back from us?" Kate lowered her eyes and there was a grim silence. "So, then. Did you accept this invitation?" He handed back Ruth's note and Kate shook her head. "Then I shall drive you home."

"Thank you, but – "

"In the course of duty, Miss Henderson."

"I see. Escort duty," Kate flushed angrily. "In case I alert someone, perhaps?"

"Not so clever, Miss Henderson. The one thing your records agree about is that you're clever."

★ ★ ★

Kate felt perfectly calm during the silent drive home. Unnaturally calm, she suspected, wondering whether her system had operated some kind of cut-out to provide an easier option than the flaring panic she believed she ought to be feeling. And meanwhile, she realised, her apparent cool would only be totted up against her by the stolid chunk of officialdom driving beside her. A pity it'd ended like this, Kate thought sadly. She'd begun to like him rather well. Vivvy would've appealed to him. She wondered if he had a family.

"You're thinking something personal about me, aren't you?" the Detective-Chief Inspector asked to her amazement as he stopped in the bus pull-in opposite Kate's house.

"Personal, but not positively hostile. That surprises me." He didn't turn to look at her.

"How did you guess?" Kate's question was as matter of fact as his. Nothing flirtatious or arch, any more than his statement had been an invitation to air her opinions of him.

"Just a feeling. We get used to all sorts of sensations ordinary people never need to be aware of. If we can – sharpen them it helps us become reasonably good coppers. Like knowing you're being watched. I learnt to use that as a novice on night patrols. Nurses must know that one too. But sensing suspicion, fear, hatred, even welcome sometimes – you get to know and you learn to distinguish. And when something's being held back." Like knowing there's someone in the room with you, Kate supposed. Nothing sensationally extra-sensory. She was grateful for the easing of their separate silences.

"Talking of being watched on night-duty – across the road you'll see a rather off-white mini, nose to tail in our neighbourhood way of parking. You see why I didn't put it back in place that Friday night, but left it over here. Not in order to be noticed."

"Point taken. But it's still more noticeable here."

"And if you want to know, I was wondering if you had a daughter." The Detective-Chief Inspector was silent for a while.

"The existence of your daughter is my assurance that you won't do – anything foolish," he said at last. "And I won't do anything or – or give orders for anything to be done before you've had time to forewarn your daughter."

A soft prickle, like the stealthy brush of Domina's fur, crept up Kate's arms and the back of her neck to her scalp. She got

155

out of the car and crossed the road to her house without a backward glance. A foretaste of horror to come, she found herself thinking as she locked herself into security. But there could be no horror for her. The Detective-Chief Inspector's basic premise was wrong, dead wrong, whatever circumstantial corroboration he might find to support it. For what could there be that threatened to destroy her life, for heaven's sake? In the end he would be shown to be mistaken.

★   ★   ★

Domina implied that her hunger was so debilitating that she could hardly crawl her sleek self across the kitchen floor. Only her voice had any strength. Kate listened to it with a grin, forking out some of the gripingly pungent food, while Domina revived enough to circle round her feet and lean heavily against her legs.

"There you are, you great fraud." Kate put down the filled bowl and some more milk. She went into the living-room and turned on the television midway through the regional news programme. The presenter's voice cut across her dull preoccupation as she drew the curtains.

' – Sinclair, who vanished at the same time as his flatmate, Peter Colebrook.' Kate turned quickly to see a blurred snapshot enlarged on the screen. Of Peter? She stood still, holding the curtain.

'A police spokesman has confirmed that a former close friend of Terry's has come forward with this photograph taken some years ago. He claims to have seen Terry in his home town of Bude, in Cornwall, yesterday afternoon. Mr. James Leverton – ' the snapshot was replaced by a new shot – 'was walking down the main street when he thought he recognised his old friend approaching. He told the police, "I think he's lost his memory. He passed quite close and I said 'Terry!' but he walked on. I ran after him and called his name again but he went into Woolworth's and I lost him. It was Terry – I'd know him anywhere and he was wearing a leather jacket like they said in the papers. Now the police can find him and prove what people are saying about him is all lies. Terry wouldn't hurt anyone."

'There have been several unconfirmed sightings of Terry Sinclair and Peter Colebrook in different parts of the country since their descriptions were published,' the presenter continued. And this one's only being given air-space because of the snap, Kate believed. 'Terry's family, who were interviewed by the police when he first disappeared, are not available for comment on James Leverton's story.

'And there's been a further development in the investigations at Morgan's Mount. The clothes found in the gardens have now been positively identified as Peter Colebrook's. As yet there has been no positive identification of the body.'

But that can't have been Terry Sinclair, thought Kate in puzzlement. Who'd flee home – for refuge, presumably – and then march openly down his own main street? Unless he really had lost his memory; in which case the incidents room should be overwhelmed with reports of sightings in Bude.

Kate switched off the television, lit the fire and sat on the rug watching the sticks catch up. Why had Terry dropped out of his degree course, she wondered. And having done so, why had he stayed on in the very agreeable flat with Peter, presumably with his family's approval? The obvious explanation came too pat to answer the first question.

What kind of a family, of a background had he? Kate supposed he must have been lured out into the world by a particularly attractive offer – yet hired hand at The Duke's Wine-Bar didn't sound very sensational. Maybe he was actually some sort of partner, if not much of a ball of fire by all accounts.

But students did drop out of university courses, some did have wealthy and indulgent parents, some did find success without a degree qualification at their backs. There was nothing so unusual in Terry's story. Only his possibly murderous involvement with Peter. How much did he benefit from Peter's friendship? Peter seemed to have some influence at the wine-bar. But Terry had been getting himself into hot water, Peter had told Linda at the party. And so, according to Gordon, had Peter himself. Was Terry the source of Gordon's information about Peter?

Domina twittered from the doorway and stalked over to the

fireside where she gave herself a searching launder. Kate watched her delicate paws move back and forth from her tongue over her ears and muzzle. It's not that they wash their faces, she decided, fascinated as always by the precise rhythm. They wash their paws and then dry them on their faces.

Domina lay back and teased at the fur on her chest and under her chin. She caught sight of Kate watching her, pencil at the ready, and stopped in mid-lick. 'Prr-rrp!' she trilled, rolling onto her side and peeping at Kate from under her arm. Kate sighed and absently reached out at the invitation to tickle Domina's drum-tight midriff. Only to remember too late the danger of that fond caress when Domina fleshed her claws in her hand.

"Tripe-hound! Vain deluding joy!" Kate sucked at the beaded perforations. "Fat twerp!" Domina fell into an ecstasy of purring and coiled herself for sleep. "I'll give you to the large policeman for a sporran."

And where did Peter get his money? Gambling? Elegantly dinner-jacketed in the hushed, exclusive opulence of some deep-pile club? Too chancy. A lucky deal on family property – an attic collection of Old Masters. Kate thought ruefully of her own attic collection of old cobwebs and scuffed suitcases. It could even have been a straightforward legacy from a wealthy last of the line in Australia or somewhere. An umpteenth cousin, far removed, who didn't know what else to do with his – his opal mine. Or diamonds in South Africa. Gold. Rubies in Burma. A pearl-fishery in Japan – Kate roused herself from her lavish dreams, threw a couple of small logs on the fire and reminded herself that once you're dead nothing is secret. Peter's bank or his solicitor would soon provide the police with the information they needed.

14

There was a letter from Vivvy the following morning, Saturday. Kate read it over a leisurely breakfast of coffee, toast and homemade jam – courtesy of Miss Lawrence and her Victoria plums, in return for a pound of Kate's almonds. The letter was just what Kate needed to put into better perspective the rather frightening bewilderment of the previous day.

'What goings-on back at the old homestead and how the place seems to have degenerated since I left! The shock of reading about the body! Nothing like that happens here, you may be relieved to know, and the most excitement we can hope for is trying not to be late for early lectures or the suspense of wondering if we can make sense of the next tutorial.

'So it's with great expectations that we turn to the papers to catch up on your daily instalments. We think your Jessica Nicholls must the absolute *bottom* and await with apprehension the day, no doubt soon, when the camera angle follows her there.' Kate blenched at the line-drawing that accompanied that. 'She isn't one of your Bosom Chums, is she? I hope? We never had teachers like her at St Wilfrid's Primary.

'However, I suppose it must be pretty beastly for you, even though you're no way involved, thank heavens, though we're inclined to believe that the *corpus delicti* must be your Peter Colebrook, mustn't it?' (Kate hadn't told Vivvy that she'd been present at the body's discovery.) 'The betting here is in favour of this Terry having done him in, though now one or two feel that la Ballonade could possibly have worked up a rival boyfriend(s) into a frenzy of murderous lust. I mean, it does look a bit sexual, doesn't it? All that *dubious* surgery. Meanwhile we await the next instalment, and though these ghouls would like to see you figure more – only to win some interest for themselves by association, I promise you, dear Ma – I hope you'll continue in your unruffled aloofness. One doesn't like to think of one's mother up to the hocks in situations so unlike the life of our dear Queen, and your calm is the world's best fixed point.

'From which you may deduce, and rightly – why not – that here I come a-buttering and your famous calm is summoned. Could you bear it if I had someone home for the vac? Only over New Year, as he feels he ought to spend Christmas with his family, but he's terribly nice. Not dishy, you know, or particularly outstanding in any way, except he says he likes cats, but he's kind. If yes, great. If no, quite understandable but worth a try. Come up and meet him some time. He may invite me for New Year anyway.'

"Oh, Vivvy!" Kate laughed out loud in love and despair. If that last sentence wasn't a pistol to her head she was a monkey's uncle. But she was happy to find Vivvy so cheerful and caring, for all her open manipulations of her mother's spinelessness where she was concerned. She'd better write back straightaway and set her mind at rest, both over the police investigations and her nameless young man. There was just time to catch the one Saturday collection.

The smile still lingered on Kate's face when she answered a ring at the front door – and looked straight into the unresponsive grey eyes of Detective-Chief Inspector McPherson. Over his shoulder Kate could see the bus pull-in lined with cars and the street seemed full of men, in and out of uniform, some knocking on doors. She couldn't believe her eyes, and for the first time Kate knew what that saying really meant. Dumbly she stepped back into the hall and he followed her in.

"Miss Henderson, we're conducting house to house enquiries in the village and we're authorised to search the gardens and any outhouses as well. The waste ground is being quartered now. In a moment some of my men will be ready to search your garden, so please unlock the door in your back wall. When my men are admitted I shall ask one of them to assist me in a search of your house. Here is the warrant. No one will know that in that respect at least you're to be treated differently. Will you go through now."

A moment of disbelief, of stupefaction, a moment of pure fear followed by anger telescoped through Kate's emotions before she turned and led the Detective-Chief Inspector into the kitchen. She reached down a key from a hook by the boiler, shrugged on an old anorak that hung on the back door and went out into the garden. Domina fled before her across the paving at the heavier sounds of the Detective-Chief Inspector's approach and leapt for the almond tree.

Kate unlocked the door in the wall and eased it inwards. Once an abandoned cooker had fallen in with it and given her a surprise bruise, but now only the summer trail of brambles lay across the threshold.

"Shall I leave it open?" And would Domina stray off?

"Please." The Detective-Chief Inspector looked thoughtfully at the brambles and then stepped over them into the wasteland. "Not a very delicious back approach."

"The high walls have made us lazy. It's worse nearer the main road."

"Used much – apart from dumping? Kids' dens, that sort of thing?"

"There aren't that many young children in the village – or many of courting age. It's a bit of an elephants' graveyard since the quarry closed down. But the blackberries are good." Kingdoms may rise and kingdoms may fall but the blackberries flourish just over the wall. This is a very black comedy and I'm merely an offended spectator, Kate told herself. I shall not jump up and down spewing forth emotions. Come, friendly bombs, and fell him now. Or blow winds and split his breeks.

Detective-Chief Inspector McPherson stepped back into the garden.

"How long have you lived here?"

"About eight years. It became my own home by bequest two years ago."

"When did you have the paving laid?"

"It was already down. We took up some to make room for the tree," Kate nodded towards Celia's almond tree, where Domina crouched glowering among the leafless branches. The Detective-Chief Inspector walked over to look at the naked square of earth at the foot of the tree. Domina fluffed up and lifted her lip.

"And over there?" He swung round, pointing to where Kate had removed the row of flags. "They've been lifted recently. There's still sand clinging to the lower edges of that pile." Where the weather hadn't reached so easily, Kate supposed, impressed by his astuteness as she looked at the pile of flags by the lean-to.

"I took them up – I can't remember when exactly – not long ago. When I – got the cat. Sometime at the beginning of November. She was digging in the exposed bits but they're full of spring bulbs. It was to give her more space and it's driest along there."

"You'd have done better to give the cat away and had the whole lot concreted," he told Kate roughly. "A foot thick. I don't like paving-stones in my job."

Kate flinched, suddenly enlightened. The head. Of course. They were looking for it. In her garden. Her house.

"Will – will there be much mess?" Kate collapsed onto the edge of a tub and gazed hopelessly round the yard, appalled at the thought of cleaning down the flags afterwards.

"Probes," the Detective-Chief Inspector muttered, looking up at the walls. "At first, anyway." He glanced at her, his preoccupied expression softening momentarily. "Come away inside. Where will you want to be? I can leave you there in peace."

"I'll wait in the living-room, then. The front room. I was going to write to my daughter."

"Do that. But I'll have to search there first."

Detective-Chief Inspector McPherson disappeared indoors while Kate cajoled Domina, unwilling and resentful, down from her perch. She was sitting with her in the kitchen, the flap bolted, when the Detective-Chief Inspector reappeared. Domina retreated angrily to her basket and flattened herself on the cushion.

"You're free to have that room now. Your writing desk has been searched. I've read the letters and bills you keep there – I had to. The only letters are signed 'Vivvy'. Is that your daughter?" Kate gave a single nod. "If you have other letters, never mind how old or who from, they'll be read too. You'd better tell me."

"I have no others," Kate snapped, outraged. She felt smeared and sticky with disgust. "But this one came this morning – you'd better read it." She pushed Vivvy's letter across the kitchen table, swept up Domina in her arms and hurried breathlessly from the room.

★ ★ ★

Kate shut herself into the living-room with a slam, a spurt of childish bad temper repaid with interest by Domina who clawed her way spitefully out of Kate's arms.

"Et tu, brute," she muttered, and gave her an apologetic stroke along her back. Domina retired to rearrange her disordered feelings under the piano stool.

Kate raked out and relaid the fire with gleanings from the log basket and hoped she could make it go. Nothing would induce her to return to the kitchen for the kindling box beside the boiler. And nothing could heal the sense of depredation in that once friendly room. The whole affair was a load of silliness. Harassment, Kate felt. She knew nothing and had done nothing to warrant such nightmarish treatment. The thought that the Detective-Chief Inspector's superiors must have seen good reason to support his application for a search warrant nudged briefly, but Kate was too angry to give it much consideration.

The fire caught up and Kate left it to Domina. She couldn't now write to Vivvy. What could she possibly tell her? 'The house is being searched, your letters read, Domina frightened out of her wits, the garden prodded and perhaps dug up – likewise all through the village – and all because some bloody specious jack-in-office has a bee in his bonnet. But otherwise

I'm not involved, dear Vivvy. I keep my cool and slam doors for a hobby.'

Kate crossed to close the window she'd opened to get the fire going, and looked out onto the road. She wondered how Anne Lawrence would cope with renewed police enquiries at her door and large men poking holes in her garden. Kate saw that the front garden next to Mrs. Harrison's was under investigation. A uniformed policeman was driving a thin rod at intervals deep into the flower-beds. Probably skewering bulbs like kebabs. Lawns could give their own proof of non-disturbance, but flagstones – ? Would all her flags be taken up in order to prod the earth below? Oh God!

Footsteps sounded along the hall and up the stairs. Someone was blundering about in the cupboard under the stairs; Kate heard the Hoover trundled out. Distant bumblings sounded from the bedrooms. A craving for another cup of coffee seized her and Kate bitterly regretted shutting herself away in the living-room. If she'd opted to stay in the kitchen she could have kept an eye on the yard as well. She heard drawers being opened and shut in the bedroom directly overhead. The house felt no longer secure, her personal things no longer her own. People feel like this after burglaries, Kate reminded herself. At least it wasn't that kind of intrusion. But was this any better?

Now Mrs. Harrison's front patch was being scrutinised and Mrs. Harrison herself oversaw the exercise. Kate could hear snatches of her warnings, prohibitions and reproofs. One of the police cars across the road suddenly broke into a tinny babble of duck-speak and the uniformed man inside could be seen writing while the radio quacked busily. The message over, he hurried up Kate's front path and knocked urgently at her door. He might have more discreetly rung the bell, but no doubt knocking produced a more suitable sound effect, Kate thought bitterly. They stood almost nose to nose, she at the open window, he on her doorstep; but as he didn't address her and seemed not even to see her, Kate concluded that his business was strictly with the Detective-Chief Inspector. She shut the window and went back to sit by the fire with Domina, noticing wearily that the bookshelves showed signs of having been searched.

Steps passed the living-room and Kate heard the front door open. A growl of talk, of which she couldn't make out a single word, was followed by the Detective-Chief Inspector's voice calling down the hall.

"Steve? Finish here now, and call the others off. Tell John to see me back at the shop." The front door closed as Kate went back to the window.

She could see that the quacking car had been pulled out of line and turned round in the road. She watched the Detective-Chief Inspector climb in to be driven off but she could hear no directions given. Anyway, the exercise was over – perhaps because some discovery had been made elsewhere? Kate longed to ask the uniformed constable – no more than a boy, surely – who knocked gently on the living-room door and put his head round.

"We'll be leaving now, miss. They're just tidying up at the back."

Kate wandered dispiritedly to the kitchen and looked out of the back window. Time enought to go upstairs and tidy things. Nothing much seemed disturbed in the yard. The exposed patches of earth were here and there freshly levelled, but that was all. Kate went out to lock the door in the wall.

She was making herself the longed-for cup of coffee when the door bell rang. Mrs. Harrison. Kate took her back into the kitchen and poured out a second cup.

"Well! What excitement! You heard what it was all about, did you? It makes me very uneasy, really. First the murder at your place and now this burglary. Exciting too, though. But it's nice to relax. Where's your little one?" Mrs. Harrison looked round expectantly. "I brought Gallardia in straight away. She's such a good mum she wouldn't have left the kits for long, but I didn't want to risk her being frightened out of her milk."

"Dommy's in by the fire," said Kate. "What's this about a burglary? I was – rather busy this morning so I didn't see much of what went on."

"My dear Kate! You're almost as uninterested in things as Anne Lawrence! Well!"

Mrs. Harrison settled herself with a little sideways wriggle, obviously delighted to have such an early opportunity to rehash the recent events.

"There's been a big burglary – jewels, you know, and old silver, so my young man was telling me. Over at Lake Haye, I guessed, but he wasn't giving that much away! We'll read about it on Tuesday, I suppose, and about our part in the search. What Vivvy's missing! Anyway, it seems that a lorry driver picked up a hitch-hiker who asked to be dropped off just up here, on the main road. And they seem to think he could've hidden the stuff – in his back-pack, you see – either on the wasteland or somewhere in our gardens. What a thing to have turned up next spring! But didn't you watch?"

Kate shook her head, wondering how much of Mrs. Harrison's story reached her directly from official sources and how much was via Mrs. Harrison's own imaginative reconstructions.

"Aren't you funny? I watched them from upstairs – you can see almost all along the backs. They spent most time in your yard. They prodded into all your tubs and they must've thought the paving would be a good place to hide stuff under, for they levered up a few slabs. Well, they may not have found anything, but I shall keep on looking!"

"But the walls," Kate protested. "Why should he spend time and effort howking the swag and himself over walls and into unknown gardens when he could find a good place on the wasteland?"

"Oh, I shall keep looking there too! There must be a reward, mustn't there? But not everyone keeps their back gates locked, you know. The Matthews' gate always bangs when it's windy, and very irritating it is! But he could always find something to stand on to get over and no one would see him in the dark. Whereas anyone might find the stuff by chance on the wasteland. It's much more exposed in the winter. And it might be someone who knows the area from his childhood, mightn't it? Anyway, I must fly and give

Gallardia a break. The little toms are getting so boisterous now!"

Mrs. Harrison was determined to believe the burglary story and had an answer ready for every doubt. Well, let her convince the others. It would clear Kate's own problem of how she could possibly go freely about the village without a guilty and apologetic expression all over her face. And if the *Herald* did show any interest Mrs. Harrison could be relied upon to make the story plausible. Kate wondered if it was a spur of the moment invention by the harassed constable or whether the burglary was a prearranged cover for the whole exercise.

Kate cleared the table and washed up the breakfast dishes, tucking Vivvy's letter sadly into her jeans pocket. It had read so fresh and unspoilt as she laughed over it. Now it was a bitter relic of a distasteful and humiliating morning. It was nearly lunch-time but Kate couldn't feel less like eating and the day seemed to stretch interminably ahead.

She debated ringing Ruth and teling her what had happened. If Ruth had been interviewed again some clue as to what was in the Detective-Chief Inspector's mind might be deduced from the line of questioning. Perhaps she could even throw some light on his 'hypothesis'. But Kate wasn't certain how Ruth might react to such revelations. She might believe there was no smoke without a fire. If she'd been questioned again her sympathies might already be undermined.

Kate was aware of a barrier, a lack of trust or honesty somewhere between them. She couldn't say whether it was one she'd unconsciously thrown up herself, or whether it arose out of mutual restraint, but generally she was content not to force it. Kate thought they were like two dogs circling stiff-legged round each other, not hostile but curious and uncertain. She cared enough not to prompt hostility by a clumsy move. Her reliance on Ruth's friendship had come to mean more than simply a chance to talk about Celia. So on reflection Kate decided to sweat it out alone. She could at least catch up with her reading.

But whatever her plans, the world seemed determined to break in. The telephone rang and Kate was jolted into apprehension by the sound of Detective-Chief Inspector McPherson's voice.

"Miss Henderson? I'd like to see you, if it's convenient. Will you come in to Headquarters or shall I send a car for you?" If she was being given the option of travelling under her own steam the visit couldn't be terminal, Kate decided, and hastily refused the offer of a police car.

★ ★ ★

"I'm sorry to bring you out," the Detective-Chief Inspector apologised when Kate was shown up to his office. "But I thought you'd maybe had enough of me at your home."

"It's your job," she reminded him stonily, herself remembering – of all details to remember just then – her moment of intense humiliation when she was so totally ignored by the constable on her own doorstep.

"Yes," he agreed wearily. "A job performed effectively only if we don't get emotionally involved. I think I've tried too hard to achieve that detachment and it's been as effective as a blindfold. Bushes have become bears. As you see, this is another meeting off the record. The information I want to give you will soon be made public – there's a news conference called in half an hour – but I wanted you to know first from me. Well, then. Two discoveries, or recoveries, were made this morning while we were at Abbots Barton. The first was the charred and badly damaged remains of a human skull, sifted from the bonfire site at Rivermead Flatts – do you know it?" Kate shook her head weakly.

"The name only."

"Yes, a bit out of the city. It was the site of a public Guy Fawkes party and obviously accessible before and after Bonfire Night. Interesting, as it happens. A small motor-cruiser was stolen from there on the morning of Saturday, November fifth. It hasn't been recovered."

"But – but do you mean it was *Peter's* head?"

"Unrecognisable, of course. They may get something from the teeth. I seem to remember you telling me Colebrook had good teeth?" Christ!

"He – they looked good when he smiled. But wasn't –

whoever it was – taking a risk? Throwing – that – on a flaming bonfire in full view – ?"

"What if it'd been put there the night before? Pushed well into the heap before it was lit? You know what these community bonfires are like – old tyres, cushions, hedge-trimmings, you name it. Who would've seen – or smelt?" Kate shut her eyes briefly.

"And you looked for – it in *my* garden, and believed *I* could be capable – "

"Was afraid, not believed. I did try to distract attention from you in case I was – I hoped I was wrong."

"What if the *Herald* gets wind of your burglary story?"

"We're ready for the *Herald* – in fact its thunder will be stolen by Tuesday. And there actually has been a verifiable burglary just over the county boundary. Like criminals, Miss Henderson, we know that if you want to lie successfully you should tell as much of the truth as possible.

"Well, then. The second recovery was reported from Bude, where the Sinclair boy lived. A heap of clothes resembling the description of what he'd last been seen wearing was found in a hay-loft after a farmer saw – rather obvious signs of trespassing. So. We'll soon have them here for tests, but their discovery does seem to support this James Leverton's story that he saw Sinclair in Bude on Thursday. You've been following the news programmes, I expect? Did you recognise the face in the photo on TV?"

"I thought it was Peter at first. It wasn't very clear. But I really don't think I'd recognise even a good photo of Terry Sinclair." The Detective-Chief Inspector nodded as if Kate had just confirmed something.

"So you see, you're no longer in the front line, Miss Henderson. I must thank you for letting me take up your time," he ended formally, and rose to his feet.

"Indeed. And for taking up so much of my peace of mind," Kate retorted. "May I not at least hear the rest of your hypothetical scenario? Am I not owed more than merely civil thanks?" The Detective-Chief Inspector stood staring at the papers on his desk. He spoke quietly.

169

"I could take the easy way and get someone else to tell you. There is one other person at least who knows why you might have cause to – to organise mischief to both Colebrook and Sinclair – "

"I keep telling you – " Kate began impatiently, but he raised his head and looked at her. The interview was over.

15

Bewildered and very uneasy, Kate left Detective-Chief Inspector McPherson and returned home. She now felt ravenously hungry and to Domina's delight fried a plateful of eggs and bacon. The rinds, cut off and crisped further under the grill, were Domina's perk for sitting around looking decorative and loving. She fell on them like a swooping hawk when Kate's own meal was finished.

The local radio station was first with the news of the latest developments in the Headless Corpse case; Kate listened while Domina slept peacefully on her lap. Top of the Pops in order of sensationalism was the discovery of the skull at Rivermead Flatts:

'The remains are badly damaged and show signs of crushing, perhaps within some kind of wrapping or container, before being hidden in the bonfire pile. Some pieces are missing, understandably in view of their fragmentation, public access to the site and their general unrecognisability.' Animals, Kate supposed in distress. 'Only dental evidence may possibly prove identity, but Detective-Chief Inspector McPherson is understood to be working on the theory that the skull remains and the headless corpse of Morgan's Mount belong together.

'Meanwhile a house-to-house enquiry and a thorough search of the Flatts area has been mounted. The Detective-Chief Inspector had given instructions yesterday for all such bonfire sites to be investigated and his hunch was rewarded by the find this morning.' So he hadn't staked everything on finding significant evidence at her house, Kate realised. "We're close to something now," the Detective-Chief Inspector told a news conference this afternoon.'

There followed an account of the clothes, believed to belong to Terry Sinclair, found in the Bude hay-loft. Listeners were reminded of James Leverton's belief that he'd seen Terry in Bude. Results of the forensic tests on the clothes would soon be known, but meanwhile enquiries were being made by the Bude Police at all local clothing stores where Terry might have bought a new outfit. The implication was that after James Leverton's much publicised sighting, Terry had panicked and tried to change his appearance. There was still no comment from his family.

Last among the local news items was a light-hearted mention of Kate's own crucifixion. That following a burglary in a neighbouring county (unspecified) local police had made a search of Abbots Barton, near where a hitch-hiker, thought to be carrying a hold-all, was believed to have been seen. Gardens and the nearby waste ground had been searched but nothing significant found.

'This is the second time in a week that police enquiries have disturbed the routine of this sleepy little village, where the attractive "Barton" stone was once quarried. The earlier visit apparently followed complaints of late-night disturbances.' So that had been the reason given on Monday. Kate was impressed by this unexpected tactfulness in the pursuit of her alibi. 'But the inhabitants of Abbots Barton are jealous of their law-abiding reputation. "We never have disturbances here," one cottager insisted. "There isn't even a public house."' Kate laughed as Anne Lawrence's ex-headmistress rasp sounded through the words. She wondered how Anne liked being referred to as 'one of the cottagers'.

But none of this story seemed to tie in with the main items of interest and the Detective-Chief Inspector wasn't mentioned in connection with the village. The skull would figure in the national news, together with the discovery of yet another bundle of discarded clothes, and no doubt the Flatts and Bude would be targets for reporters looking for a change from Morgan's Mount, where their activities were so circumscribed. But the village would sleep undisturbed once more.

* * *

The next morning Kate made her weekly trip down the road for her Sunday paper, prepared for May's friendly enquiries after Vivvy. The wind blew tempestuously and she had a struggle with the paper shop door as it threatened to blow out of her hands. She was vaguely aware of someone else in the shop talking to May, but by the time she'd triumphed over the door he'd moved away to the book rack where he stood with his back turned.

May had Kate's paper folded ready and asked when Vivvy was expected home for Christmas. Kate's reply was momentarily distracted by May's twitching eyebrows and jerking head. When she construed these contortions as indicating something interest-worthy about the stranger at the book rack, Kate half turned to lean on the counter while she studied him more closely.

"Term finishes on the eighteenth," she told May, scrutinising the back of a grimy Gannex driving jacket and dark trousers. "She's inviting someone home for New Year." A well-fingered tweed hat brim nearly met the greasy turned-up collar. Kate turned back and arched her own eyebrows at May, inviting enlightenment.

"Oh? A romance, do you think?" May pronounced it ro-mance and expected to see it round every corner. Kate's illegitimate motherhood had appealed to all her repressed yearning for exotic and lusty adventure. She mouthed something, like a goldfish swallowing a golf-ball, but Kate crossed her eyes in village-idiot non-comprehension. "Reporter," May mouthed again, her own eyes starting with the effort of communication.

"Well, you know Vivvy." Kate sneaked another glance at the seedy-looking back. A reporter. Hell! She wrinkled her nose in distaste at May. "She's usually over the moon about somebody." May smiled in agreement and clattered the till noisily for change. She stared meaningly at Kate and then at the reporter. Kate looked round in time to see him replace the book and half turn to mumble 'Good morning' as he left the shop. Kate registered tinted glasses and a woollen scarf as the old-fashioned door bell jangled irritatingly after him.

"He might at least have bought it," May remarked sourly.

173

"What was he after, May?"

"Search me! He seemed to think he was on to a scoop. Wanted the inside story of the police search – was anywhere particularly thoroughly searched, who was questioned and which gardens were dug. I said no, pretty well everyone and none. So then he said he didn't want other reporters getting wind of his visit and he'd *pay* me not to blow his cover. Well, really! I was just asking him if he was with the *Herald* when you came in, but he'd been here almost since I opened up reading that dratted book. Just standing there while people wandered round him – hoping to pick up something, I suppose. When things quietened down a bit I asked if I could help him and he gave me this spiel."

"He should be down at Rivermead Flatts if he wants a scoop," Kate said, her mind elsewhere. "But come to think of it, isn't he a bit off course chasing the tiny story of the burglary here? He can't have been detailed by his paper, he must be doing it off his own bat, to be so fussed about others following up the same lead. What can he think he knows, May? What on earth kind of scoop?" There was nothing to know. Their local connection with a distant burglary was pure fabrication. Unless. Unless he'd somehow picked up a clue to the real purpose of the search. "I suppose he *was* a reporter?" Kate added, as a new and unwelcome thought suddenly struck her.

"Well, he wasn't a tourist," May returned tartly. "He claimed he was – or anyway hinted he was a reporter, and he had all the gimmicks. You know, tatty clothes, notebook, flashy – "

"You don't think he might've been someone following up the police search on his own account?" Kate wondered uneasily. Even a reporter would be preferable to someone sneaking over her wall to finish the job of lifting her flagstones on the off-chance of finding buried treasure.

"Kate!" May gazed back with round, brightly excited eyes. "You've got something there! He could be the – the advance scout for the raiding-party! Well, he didn't get anything out of *me*, but there's some would talk the hind legs off anything that moved to get their names in the papers. You leave this to me," she advised importantly. "I'm going to get straight onto the

Herald – darn! It's Sunday! Do you know the editor?" Kate shook her head, smiling. "Okay. I'll ring the cops and they can sort it out. They never should've published the search in the first place. I'm *sure* you're right, Kate! Now, you just go home and keep buttoned," as Kate opened her mouth to speak. "And not a word to Ma Harrison. I'll handle this. With any luck it won't come to a shoot-out."

"Okay, pardner," Kate laughed. "Give my regards to your mother, May, and tell her I'll come and see her with Vivvy when she's home again."

Kate hurried back to her house, trying to steal a march on the wind and read the headlines. The rest of the paper would wait till later but the headlines were fair game, if only they'd hold still. She had to write to Vivvy and post the letter to catch the first Monday collection; and there was one other thing Kate wanted to do before she could switch off her head and laze with the weekend news.

   ★ ★ ★

The telephone was in the hall. Kate didn't stop to take her coat off but turned up Ruth's number and dialled. If by some chance the *Herald* or any paper had been given a clue to the one detail concerning the murder enquiry that had so far escaped publication, the names of the corpse's finders, then Ruth ought to be warned. If May's reporter was genuine, Kate's name and the fair assumption that the police search in her same village must be linked with the murder investigation at the Department would be a good enough reason to attract reporters. And if he wasn't genuine, but genuinely misled about the supposed cache, then certainly the police ought to know. But meanwhile Ruth might have some information.

"Hullo, Ruth?" Kate heard the receiver picked up at the end of the line. "It's me, Kate Henderson."

"Kate! Is everything all right? What's all this about the police practically camping in the village?"

"Not quite, but they had a bit of a poke round yesterday. It made the local news, that's all. But – "

"Poor you! You can't escape them, can you? Margaret O'Hare says they're still crawling all over Morgan's Mount."

"Yes, they were around on Friday." Kate took a giant stride, hooked a chair nearer with her foot and sat down. "But we're not told anything more than you read in the papers. Look, Ruth, what I wanted to ask – have you mentioned to anyone that we – that we were at the pond when the body turned up?"

"Lord, no! We agreed not to. Why?"

"Just there's been a stranger snooping around here this morning, apparently a reporter, and I wondered if we'd been leaked. Anyone lurking round about you?"

"Oh, hell! No, I haven't seen anyone I couldn't account for. But even if there were, it would be difficult to lay siege on campus. It's different for you, though. Someone's been indiscreet, I suppose. Do you want to spend a few days here?"

"Oh – no, but thanks for the offer. I can't leave the cat and she's not as transplantable as Hermie. It may just be a false alarm and nothing to do with us. Er – have the police seen you since that first time?"

"No, but I wouldn't expect them to. I was only an innocent passer-by, after all." Don't you believe it, thought Kate grimly. You were damn near an accomplice. "They've talked to you again, have they?"

"Oh, several times," Kate replied casually. "They drop in and chat to us in ones and groups. I was just wondering if there was a common line of enquiry that might give one a clue how their minds are working. But if they haven't seen you since you can't help there."

"Kate, are they giving you trouble? I detect a slightly too throwaway tone. Though obviously what's been discovered about that poor, wretched boy must convince everyone that you were no more than friends – for all he seems to have developed a post-mortem fiancée. Did you know about her? Is she the silly woman you mentioned?"

"Mm. Not that she was ever his fiancée, whether or not the rest is believable. Which means I didn't know *that* about him either. In fact I seem to have missed out on several rather pertinent facts. Er – how can they tell, Ruth?"

"The homosexual thing? Heaven knows! The imagination boggles. As for being active or passive, or positive or negative

– if asked they can probably tell your taste in literature from the shape of your knee-caps these days."

"Only if it's devotional literature, I expect. I just wondered if they were ever wrong."

"Well, there was that poor devil, not so long ago – do you remember? They had to re-try, or at least reconsider some of the cases where he'd been the forensic expert."

"Vaguely, yes. Oh, well. Anyway, you haven't been and aren't further troubled, and that's all I wanted to know."

"If that keeps you happy. When are you coming over again, Kate? Chris Lowther was asking after you the other day."

"Nice of her. Give her my regards. I think I'll hang on, though, till this business is settled. The – the fact of the police still being at Morgan's Mount and my own connection with the place could give any conversation an awkward turn."

"Are you including me among all that as well? You aren't forgetting I was with you at the beginning? Kate, are you trying to tell me there's something I don't know?"

"I wasn't trying to," Kate admitted carefully. "But something peculiar and – er – inexplicable seems to have cropped up and I rather think I ought to – to get it sorted out first."

There was a long silence, during which Kate wondered if Ruth had left the 'phone for some reason. She waited.

"Something personal, do you mean?" came Ruth's voice at last, muffled. Kate imagined she'd lit a cigarette. "Or something to do with the case?"

"Bit of each, really. But – "

"You know I'll do what I can to help."

"Of course. But it isn't that simple."

"And nor am I. Have you found out something and you're not letting on? I suppose it incriminates someone at Morgan's Mount," Ruth continued without waiting for Kate to answer. "It can only mean someone you're – emotionally entangled with. Kate, you sound just like Donald Duck."

"Because I'm failing to get a word in edgeways," Kate laughed in exasperation. "You're wrong all the way. That much at least I know and can assure you about. It's what I *don't* yet know, and who else it involves and how, that's – er –

confusing. When I know all that I'll tell you. If you're still interested."

"Is someone trying to get at you? Kate, are you being *blackmailed*? Over that boy?"

"For pity's sake – ! There's nothing there to blackmail me about!" I have it on the best authority, thought Kate wearily. "Are you a secret Mills and Boon addict, or something, Ruth? Absolutely and finally no. N.O. Someone has tried to get at me, yes, in a way, and almost succeeded in making trouble, but until I know the whole story and can see how far it's gone the rounds – I'd prefer to sort it out alone."

"You can't afford not to need friends, Kate – like one of those awful front parlours kept dusted and polished for someone who'll never use it again." Ruth stopped suddenly and then continued with greater calm. "I just hope you know what you're doing, that's all. You could try trusting me, instead of wondering if I'd given you away over our agreement. I take that pretty badly, I may say. And you might at least know I wouldn't believe anything discreditable about you."

"But listening to all you've suggested so far, it seems you might believe anything!" Kate laughed outright. "If I thought you might be able to help – never mind whether you wanted to or not – I'd come to you, really. But I've got to find the clue to all this nonsense first. Until then I don't know who might get hurt. It could all be cleared up by Friday's lecture when I'll see you again."

"If that's the way you want it I'll have to abide by it, I suppose," Ruth capitulated grumpily. "But you know you can give me a call any time you change your mind. And if that reporter does become a nuisance, the invitation still stands."

"Thank you, then. But I hope for both our sakes he'll run away and play somewhere else."

Another beautiful friendship up the spout, thought Kate gloomily as she replaced the receiver. Ruth's reactions had been as lurid as May's imagination. Kate was convinced she'd been wise not to cloud their relationship with more smoke until she could at least see the source of the fire. Suspicion of murder, or even complicity, and search warrants could only add fuel to Ruth's uncertainties about Kate, whatever her assurances of belief in her. 'You haven't convinced me. Academically speaking.'

* * *

Kate went through to the kitchen to make herself a mid-morning drink and walked over to the window while the coffee percolated, pondering over the 'phone conversation. Outside, Domina stalked a sparrow come close to the backdoor for crumbs and scraps. Kate looked on vacantly, trying again to anticipate what the Detective-Chief Inspector could possibly have to tell her. Obviously more than the fact that he'd caught her out in withholding minor snippets of information.

Domina lurked in the shelter of one of the tubs, betrayed only by the scarcely perceptible twitch of her tail-tip and the wind ruffling her fur. A shadow within a shadow. Her jaws gibbered a silent threat. The blustering wind and the little bird's preoccupation offered her a quick kill, if she chose, but Domina wasn't hungry. It was the fun of the hunt that drove her, not an empty belly or a litter of kittens awaiting her return. Kate watched her inch out of cover, sleek, flexed and armed; whippy steel sheathed in velvet. Lethal.

"Playtime's over," said Kate aloud, and rapped sharply on the glass. The sparrow took off, an almost vertical brown streak, while Domina, caught in mid slink, turned her head to glower greenly at the window.

The 'phone rang as Kate poured out her coffee. Instead of the half-expected voice of Detective-Chief Inspector McPherson came the Principal's surprising announcement that he proposed to call on her after lunch 'on a matter of the utmost gravity'.

"I'll be in," Kate replied faintly, wondering if the corpse's identity had now been officially established as Peter's and the news was to be broken to her gently. She reckoned she had a couple of hours to knock up something for lunch, set the living-room to rights and get it warmed up, and try and find time to dash off a curtailed note to Vivvy. The Sunday paper would have to wait a bit longer.

When he arrived Professor Edwards seemed flustered and ill at ease.

"Miss Henderson," he sat carefully and precisely, paying close attention to his trouser creases. "I was yesterday advised of events so disturbing that I must ask you to be perfectly frank with me. Believe me, much more than mere – personal embarrassment or inconvenience depends on this. Gordon Watson, my informant, has persuaded me that you are in possession of some, if not all, of the following facts. He came to see me initially because he was aware that further investigation of the murder could endanger his own position at the Department. Even his whole future." The Principal sighed heavily. "I could only assure him, as I assure you now, that I and my staff would deal with any of my students strictly on the merits of their own achievements at the Department. However, police prosecutions arising out of these investigations would be beyond our sphere of influence." He looked intently at Kate. "You understand me, Miss Henderson?"

"But I've no idea what we're discussing," Kate protested. "Gordon has made some odd observations to me, most of which left me confused. I'm at a loss to know how I can possibly – " she flapped her hands. Even the Principal was at it now, Kate thought in despair.

Professor Edwards gazed at her over steepled fingers.

"Gordon is aware of my meeting with you and I am not breaking any confidences when I tell you the facts he set before me. As I said, he believes you to be aware of at least some of them. They are, then, that he knew this Terry Sinclair during their first year at the university. That, in fact, they entered into a – an intimate relationship. Peter Colebrook was a First year undergraduate with them and even then showing signs of – of an advanced sophistication. He discovered their relationship and I am afraid to say he used this knowledge for his own ends. Because at the time there could be no profitable blackmail of Gordon, Colebrook apparently told him, 'I'll wait till you're earning. You'll be glad to pay me then.' Gordon, as you must know, is a quiet, caring lad, and he knew himself unable to defy that kind of threat, even in these more permissive times, as certainly as he knew that the threat was seriously intended.

His fear is now that he is unequivocally placed with a motive for – the murder of Peter Colebrook if even one other person knows this story. He believes you do."

It sounded very like the cat-and-mouse game Peter might play. That Gordon might be a murderer wasn't worth Kate's consideration and she was surprised that he or anyone should think him 'unequivocally' suspect. It seemed more in keeping with Gordon's uncharacteristically hysterical outburst of the day before than his better known sane image.

"Poor Gordon," she said at last, wondering where the Principal was leading. "But I didn't know."

"Indeed? But what of your own position, Miss Henderson? Please – I am not here to sit in judgement or idly question to satisfy a morbid curiosity." Kate continued to look blank. "Have you really no knowledge of the other details? That Colebrook so worked on this boy, Sinclair, a poor creature by all accounts but likeable enough, that he persuaded him to attempt a rape? You are unaware of that? Then listen to me for I believe it to be true, and I know that Gordon has given the police officers these details as facts. Colebrook drove that miserable boy to make an unspeakable assault upon a lady of good reputation. The lady selected for this – exercise was single, apparently virginal and certainly admirable. These qualities and Sinclair's homosexuality added spice to the circumstances and no doubt gave greater satisfaction to Colebrook." Kate felt an incredulous disgust.

"You look outraged, Miss Henderson. Even in the retelling there is a shocking ring, a whiff of old evil. The reduction of goodness into the dirt. Gordon claims that he was unable to prevent Sinclair going through with this wicked plan, and indeed a night was secretly chosen when Gordon was engaged elsewhere. But, as if what was planned were not enough, something went dreadfully wrong. There was a car accident and – the lady died in it."

The first wave of realisation brought Kate to her feet in a surge of disbelief and loathing.

"Celia! You can't mean Celia!" But suddenly all that had been puzzling slotted into its new, hateful logic. "Terry Sinclair was taking the History course. It was Celia they fixed on, wasn't it? Oh, if I'd known that much – " Kate halted in anguish as she saw the Prinicipal's expression and sank back in her chair. She felt weak with horror, gutted, yet a creeping fury screamed for release. Kate bowed her head into her hands before the gale of violent emotion and fought herself for control. Knowledge. She needed knowledge; the fuel for her release. "You must tell me what you know. I am right, aren't I?" Kate heard her voice shaking, barely recognisable as her own.

She looked up to see the Principal's pitying appraisal.

"Yes, I'm sorry. This is a grosser enormity than anything – I only knew Dr. Rowland by repute, as a brilliant academic and a good woman. I heard of your – long association with her only recently. You tell me that you knew nothing of this, of what happened?"

"No, how should I? We all understood – the police – it was an accident, the car out of control. But Gordon knew the truth?"

"To his own great horror and distress. He said nothing because of his attachment to Sinclair, but he had cut all connections with him until recently. In contrast to his own circumstances, Sinclair's family is rich and Gordon says that Colebrook traded on what happened to profit at their expense. He kept Sinclair close to him. But this term Sinclair sought Gordon out in desperation and when he recognised you, as it seems he did, he believed you might be used to expose Colebrook in some way. You did not realise this either?" Kate shook her head.

"Sinclair was intending to speak to you. But when both men disappeared Gordon believed you to be responsible, directly or indirectly. Because Gordon has already told all this to Detective-Chief Inspector McPherson, I have to warn you that you may find yourself closely questioned."

"My house and garden were thoroughly searched yesterday," Kate said dully. "I had no idea then what their reasoning was based on, but I see their frightening logic now. I wish it was true. For all the fear I should now be feeling, I wish I had – been responsible and free at least of this – frustrated – hate. She gave me everything, you see. She saved me. You're too civilised – " Kate heard her voice rise and break. She sat amazed, not at the violence of her feelings, but that she should have disclosed them to the humane and cultivated man sitting opposite her.

Kate hardly listened to what the Principal said after that. No doubt they were things he felt it proper to express, but they didn't touch Kate or comfort her. It was as if she was rid of all softness or concern for anyone. Those were feelings – weaknesses – that might be clung to from outside and weigh her down. Kate was filled wholly with a flaring rage that saw its target and held itself in check only to fix the range.

"This will pass," the Principal interrupted her frantic musings. "And let it pass, my dear Miss Henderson, or you will end by hating yourself and bring about your own destruction – the destruction of whatever her friendship for you may have created. Remember you have your future and your daughter, and others who respect and care for you. The law must take its true course now, and Sinclair will be made to answer for the goodness he so wantonly destroyed. As for Peter Colebrook, that vicious young man – he is beyond all thoughts of help or revenge. But I must beg you to restore your own balance. Talk to Gordon, if you care to. He has borne a terrible weight out of his misguided loyalty, and his conscience is uneasy at the thought of trouble he may have brought on you. If you need clarification of the facts go to him, rather than brood on events you could not have averted two years ago. It was not because you failed your friend that she died."

16

The need to see Gordon, more than her own conscientiousness, drove Kate into the Department that Monday. She'd put herself to sleep the night before – or rather, knocked herself out – with whatever she could find in the sideboard. Kate knew there had been no other way to win any peace that night.

Like herself Gordon was free on a Monday afternoon, and when they were all gathering for the Principal's lecture Kate told him she wanted to see him at the end of the morning.

"With or without Jeff, I don't mind. Let's meet at The Happy Man. It's the nearest and I want to get it over." Gordon agreed readily enough, though he looked at her pretty sharply. Probably he felt self-conscious at being seen in such ravaged company, Kate guessed, and she didn't care. He should be so lucky. But several others did a double-take on seeing her face that morning and might have paused to question, but for the blank gaze of withdrawal that warned them to hurry past.

"I've heard the gist of what you've told the Principal and the police," Kate began abruptly when Gordon came to sit beside her in the pub. "It might've occurred to you to tell me too. If you had, I'd have reassured you on every single point and saved you twitching. I knew nothing of all this." Gordon glanced with relief at Kate's glass of orange juice and for the first time she noticed how distressed he looked. She felt a momentary pity.

"Are you sure you want to talk about it now? You – you don't look very well, you know."

"If your head ached like mine, you too might appear less than usually lively. But I'll get what I came to hear if I have to beat it out of you. Just answer my questions. I fully accept what the Principal says about being bowed with grief, shock and horror and we'll take that as read. Just now I'm not too much bothered by feelings, I want facts. Right. First. How was this disgusting plan supposed to work? Celia wasn't an easy person to lead up a dark alleyway."

"Look, I want you to know I'm sorry, really sorry you ever had to hear any of this. But my own position – I thought you must know already – "

"Get on with it," Kate muttered in a savage undertone. "What on earth can you know about how I feel?"

"I had to stand by and bear losing Terry inch by inch," Gordon answered quietly. "I – he was – I'd never known anyone so innocent and so – gentle natured. But I had to watch him – desecrate himself. Then the accident. And now – "

Kate suddenly felt ashamed of her anger. The real shock of her loss was over and done with two years before, a swift and sudden cautery; but Gordon had to bear a piecemeal separation, each step more distressing than the one before. And each accompanied by its own stresses of inadequacy and failure. Like a limb being twisted off. He hadn't even the relief of rage.

"I'm sorry, Gordon. I daren't get emotional and it's making me inhuman. It must be bloody for you. The Principal told me – "

"He's a wonderful man. You were right about him. I'm glad I went to see him about this. But I'm sorry I had to drop you in. Really sorry. It was just – " Kate began to despair of ever getting Gordon up to scratch. She decided to try an oblique approach.

"How did Terry know who I was?"

"That day you and Elinor came in here," Gordon turned his glass gratingly round and round on the table-top, "he asked who you were. He grew excited. He was pretty low before that. Anyway, he was sure he'd seen you before – with Dr. Rowland, though neither of us could remember her name and Jeff never knew it, of course. I knew who he meant, naturally." Naturally. Kate felt her anger return. "In a carpet shop. The beginning of our second year, when he was furnishing the flat and – and Peter was getting a tighter grip on him. The original idea was to find out where she lived and – and do it there. But when he heard how you two talked he realised she didn't live alone."

The new stair carpet, Kate remembered. It had been laid not long before Celia died.

"I remember the shop. Go on."

"So Terry told Peter it was all off. But Peter wouldn't let him back out and Terry – Terry was bewitched. He was to get her to his flat somehow instead. It was then I realised it wasn't just stupid talk. Peter was serious. 'Invite her to an innocent party. No one deserves to be so untouchable.' Terry admired her, you see. More than that. Peter mocked him for what he called a medieval romanticism that identified the Virgin Mary with any unobtainable woman. Only emotionally retarded adolescents could make that mistake, he said. But there was a cure. But everyone liked Dr. Rowland and she'd been to a few student gatherings. But she wouldn't accept Terry's invitation. Apparently. I think Terry never had the nerve to ask her, or was genuinely unwilling to.

"Peter said, 'She's probably guessed you're a raving queer. You'll have to go through with it now to put the record straight.' I hated him. He smeared everything. So he told Terry to waylay her on her way home one evening. In the end I didn't know what they planned or when for. I was doing a weekend job and didn't hear any more about it till the Saturday when Terry came to me looking like death." Gordon flicked a glance at Kate, acknowledging an unfortunate choice of words.

"Don't excuse yourself." Kate's voice shook. "You could have warned Celia at least that mischief was planned. You knew that much. You could've done *that* much."

"It's easy to look back and say that. *I've* said that. But at the time I hoped nothing would happen. I couldn't believe Terry'd go through with it. I thought I knew him. And – and I was afraid of Peter, of what he'd do about my – my relationship with Terry."

"All that's only another way of admitting you let it happen," said Kate deliberately. "You listened to rape being planned and you did nothing. Good God, even today you don't get away with a smacked wrist – and bystanders who plead 'I just hoped he wouldn't get it up – ' It's all right. I'm not going to make a scene," Kate added as Gordon threw a hunted look round the room. "I want to know what Terry told you."

"He'd got into the back of the car, you see, and hidden himself. Just parked unlocked in the staff car-park. If only she'd kept it locked," Gordon tugged at his moustache. "He might easily have been killed as well, you know." Celia's old Ford Estate, so handy for chauffeuring Vivvy and her friends and Celia's own piles of books and papers. It'd been written off in the crash. They'd gone touring in it, camping with it, exploring. It was their family stand-by.

"Then?" Kate prodded.

"The back seat was down and there was stuff in there. Terry wedged up against the front seats and pulled a rug over. It was dark, about six, when Dr. Rowland came. She didn't even look in the back. If she had she could've prevented – but she just chucked her brief-case on the passenger seat and drove off." In a hurry to get home.

"Go on," said Kate harshly.

"When they were out in the country Terry tried to stop her. You know, he could never've gone through with it," Gordon turned to look at Kate directly for the first time. "He didn't have the – the aggression or the strength, let alone the – the willingness. It would've been a farce – "

"Instead of a criminal tragedy?" Kate snarled.

"It was that, of course, but I think Peter always knew it'd be a pathetic failure and that's why he pushed Terry. He liked to see him wriggle on the hook. I don't know what – incentives he held out to him. I thought then Peter wasn't gay and what I knew of Terry – But Terry would've done anything to prove he was – worthy, I suppose, just for Peter's friendship."

Kate finished her drink and snapped the glass down on the table. Terry's hopeless feebleness was not what she'd come to hear about.

"Well, anyway. He startled Dr. Rowland and she lost control of the car. It had been raining, but it was a big car and she was going fast. She hit a tree. Terry was all right, crouched behind the front seats, but in her hurry she hadn't put her belt on and he found she – she was – she wasn't alive. He legged it through the fields back into town and went to earth till the news broke the next day. Then he came to me. I promised not to say anything. It was an accident and – he was devastated. We could only hope Peter would keep quiet too."

There was a long silence while Kate struggled with her emotions.

"He didn't deserve that much consideration," she began tightly. "I'd have – "

"You couldn't have thought up anything worse than what happened to him," Gordon told her sadly. "You know he just dropped out? I couldn't stop him doing that. Peter said, 'You've actually done something I haven't, killed someone.' He moved into the flat with Terry, supposedly to help him through, but he's lived there for nothing ever since. Terry's father paid him heaven knows how much to keep his mouth shut. Why do you think he stayed on for his training year here when he could've gone to any of the more prestigious departments? It was a good way to stay in command. He liked that. And he could keep tabs on me as well. He'd have got at me too when I was earning. So I had a motive for – getting rid of him, and no one but Jeff to give me an alibi. They don't keep watch on us where we work. But I thought you had a better motive – for both Peter and Terry. That was why you'd started this course. When they started asking about Terry, I – I had to cover myself."

Kate considered all that Gordon had told her. Her headache had stilled to a dull thump and the orange juice had settled her queasiness, but her anger and the need for information to give her anger direction was still overwhelming.

"So the worm turned in the end," Kate broke the silence. "And the worm was intending to use me somehow?"

"I'll get us another drink first." Kate watched Gordon at the crowded bar. Quiet, calm, drilled, he was apparently able to cope with anything. It had been a revelation to find he had such blind spots and to see how precarious his self-sufficiency was. Quite different from Peter. Yet neither of them had been able to cope successfully with bloody Terry. Worm? In his own spineless way Terry had been the rock that Celia's and

Peter's lives had smashed on, and Gordon's all but ruined perhaps. And her own. And her own.

"That wine-bar's a pretty squalid place behind all that chic," Gordon began when he returned with the drinks. "All I know is from hints Terry's dropped since he looked me up again this term, but someone there's tied in with the local drug scene. Someone there recruited Terry – he's a pusher now – and that's where he meets his clients. I think he's been experimenting himself. It'll be the end of him if so. Anyway, Peter found out. Terry made the mistake of getting him interested – trying to get his money back – but Peter would never pay out simply for the privilege of dependence. He played along because he wanted something more. He wanted a share in the business.

"Well, he tried to get behind the scenes using what he knew of Terry as a lever. That's when Terry came to find me again and Jeff and I tried to interest you. None of us knew then how closely you were involved already. I was afraid for Terry that Peter would make known what happened two years ago. But Terry was even more afraid of his masters and he daren't let Peter in just like that. Then he saw you here and decided to tell you what happened that night, how it was Peter's fault. He thought you'd expose Peter and he'd have a chance of freeing himself. He daren't go to the police because of the drugs business, but he was prepared for even that to be known if it would get Peter off his back. What he really hoped was that you'd say something publicly at the party, and then Peter might've been persuaded to leave quietly. It seemed worth a try.

"I didn't know where you lived and Terry only knew the general direction of that ghastly car ride, but it was his half day on Thursdays and I told him you were free in the afternoon too. He never got to you?" Kate could only shake her head. She'd been expected to help a pusher and a killer? "He tried to contact Linda Mayer too. We'd all been friendly once and he just needed support. I left a message for her. I don't know why he didn't reach you, or what can have happened that weekend. I never saw him again."

Kate finished her second drink, maddened by Gordon's naïvety and beginning to feel an intense dislike of him, his shuttered mind, his selfishness, his criminal weakness. She was ready to suspect his 'nice guy' image.

"At least now you know I had nothing to do with this. So, what did happen that weekend, do you think? Terry's still alive. He killed Peter? Or the drug fiends did? And I really can't believe in them. You'll be talking about Tong warfare down at the docks next."

"Would that be any more incredible than what's happened already? But neither seems to fit in. Before all this I wouldn't have believed Terry could've done – what's been done. Somebody must've been behind him threatening him with worse. Or they made sure he was somehow involved. For all I know, the others – his business associates – might well be capable of doing that to Peter. Terry was really frightened of them. But why bother? Why not just kill Peter and dump him? To encourage the others, I suppose. Either way, directly guilty or not, Terry's on the run and he'll be frightened into doing something silly."

"I'm not breaking my heart over him," Kate commented grimly. She gathered up her things from the settle.

"Have another drink before they close?"

"No, thanks. This stuff's as sour as hell and you'll probably find 'Seville' engraved on my heart already. What do you think Terry'll do now he's been flushed out of Bude? Come to you?"

"There you are, you see." Gordon was exasperated. "It's just the sort of idiot thing he'd do – rush home right where they'd be looking for him. All his – his badness is really frightened silliness."

"And it was at least Celia's own fault that she died? Loyalty binds you, Gordon, hand and foot. It wouldn't surprise me if you gave all this to the police to divert attention from Terry, using me as an all too handy red herring, not to protect yourself. But will you let me know if you do see him? I'd like to hear his side of the story. It's only fair."

I'd like to cut his heart out. Kate surrendered to engulfing waves of gratified revenge. Terry, cornered and pleading, while Kate savoured the heady power of life and death. Terry, limp and fainting, a poor, drooling apology for a man, while

Kate lashed him into even more abject terror and flayed him with her hatred. Terry, festooned across a rock-face while the vultures pecked out his liver – his eyes, his tongue and anything else available. Oh avenging Furies, she almost cried aloud as she walked sedately down Carriage Hill; Medea, Clytemnestra, Lady Macbeth – unsex me now and give me the guts not to miss my chance.

* * *

Domina pinned Kate with an accusing look as she elongated herself sleepily, leg by leg, out of her basket. Kate had been nearly too late to catch the bus that morning and she'd hurried off without putting Domina's food down. She forked out some for her now and heaved at the smell of it. A quiet sit-down for much thinking was indicated. Some thought first about what and how she was going to tell Vivvy. Luckily she'd written the letter and posted it before the Principal arrived the day before, so she'd have time to sort out her ideas before the next one was due, and not blurt out anything ill-advised.

But need Vivvy know anything at all? That old tragedy and past misery was only incidental to the present case. It had been dragged out simply as a possible motive for herself. And given the way she was feeling now, even two years old the motive was plausible. Two years ago, if she'd known the truth, she'd have gone for them with everything she had. But surely none of it need be made known in the course of police revelations concerning this murder?

Kate wanted to believe that her own relationship with Vivvy would survive, whatever was revealed. She was more bothered by how Vivvy might be regarded – the illegitimate daughter of a lesbian mother mixed up in a nasty murder case. And how would Celia's old friends remember Celia then? Would their live and let live philosophy survive?

One would just have to wait and see. There would be time to warn Vivvy later if everything looked like hanging out. But meanwhile concentrated thought was impossible and it would be unwise to try to come to any firm decisions.

With a sigh Kate turned to her daily paper. As far as the

murder was concerned it merely reiterated the details that had been made public over the weekend, the discovery of the skull taking its place in a few calm paragraphs. The *Courant*, however, which Kate had read during the coffee-break, had hustled together an article purporting to deal with the forensic aspects of the case. It assured its readers that records of dental treatment could be used to establish identity when all else failed. However, if the skull had been too severely damaged, dental evidence might not be possible.

She hadn't bothered to continue with further non-information regarding forensic tests on clothing and the details of possible murder weapons and possible methods of decapitation merely sickened her. It seemed that the *Courant* was simply filling a silence with something appropriate while the police kept their own counsel.

The only thing that made Kate pause was the *Courant*'s mention of psychograms, a psychiatric profile of the supposed murderer. Not that it produced one – that would be for a later issue, no doubt, if it was even possible on the strength of one murder. Multiple murderers, like the Boston Strangler or the Yorkshire Ripper, dropped enough hints as to their psyches to allow some sort of lucid deduction from them to the whole; but what could you learn from this kind of single murder that seemed to hint in every direction at once?

All the same, Kate was reminded that those who'd known Terry agreed that such a murder – any murder – wouldn't have been in character. So? We all seem to have acted out of character since it happened, she reflected. Who'd know for certain about anybody till it came to the crunch? Rage, panic, uncontrollable impulse, derangement – none of them were necessary goads, she realised. Cold revenge was its own imperative. She knew that now. Putting it baldly, anyone who loved Celia – who loved Terry – who saw Peter as a threat – had a motive.

* * *

But all very melodramatic and profitless without opportunity, Kate reminded herself, and meanwhile the agony back again in her head was scarcely to be borne. She considered ringing

Ruth again, but decided against it. She hadn't made up her mind what to say to her about Celia. Ruth might come to know in the end, but Kate didn't want to be the one to tell her. Not just yet, anyway. She might disclose too much about herself which never could be reconciled with 'live and let live'.

Instead Kate watched her neighbour, Anne Lawrence, wellied and sou'westered, march her dog past the house and cross the road into the fields through the wooden wicket. Someone came up the road, nodded and raised his hand as they met and passed, but in the fading light Kate couldn't see who it was. Anne was out early this evening, Kate realised, trying to beat the downpour no doubt. As she watched, the first of the rain streaked the window. The dog wouldn't get his usual half hour out. Kate saw the gaunt, caped figure trudge purposefully into the gloom as she drew the curtains.

The early onset of darkness, emphasised by the heavy rain, brought with it a cloud of depression. Kate's own 'high', hyped up as it was by her rage and hatred, seemed to have fizzled out and left her feeling limp and purposeless. Ruth's company would have been very welcome. It was a mistake not to share, even if sharing brought responsibilities. No man is an island – and you never wanted to be a recluse, Kate reminded herself. Look how bloody hard you worked to retrieve your social respectability. But that had been as much because she felt she owed it to Celia and Vivvy as for herself. And, Kate supposed, it was out of an inculcated sense of duty that she owed her own parents as well.

It had been a blow, though not entirely unexpected, when Kate's parents had silently refused to entertain her apologies, explanations or advances. She knew they'd be hurt and angered by her disturbance of their own social ease.

Kate had written from Reading explaining why she'd given up her post-graduate year and telling them what she was doing instead. When Vivvy was born Kate wrote again, and after that annually sent a letter and a photograph on Vivvy's birthday and another letter at Christmas. She felt she owed that much contact on Vivvy's behalf. But there had never been any reply and Kate knew better than to invite herself home. She assumed that at least one parent was still alive since her letters weren't returned, but she didn't expect to hear anything even if they were both dead. The hurt must have cut deep.

The door bell trilled across Kate's reverie. She hurried to answer it and found Anne's caped figure on the doorstep, gleaming wetly in the hall light. Her dog was in her arms, limp and soaked with blood and rain.

"Dear God! Come in, Anne! Whatever happened?" Kate dived for the 'phone. "Which vet?"

"Leave that!" The front door slammed and Kate turned, startled. Peter Colebrook raised his mocking face to meet her dawning horror.

17

Peter threw down the carcass and pulled off Anne's sou'wester.

"'At last we are alone'," he mimicked, and laughed as he stepped over the dead dog, stripping off his sodden gloves and unbuttoning the wet cape. "It's the end of your line, sweet Kate." As Peter dropped the cape on the floor Kate saw that his trousers were tucked into Anne's old boots. She stood gaping, her brain and body paralysed with shock and bewilderment.

"Kate! This is no welcome for a friend returned from the dead!" Peter put his hands on her shoulders. Abruptly, that contact broke the spell.

"Is the dog dead?"

"I imagine so," Peter replied indifferently, though surprise at Kate's question wiped the smile from his face and he dropped his hands. Kate didn't need to know anything more. She looked away from his excited eyes, fear for herself flooding her whole being. It was the end of the line. "Ahah! You're frightened now, aren't you? Calm, confident, ever-watching Kate! A small success but mine own. I'd almost despaired of ever getting any stimulating reaction from you. Such a challenge!"

Peter stooped and wrenched the telephone line from its connecting-box on the skirting.

"I had to get in somehow, you see, and your walls and double-glazing make life very tedious for uninvited callers. Not to mention the gent who's been tramping about ever since yesterday afternoon. Didn't you know you were under surveillance? Naughty Kate! What have you been up to, I wonder? But he doesn't matter now. By the time anyone looks closely, dear Kate, you'll be past giving any answers except the ones I've scripted for you. Is that a fire I hear crackling? Oh, do let's go and sit by it!"

Kate turned hopelessly, shocked and incapable of resistance, and led Peter into the living-room. Her bright citadel was stormed.

"Much more comfortable," Peter approved, glancing round. "Really, from outside one would imagine you still slept on rushes. But don't look so frightened. It won't be half so much fun if you just cave in."

Kate looked towards the door. A faint sound from the hall made her wonder with anguish whether Anne's dog at least might still be alive. Or perhaps Dommy – ? With all her might she willed Domina to keep away. Peter had left the door ajar but Kate knew there was really no escape for her there, and she was determined not to make such an obvious attempt. The open door was a lure, she was convinced, and in all the dizzy distortion of her emotions one thought remained firm, that she would deny Peter as much enjoyment of the situation as she possibly could. It was her only defence against a total collapse.

"Why have you come here? You must know – " Kate could hardly speak for the dryness in her mouth. She wished she hadn't forced herself to that much autonomy when she heard the tremor in her voice. Peter smiled back.

"That they're looking for Terry? Of course they are. I left them no alternative. *I'm* quite dead. While he, poor fool – that's what I called him as I hit him. Or was it just after?" Peter parodied meticulous recall. "He thought he'd achieved a moment of triumph and it almost seemed a shame to deny him, but there. We can't always consider other people, can we? He was going to see you, you know, and tell you things you oughtn't to hear. Though I did wonder for a moment, such an enigma as you've made of yourself, whether – but you aren't that clever. He expected me to quake, poor fool – as I've said – but I'd been planning his – his translation for the past week. Oh, with incredible subtlety. That day, the day before my lovely party, was to be the end of his line anyway. And so it was. You don't ask me why or show any interest, dear Kate.

It's always been one of the traits I've liked least about you, your arrogant disinterest. But listen you shall."

Peter leaned back comfortably, kicked off the boots and propped his feet on the fender.

"There were reasons why I had to disappear. Such vulgar, unfriendly people around, aren't there? But wasn't it a clever way to contrive it? Come now, Kate. Admit it! Ah, well. You can't expect everything at once. So Terry was already dead, wrapped in plastic and stowed under the bed where you left your coats. A piquant situation, don't you agree?

"And so many old friends ready to wish *me* dead by the end of that evening, yourself included. But you eluded me, you know. Yes, you did. Almost. And it made me quite angry. I wanted to leave him somewhere near you, his head at least. Also wrapped in plastic and run over several times, it was reduced to a discreetly portable size and quite incapable of giving any information at all.

"How I laughed when I heard about all that searching round the gardens here! But I was forced to miss using that chance because you turned coy about your humble address. Just imagine your feelings if they had found it in your garden! Still, I'd set a piece in motion and it was gratifying to see that everything otherwise followed like clockwork. But soon it must stop and I shall stop it when I'm ready.

"So, it had to be the pond where you were known to sit so often – smiling at grief one must suppose – and the bonfire. Of course I hoped you'd find him. Just an artistic, rather self-indulgent little touch. It would've made all that disgusting thrashing about in the water worth the discomfort. Do tell me, who actually did make the gruesome discovery? I was surprised they managed to keep that tit-bit from the news-hounds. It can't have been anyone dramatic or they'd have winkled it out of Jessica."

Kate involuntarily glanced towards the door again as another sound, a soft thud, came to her ears above Peter's gently conversational voice. It was a mistake.

"Thinking of making a break for it, Kate? Remember Atalanta. You can try to run, but you're weighted out of the race. I've loaded you with so much – not gold, I'm afraid, but dross – that even that blockish chief flatfoot must follow my clues and find you. I was so glad in the end that they held off the inevitable arrest. Of course they're torn between you and Terry, and for the moment Terry must be the favourite. Wasn't it marvellous fortune that I should've run into his friend? I was hoping someone would spot the clothes, naturally. It's why I was there. But that was a bonus. I won't let him stay favourite much longer though. Another little twist and – voilà! A new favourite. The obvious one all along. Which is why I wanted you to myself for a while, and here we are!"

"Why – why inevitable arrest?" Kate croaked. "As you said, so many wished you dead."

"Clever, wasn't I? Such a positive swarm of clues for them to chase. It was really quite exciting laying all the false trails. But after the party I felt you needed a lesson, so I left a special clue just for you. Haven't they told you? *Don't* say they overlooked it! I left a note, not headed but explicit all the same, negligently lying under the spare room bed. Just to the effect that I'd be at Morgan's Mount after the party as requested. I signed it 'Petrucchio' and that should've suggested something, don't you agree, my little shrew? Haven't they faced you with it? Perhaps the reference was too intellectual. Really, their standard of education makes one quail! Never mind. The conclusion I've provided for them is quite inescapable."

Peter obviously didn't know about Terry's contact with Gordon, Kate thought confusedly. The police hadn't needed the note to point at Kate. She found the will-power at last to look at Peter directly. She saw that though his hair had dried by the fire it wasn't the sleekly-groomed colour of ripe corn but a dull, indeterminate brown. And in other ways he looked unlike the soigné Peter whose appearance she used to admire. His light-coloured jacket was rumpled and grubby and his dark trousers were loose and ill-fitting. He was the supposed reporter in May's shop, Kate knew then. Peter, catching her look of realisation, gave her another happy smile but remained silent.

But Kate didn't need time for all the implications to sink in. They swarmed upon her in a rush. Peter had never stopped hunting her. The report of searches at Abbots Barton had given him the vital clue to her whereabouts. Peter was expecting searches somewhere in Kate's vicinity – he'd laid that trail. And his puppet-mastering behind the scenes had been successful, though not precisely for the reasons he believed. Then he'd merely hung around long enough for her to appear and show him where she lived. If she hadn't gone to the paper shop, her later visit to the post-box with Vivvy's letter or the Principal's arrival would have given him all the direction he needed.

But surely he must have known where to reach her, through the 'phone directory, once Terry had reminded him about Celia. Kate's number wasn't listed under 'Henderson' but he might have known then to look under 'Rowland'. Sentiment had prevented her changing it. It would always be Celia's house. Why had he waited so long? Kate felt her reasoning retreat in the face of her imagined horror at what Peter must have been planning.

And she hadn't recognised him. Hadn't seized that chance to save herself. Of course not, cocooned about in such clothes and presumed dead anyway. He was as effectively disguised as a bandaged mummy. Kate's eyes dropped from Peter's mocking grin to his hands; those beautiful hands which had almost certainly killed a harmless old woman and her dog, killed the youngster he'd ruined and hacked him about. The blackened thumbnail was the only blemish.

That thumbnail! It never was a cut. The Detective-Chief Inspector had been misled from the start, Kate realised, by her colleagues' insistence on a cut – which she could have corrected had she been half as alert as she believed. But she'd described Peter's hands in a signed statement days earlier. Detective-Chief Inspector McPherson must have known for the past week that the corpse wasn't Peter's, if the hands had retained any recognisability. But only then if he'd believed her description, Kate corrected herself miserably, or could have found anyone to corroborate it. Peter's note would have undermined anything Kate had ever told him, would have supported any suspicion that she was personally involved in the murder of either or both of them. Devil! The word nearly escaped out loud.

"At a stand, resourceful Kate? You see I've blocked every exit from your burrow – which I was determined to find, by the way. I could've lurked about and tracked you from Morgan's Mount, but I might've been recognised and it was an unnecessary risk when everything else was working out so well. You didn't recognise me though, did you? I felt quite a childish triumph then. I'm surprised you and that bucolic hayseed friend of yours didn't sense it

"I've been watching you from that phone-box on the main road ever since. You can look right down the street from there. I saw you run for the bus this morning and I saw you come home. I saw our revered Principal arrive yesterday. Came to lend you support, did he, with his prepared speeches and balanced periods? Or to give you a stately boot? The latter, I hope. It'll make my final solution just that more credible. You know. When our self-sufficient Kate takes her own life – out of guilt? Remorse? Fear of imminent arrest? I shall read all about it. And what will your daughter feel, I wonder? Shall I insinuate myself into her friendship? Shall I? Out of kindness of heart and desire to comfort?" Peter gazed appreciatively at the drawing of Vivvy above the fireplace.

Of all the things he'd done or said, Peter's last words filled Kate with the greatest horror and fear. Fear for herself was swiftly replaced by her determination somehow to prevent him from damaging Vivvy. How then? Where in the house could she lead him to help herself? The kitchen – knives. At worst she could force him to spoil his planned suicide for her by making the murder more obvious.

Kate's frantic thoughts spun to a stop. She had no wish to die, either as a passive suicide or brutalised victim. She thought again, more coherently. The car. He didn't know she had a car. If she could get to that –

"You seem not to care for my suggestion," the hateful voice cut in. "How wounding! But your daughter may have better taste than her mother and fall into my open arms. You think not? I'm not that passive queer in the pool, remember. Incidentally, what did dear Jessica make of that? I must admit that the extent of their – scrutiny surprised me. And how romantic her engagement – a secret even from me! I almost feel she needs a lesson too, for vulgarising me so publicly. But a siege of your daughter might please me extremely. It'd round off the story, lovely Kate. I'd love to explain just why but I'm saving that for later. Meanwhile there's – "

"Oh, I know why," Kate said wearily. "And you're not so very clever. You'd go for Vivvy like you went for Celia, to despoil. To take for yourself – by force, because it would never be willingly given – something that pleases others but that you envy." Kate saw Peter's eyes flicker and register a hit. She continued, carefully assessing and feeling a return of confidence, "It's a trait shared by vandals and little vicious children."

"So you did know," Peter said softly. "I wonder how? But wasn't it frustrating? Neither Terry nor I could remember her name. It never meant anything to me, of course, but you'd think Terry might have remembered that much. Perhaps if I'd given him more time and – incentive. But it's landed you with such a motive, dear Kate, and really, I was quite grateful to Terry for dropping it in my lap.

"Two lovely birds with one well-aimed stone," Peter went on dreamily. "I need a surrogate, you see, and there you are simply asking to be used. You shouldn't have despised me, you know. Oh, I'm sure you despised us all from your lofty perch, but I was always different from those dull yokels and you should've seen that. No one should be quite that unapproachable, dear Kate, like some latter-day ice maiden. I was always certain what you were, before Terry provided that added confirmation, but admittedly I was looking carefully behind your superior respectability. Now you must melt at last – I was determined you should – so that I can go free. Properly speaking, of course, sacrifices should be virginal, but there. It's petty to quibble. Especially, as it now seems, others may be aware of your motive and come for you before I'm quite ready. I do so hate to be bustled." Peter stood up and took a small package out of his jacket's inner pocket.

That had been another mistake, Kate realised with cold dread. Instead of throwing him off balance she'd merely confirmed his subjection of her. There were things she might do, in the heat of anger or panic, to try to save herself, but his glacial calm hypnotised her and chilled her physical reflexes. The earlier cold steel promptings of revenge at which she'd warmed herself were frozen, suspended by petrified terror, and hadn't now even the power to thaw one independent movement in her own defence. Revenge, after all, was possible only with power; and Kate hadn't even the power of surprise.

She couldn't either consider screaming in cold blood, had there been the faintest chance she might be heard, for dread of what Peter might do. And while he spoke so fluently and temperately, however frightful the subject matter, she found it hard, intellectually, to believe in the reality of his intentions though her senses screamed 'Danger!' To keep him talking seemed her only safe option, though it froze her into greater immobility.

"Why don't you mind your – image left so – so shattered?" Kate asked quietly, making a despairing attempt to establish some sort of last minute rapport through Peter's vanity. He paused in the act of taking off his jacket and looked at Kate, again surprised. "That body – Terry's – the post-mortem findings, all the other details about him that'll be made public when my – my suicide is accepted. They all reduce you in Terry's persona."

"But my dear Kate! What's that against winning? You don't have to be admired to be successful – in fact it can even be a positive hindrance. Where's your historical understanding? Of course it's a pity I have to continue being that corpse and not let everyone know how clever I've been – in spite of what you say – but it's all for the best in the end. Fancy you showing this much interest, and at such a time! You amaze me!" Peter laid his jacket on the chair.

"But – but you won't have won. You've had to give up everything."

"Don't you believe it! It's been a valuable exercise and I've learnt a lot. And I've always planned for a swift withdrawal, you know. Not a retreat, a withdrawal – with one or two irons still left in the fire. What else can I tell you about myself? What I'm going to do after this, for instance. Don't you want to know? With my gifts you'd expect me to go far. In fact, in the circumstances I'd be advised to for the moment. Wouldn't you agree? I'm not tied to one element you know, like a clod of clay. I'll treat myself to a holiday first. A little coastal touring to familiarise myself. The world's my oyster and it owes me a pearl or two. What a pity you chose to ignore my hints, doubting Kate. You should've known that I don't talk merely for effect. I've always believed you were the only one who'd appreciate my cleverness. If only you could've believed what a natural pair we are. I don't mean romantically, of course. But that was really – yes, it really was an unforgivable rejection. As if you were and had everything that mattered. And now you have nothing – and that, sweet Kate, you can't reject."

Peter picked up the package and stowed it away in the writing desk. Planting something, Kate realised, and she racked her brains for some question that might yet distract him. But in the effort her mind went blank and the hard-won initiative slowly ebbed from her as the silence grew. Peter laughed down at her.

"Always so determinedly incurious! So arrogantly aloof! It's Terry's signet ring. His loving father'll identify it. Don't you even want to know what I intend to do with you?" Kate slouched lower in her chair and stared hopelessly up at him. "Quite right. I never discuss such things myself. It tends – not to relax one." Peter's eyes glittered, and Kate saw with sick loathing his ill-fitting trousers strain at the fly-zip. She remembered suddenly his plan for Vivvy – his plan for Celia. Whose name he couldn't. Even. Remember.

"We'll need to move out of here. Come." Peter moved a step towards her and held out his hand. Kate shook her head and sank lower in the chair. "You think I'm going to manhandle you," Peter complained. "I'm not. I don't want to leave unnecessary marks. Come on." He waggled his fingers impatiently and took another step.

Kate kicked up her foot with all her strength and caught him high between his straddled legs. Peter fell to his knees with an animal scream that terrified Kate and almost distracted her from her rush to the door.

Her blind impetus carried her into the hall, and there proved her downfall. Literally. Kate had forgotten the discarded cape, and she fell heavily with her feet enmeshed in its wet folds. She recovered herself but was still snatching feverishly at the foolproof lock on the double-glazed front door when Peter threw himself upon her, panting like a sprinter.

"Gotcha!" he grated through painfully twisted lips, as he spun her round.

There was nothing Kate could do but cling to the edge of the stairs in her effort not to be pulled down. Peter's whole weight, as he bent double heaving and gasping to recover himself, hung on the fistful of her hair twisted fiercely round his fingers. Kate's head strained agonisingly backwards while she clawed at the banisters and tried to avoid treading on Anne's dog, now stealthily stiffening somewhere at her feet.

"Better now," Peter grunted at last as he eased himself slowly upright. "Almost you tempt me," he stroked Kate's arched throat with his free hand, "but I think we'll keep to the blueprint. With a few extras for your bad conduct. I'm afraid the finished product may not look so – authentic, but I shan't be around to explain. We need to go up those stairs – I suppose this mean little hovel does have a bathroom up there? Let go!"

But Kate clung on. Another mistake. Peter thrust at her head as if he were putting a shot. Kate's face smashed defencelessly against the banisters. She released her grip to put her hands to her face, half blinded and in obscene pain.

"So. Now we move slowly up the stairs. It'll be added to your account, but thank you for what you did all the same," Peter murmured as Kate shuffled up the stairs ahead of him, his fingers still clamped in her hair. "I was finding it surprisingly difficult to get going. We shall proceed decorously to the bathroom, where you will undress and fill the bath with warm, soporific water. You perceive the direction of my intentions? It's a method much recommended in the past. I could've cut your throat down there – Oops! Careful! Mustn't fall and break your neck! – but I'd prefer to watch you watching your life drain away round you.

"One is assured you'll die in blissful lassitude. One will see. I may need to rape you first. I wasn't going to, in the interests of verisimilitude, but I may. If you haven't prevented that –

that consummation with your spiteful kick. Perhaps when you're a little weaker. You're very strong, you know. Some lumpish Amazon in your ancestry, no doubt. Which way now? And I'm not one of those macho he-men. Perish the thought! Though at school I bitterly resented being used and abused as a twee-man. Yes, I have much to forgive, and I don't suppose I ever shall."

Kate heard the easy chatter as she tried to bear the rending pain in her face. Breathing was difficult. Her nose poured blood down the sides of her upturned face and into her collar. Her eyes streamed with tears in response. Her mouth too, forced open by the steady pull on her hair and her gasping attempts to breathe, was filling with blood from loosened teeth and pulped lips. It was almost impossible to swallow and Kate was aware of incipient panic at the threat of choking. The strain on her neck was intense.

"Why, quite a civilised little room," said Peter cosily as they edged into the bathroom. "Small, of course, but adequate. Observe your face in the mirror. No longer a thing of beauty, lovely Kate, but a joy to me nevertheless." He released her hair and Kate straightened her neck slowly and painfully. She saw her battered face and Peter's grinning almost mischievously over her shoulder as he rubbed his hand. "And not a single protest, though your probably pained expression is admittedly masked. I know how it must hurt. Be careful not to make me hurt you worse so that you do cry out. Though I might actually quite enjoy that."

"I want to wash out my mouth," Kate mumbled indistinctly.

"Do that. Then undress."

Kate opened the mirrored cabinet and reached down a tumbler. She rinsed out her mouth as well as she could with such minimal control of her swollen lips.

"Hurry up!" There was a new note in Peter's voice, a charge of tension and urgency.

Kate turned and saw him fingering a knife, the kind found in any kitchen. Its blade was honed narrow by age and use.

"Just the simple domestic gadget you'd expect to use," he smiled happily at Kate's expression. "Don't worry. It's quite sharp. I tested it only this evening. I can't wait to hear what motives they'll dredge up for that one on your behalf. Now your clothes. Throw them through the door onto the landing."

Kate undressed slowly. Peter stood between her and the doorway. The window, no bigger than a porthole, offered not even a despairing leap. Her only retreat from fear and pain was the bath after all. Kate was reduced to hoping Peter wouldn't hurt her very much more.

"Hurry up!" Kate peeled off her blood-soaked blouse. Her face dripped blood on the floor as she bent to slip off her tights and pants, tossing each garment through the doorway after her trousers. A quick glance at Peter's face showed excitement but not lust. So that, at least, she might be spared, Kate prayed wondering irrelevantly why a clichéd dread of such a violation should attack her virtually at the graveside.

Kate stood naked, the blood still running down her chin and dripping onto her breasts.

"Yes, well. Obviously you're not at your best. No longer the cool, unassailable Kate we were all a little in awe of. Respect and obedience are painful lessons to learn. Turn on the taps."

Kate moved to the far end of the bath under the window, brushing against Peter in the restricted space. He took her place by the wash-basin, pushing the door to as he went. There was the usual knocking and hammering in the pipes when Kate turned on the taps, and as the bath filled the room swirled with steam. Peter edged the door open again to clear the atmosphere and bent to feel the water.

"Just right, I'd say. Turn off the water and get in."

He came towards Kate as she stepped into the bath. Drops of blood plinked into the water and fanned briefly.

"Sit down and hold out your left arm." It was the arm furthest from him. Like an automaton Kate's body obeyed the signals relayed by Peter's voice, but her brain strove desperately with counter-signals to resist. If she could lock her hands behind his neck and force his head down under the water – something glittered, held her gaze, and reduced her again to acquiescence.

Kate watched Peter bend over the side of the bath and saw the little knife held ready to slice. He took hold of her left arm to steady it. Kate pulled against his grip in suddenly awakened panic.

"Do that once more – and, well, that's one of your eyes gone," he snarled, and held firm, his delicate looking fingers as strong as iron bands. Peter stooped again while blood boomed through Kate's skull. Now she prayed for an early release.

The door, thrust inwards hard from outside, caught him against his left hip and sent him sprawling over the taps and the lavatory. Kate saw the knife-blade gleam in a shining arc down into the water as with a curse Pete drove his outflung hand against the wall. Wonderingly she reached for the knife, as the room filled and heaved with panting, stumbling bodies.

Someone fell against the side of the bath and stepped over into the water with an oath, treading heavily on Kate's shin. She became aware of the lethal potential of the knife in her hand and looked vaguely round for somewhere safe to put it. She sat on it.

A strange woman stood on the landing just outside the door. She seemed anxious to get in with the others, but there was no room in the confined, turbulent space. She was further impeded by the door continually slamming shut as frantic shapes bumped and rebounded in the steam. The woman resigned herself to mouthing and gesturing through the intermittently open door. She appeared to be beckoning, yet Kate didn't know her. She hadn't invited her. She hadn't invited any of them. She turned to her own affairs.

Kate sponged her face and neck of the sticky blood, grateful for the soothing warm water. "Soon be over," she heard herself crooning, like she used to encourage Vivvy when she fell and hurt herself. "Soon be over." She wanted to sink her head right under the water, but was afraid someone else might step on her.

Instead she soaked the sponge under the cold tap, drew her knees warily up and leaned her head back against the edge of the bath. She balanced the cold sponge over the bridge of her nose and shut out the scene around her. If only they didn't make so much noise she could fall asleep like this, Kate thought tiredly, mildly irritated by the sound of Peter's high-pitched screaming above the grunts and thuds.

The bathroom suddenly stilled, to Kate's relief, though the noise continued down the stairs.

"You were told to get her out of here! Great God – !" A vaguely familiar voice.

"I couldn't get in, sir, and she wouldn't come out." A woman's voice, stiffly in reply.

"Well, let the water out now at least and get her wrapped up and moved. That knife's got to be found. It's in here somewhere."

"She's sitting on it."

"What!"

The sponge was whipped off Kate's face. She opened her aching eyes, crossly squinting in the sudden light.

"I thought you'd fainted," muttered Detective-Chief Inspector McPherson, turning hurriedly away. "Can you understand me? W-P.C. Potter will look after you. Give her that knife, please." Kate reached for it under the stained water. Then she settled her head back and closed her eyes.

"Sir, I think she's – I think she's non compos."

"I can see that. We're still waiting for another MO. Get her into bed, for God's sake. But if he doesn't show up soon we'll have to risk blowing the gaff to call an ambulance. Christ, what a mess!"

"*Come* along, dear," said Woman Police Constable Potter brightly, and she pulled out the plug.

18

Kate knew she hadn't been asleep, although she felt rested enough to cope with her remembered nightmare and the sadness it left with her. Her face still hurt disgustingly, her neck was stiff and she felt as if she'd been scalped, but the nightmare was over.

W-P.C. Potter sat by the bed and watched as Kate cautiously tested her teeth with her fingers. She adjusted the bedside lamp so that its light didn't fall directly onto Kate's face.

"All there?" she smiled.

"Just about. Thank you for putting me to bed."

"I hoped you'd sleep. How do you feel?"

"Conscious." They both laughed.

"You did flip a bit," the policewoman agreed. "Had me fussed for a while. The doctor'll be here soon."

Kate was considering that when Detective-Chief Inspector McPherson came softly into the room.

"How is she?" he asked, as W-P.C. Potter stood up.

"Awake," came the warning reply. The Detective-Chief Inspector walked over to the bed.

"I need to know things," Kate explained. "I can't sleep without. The – the dog – " She'd developed a dismaying tendency to lisp.

"All taken care of," he said quickly. "Just try and rest now. The doctor will see you soon."

"So I'm told. The least interesting information." Kate grinned feebly, feeling her lips stretch and split against the bruising.

There was a gentle knock at the door and Detective-Sergeant

Breckon put his head round. Kate closed her eyes between their swollen lids against his familiar expression of distaste.

"Sir. They've dug out old Galeforce. He's with the prisoner now. I'm sorry, sir, but they've brought him straight from some beanfeast – "

"Surgeon-Commander Bellew is a very experienced medic," the Detective-Chief Inspector warned repressively, and Kate heard him move away towards the door. "Is he sober?" he asked quietly.

"Not more'n you'd notice. But Blandford's still busy with – the other one and Galeforce was the nearest, so the driver was told. He's new, sir."

"I suppose he can still give a shot as well as anyone."

"Buckshot. But they went home for his bag, so he knows he's supposed to – er – behave professionally."

"You stay here, will you, John. I'll go down and recce."

"Yes, sir. The meat-van's arrived too. All discreet."

"She's awake," the Detective-Chief Inspector said curtly and left the room.

While Kate listened as well as she could to that exchange, she'd become aware of a distant roaring. Some major altercation downstairs, she supposed uneasily, until a great booming laugh echoed up to her room. Kate opened her eyes.

"Tsk-tsk!" muttered the Sergeant predictably. "Very glad to see you all right, miss. Very nasty," he added ambiguously.

"Is Peter – ?"

"Quite safe. He's being – looked after."

"He's mad, isn't he?"

"I hope not. That is, I can't say, I'm sure."

Outside Kate heard cars start up and drive away, their sound drowned by a thundering up the stairs. Detective-Sergeant Breckon went out onto the landing.

"In here, sir."

"This is the sick-bay, is it?" roared a deep voice as a great bull of a man with a carmine face erupted into the room. His evening-dress hung haphazardly round him, rather as if he'd stood in their way in a strong wind that left him roughly draped and inadequately buttoned. His shirt-front flapped like a sail over his straining cummerbund.

"Gracious me! Let's have some lights! Can't fumble about in the dark! Now then, my dear." He collapsed heavily onto the bed, little puffs of alcohol wafting from him. "Let's have a look atcher. Hm. Painful." He reached out a hand like a bunch of bananas and seized Kate's nose. Before she could even flinch, there came a grinding, an excruciating flare-up of pain and a rush of tears to her eyes.

"Ow!" Kate protested violently, jerking upright. The W-P.C., who'd stood at the doctor's entrance, moved closer to the bed.

"My speciality," Surgeon-Commander Bellew shouted proudly. "Fixed any number of 'em! Won't spoil yer pretty face, promise yer. Tissues!" He held out his hand peremptorily and the flustered W-P.C. yanked at the box on the bedside table. The doctor dabbed at Kate's nose and mouth as delicately as if he were restoring a Titian. "Not much. Not even worth packing, but best to lie back. Soon stop. Any other damage?" He hauled himself to his feet and without warning whipped back the bedclothes. Oh, well. Come one, come all. Kate shut her eyes again. "Hm. Nothing to jump up and down about there. All shipshape and – um. Back? Pains anywhere?" Kate opened her eyes and shook her head carefully.

"Only in my face and head."

"Soon go." The Surgeon-Commander examined her scalp closely for a moment, barked "Antiseptic hair-wash," and seemed to lose interest.

He turned away and picked up his bag, while W-P.C. Potter threw a shocked look at his back and pulled the covers over Kate's wilting body.

"That's all here. Leave her to rest," he blared, and tramped noisily to the door.

"But sir – " the Sergeant wallowed like a coracle in pursuit of a man-of-war.

"Finished, have you?" the Detective-Chief Inspector intercepted the terrifying man at the door. He glanced anxiously at Kate, muffled behind her fistful of tissues.

"Set her bowsprit, that's all. Nothing to it. She'll live."

"But – sedatives? Hospitalisation? What instructions – "

"Yer getting to be an old woman, Alex. Give the gal a

mansized tot or one of her own sleeping-pills and she'll kip like a baby. *She* ain't suffering from heebie-jeebies or missish swoons. What more jer want? A splint on her nose? She's a good, strong woman. Healthy. Look at the colour of that blood."

"I don't want to go to hospital," said Kate strongly.

"There yar!" bawled the doctor triumphantly. "The lady agrees with me. Give yerself a day in bed, my dear, then go and see yer own man."

"But her mental condition – "

" – will take care of itself, given peace and quiet," came the answering bellow. "'Strornery feller yar, Alex. Jer want her sliced? She'll have a brace of black eyes – colours any man'd be proud to fly – and there's a bruise coming out on her fetlock, but gracious me! What's a few bruises? Did he kick you, my dear? Undersized little runt!"

"Someone stepped on me in the bath." Kate looked accusingly at the Sergeant's wet trouser-leg. She watched with glee as he blushed rosily.

"In the *bath*! Good gracious heavens! What was it all about, anyway? Spot of wife-beating, was it? Cockteasing? Hey?" Surgeon-Commander Bellew goggled at Kate, his round, innocent blue eyes interestedly awaiting her answer.

"*Sir!* Your other patient – "

"Gracious, yes! Much more bothersome. Couple of broken fingers on one hand, fine lacerations on the other. Yer've been riding bareback, me lad, I thought at first. High as a kite! Gave him a jab, all right and tight. Better have old Bugger-lugs look at his onion. Get him certified. He ran up some very odd signals to me."

"Please," said the Detective-Chief Inspector, almost despairing as the Sergeant cast up his eyes. "We'll need your report in writing."

"Yer'll get it, Alex. Don't fuss. Call me any time," he hollered, as the Detective-Chief Inspector finally succeeded in herding him out of the room. Release of tension was almost audible.

"Surgeon-Commander Bellew," groaned the Sergeant disgustedly to W-P.C. Potter. "The best we could come up with. He should've been struck off at birth or tipped into the drink before he ever came to retire on his ancestral midden. Miss Henderson, I – I made use of your 'phone – testing it – to let Linda – Miss Mayer – know you're all right. She says she'd like to see you tomorrow, here or at the hospital. What shall I tell her?" Kate gawped in amazement at Detective-Sergeant Breckon's scarlet but determinedly impassive face.

"Of – of course I'd like to see her. How much does she know?" Kate peered suspiciously through her swollen eyelids. Not that it mattered now. If the case came to court everything might be known.

"She only knows you've been threatened but are safe. The late bulletins will give more details."

"What's the time now?"

"Nearly nine o'clock." It felt like a lifetime since Kate had opened her door and let Peter into her security. The Sergeant smiled quietly at her surprise and left her to digest his reference to Linda.

"Do you have any sleeping-pills?" W-P.C. Potter asked. "They've finished with the bathroom now. I can get them for you."

"There aren't any," Kate glanced at her uneasily. What she really wanted was a stiff drink, but thanks to her depredations of the night before there was none in the house. "But my cat – her food – I think I've rested long enough."

"Nothing like. You ought to get off to sleep properly or something really will snap. But I'll see if I can find the Chief and ask what I should do about you. Here. Better have your dressing-gown if you're going to sit up."

★   ★   ★

Kate was left restlessly on her own for what seemed like endless hours. At last she heard the slow tread of feet up the stairs and the welcome chinking of crockery. Never mind Domina, she was hungry herself, Kate realised.

But it was the Detective-Chief Inspector not the police-woman who came into her room balancing a tray.

"Pansy's worshipping your cat and making herself something to eat. I said she might on your behalf and she sends thanks on her own. She rustled this lot up for you. Fair enough?" Kate smiled carefully, uncertain what her social rôle should be in the circumstances. "When you've finished this we'll lock up for you and leave – unless you'd like her to stay the night? The 'phone's fixed if you want to call anyone."

"No, I don't need baby-sitting, though I might ring my daughter later."

"Well, Pansy recommended bread and butter and chicken soup. It'll still be red-hot. And there's Horlicks or something in the thermos."

"Thank you," said Kate, touched by their thoughtfulness. "How odd she's called Pansy."

"It's what they call her at the Station. I believe she's Joy really. A good copper. You'd find a lot in common, I think." His eyes slid away. "We couldn't follow doctor's orders and give you a dram. Your guests seem to have drunk you dry."

"Guests?"

"Didn't you have a party? Pansy said the kitchen bin was full of dead men – empties." Kate felt her cheeks warm uncomfortably round the swellings.

"That was me. Last night."

"Oh." He looked quickly back at her. "Not habitual?"

"No. Professor Edwards called yesterday – about – about what Gordon Watson told you both." There was silence while Kate nibbled tentatively at a slice of bread and butter.

"So you know about the car accident?" Kate nodded.

Detective-Chief Inspector McPherson gazed stonily at the bookshelves while Kate gratefully bit into another slice of bread and butter.

"Your daughter seems a very pleasant person, judging by her letters," he said at last, following his own line of thought. "Happy and affectionate."

"She is," Kate replied quietly, regarding the crust in her hand. "I think her existence once – innocently – gave you a false impression of me, however. But – you can't go around with a placard." She chewed carefully on the crust.

The Detective-Chief Inspector suddenly smiled and sat in the chair by the bed.

"Try some of the soup." He passed Kate the steaming

pottery mug and she leaned over it, feeling its rising warmth soothe her aching face. "He should've given you something. Old fool. At least you'll take a few days off?"

"In self-defence. It'll be pretty hairy for a bit, I imagine. Er – Surgeon-Commander Bellew called you Alex, I noticed, but one of the papers referred to you as Sandy."

"Entitled neither by fact nor by familiarity to do so. You'll be pestered to death if you do go out. John tells me your friend, Linda Mayer, will be with you tomorrow at least. I can't think of a better watch-dog. Poor old John! He's too darn impressionable! But it just might work out – for all she hasn't red hair. He was here, in the house, you know, when Colebrook arrived."

At last it seemed that the Detective-Chief Inspector was prepared to discuss the night's events, which Kate had almost despaired of hearing about except through second-hand reports. Now that she realised the cause for his suspicion of her she felt uncertain, not because of what he'd learnt but because their former easy relationship was altered. She couldn't tell how he wanted it now to be. But she was mystified by what he said.

"How on earth – ? Look, if there's a way in here I don't know of – "

"Not a readily accessible one," he reassured her, absent-mindedly helping himself to a slice of bread and butter. "I don't know how much you know of recent events here, but your paper shop lady – Miss Simmons, is it? – rang through about a suspicious stranger. She'd thought at first he was a reporter, but then he offered her money to keep quiet about his visit. So then she decided he must be one of the gang involved in that supposed burglary. She was very insistent that some-one should check his credentials. It sounded odd enough to follow up and the Duty Sergeant had the wit to let me know of it.

"I sent John down to the shop to question her and she'd noticed the man's watch. She thought it told the simultaneous times in different parts of the world – just the sort of gadget, she believed, a globe-trotting reporter would need if he was genuine. She couldn't give a decent physical description of the man, but the watch – on his right wrist – sounded significant and what you'd said about Colebrook's persistence in trying to find out where you lived looked suddenly very sinister. But he'd vanished by the time John arrived. He had a car, of course.

"Miss Simmons was warned not to say anything to anyone. I left a man for the rest of the day rather ostentatiously patrolling the village and watching your house, while a few others took more careful Sunday walks in the fields and on the waste. The Prof s visit was noted, but there was no sign of Colebrook and we still couldn't be absolutely certain even that it was him.

"All we achieved was to annoy Miss Lawrence, who accosted one of my men and demanded his business. He brought her to see me. Well, you told me she kept tabs on the place, and I already knew she was discreet from when we tried to question her on Monday, so I told her roughly what was up in the hopes she might've seen something. I said we didn't want you to know because we didn't want you frightened and it might be a false alarm, not – "

"And you still weren't quite certain of me, perhaps?"

"Something like that," the Detective-Chief Inspector grinned ruefully. "Well, she surprised me by promptly offering the use of her house because it gives access to yours. You didn't know?" Kate shook her head in amazement.

"But there are no cellars or hidden doorways. Surely I'd have found – "

"She discovered the way, though, when she first came to live here. Some years before you, I understand. Pairs of houses in this terrace share a common attic. That is, every other party-wall only goes up so high. Sometimes these cottages were built with a common attic right along, I suppose for ease of maintenance when they were tied to some landlord. Anyway, Miss Lawrence had her access to your house boarded up. Only plaster-boards on uprights, but effective enough. So, when it was dark last evening she let us in through the back, and from then on there was always someone in your attic with your landing trap propped ajar. Only as a precaution, but thank God!"

In her alcoholic state the night before, Kate realised, she

216

wouldn't have noticed if a whole army had tramped through her attic. She'd been afraid that a door or window had been forced for entry.

"He killed her, didn't he?" Kate asked unhappily. "I saw her go out with her dog. After all she did to help, it's she who's dead." The Detective-Chief Inspector closed his eyes briefly.

"That was something we didn't – couldn't have anticipated. I'm not making excuses. I'll never forgive myself. We located him today – in the 'phone-box up on the main road. I thought we had him isolated. There was a man watching him and it's an open approach. We'd know if he moved out – but equally he could see if we tried to close in. He took off in his car once when a perfectly innocent passer-by pulled in to use the 'phone. It was that that convinced me he could bear watching even if he wasn't Colebrook.

"Perhaps if we'd had marksmen – but I believed that as long as we had you safe indoors and the house covered, inside and out, we stood a good chance of mounting a successful snatch if he moved or when it grew dark. But he out-thought me. He lit out when he must've seen the old lady set off with her dog, and instead of making for the village as my man expected, he cut down into the fields. The storm was moving in then too. It wasn't till Bates practically fell over the body that he realised what he'd allowed to happen. He's got a lot to blame himself for as well. She couldn't have known anything about it," the Detective-Chief Inspector added gently, as Kate nursed her face against the warm soup mug and let the stinging tears spill over.

"Do you want me to go on?" Detective-Chief Inspector McPherson asked after a moment. Kate nodded. "Well, then. As it happened, it was John on duty at your trap when you came home after lunch – safely home as I believed. He heard your door bell and then you invited someone in. When he heard what followed he alerted me on his two-way and spent his next uncomfortable stint wedged in your hall cupboard. Then the wretched Bates reported in." The Detective-Chief Inspector leaned forward and rested his elbows on his knees, dropping his head in his hands. "Right under our noses," he

217

muttered. "It was then I realised, too late, that we were tracking something very special in villains. We had him, all right, but the real question was whether he had you. Three more of us inserted ourselves into your attic and John kept us informed of what he could hear in your front room." He leaned back and relaxed. "Try and drink that while there's still some warmth in it."

Kate sipped cautiously as she peered back in her memory to the time of near-paralysis spent with Peter. And she'd looked forward to cornering Terry Sinclair in just such a situation, she remembered miserably.

"There was nothing Detective-Sergeant Breckon could've done," she murmured, dabbing at the soup smeared over her battered mouth.

"We knew – only too well – that he had a knife. I daren't take any more chances, daren't alert Colebrook by moving closer, daren't put you or John at greater risk, though John was ready to come thundering in. I ordered him to intervene only if things looked like becoming – terminal. I've never felt so *useless*! When John heard the scream he thought it was you and he was desperately struggling to uncramp himself and come to your help when you hared into the hall. Then that maniac grabbed you and put you in balk again. We could hear the both of you when you passed below us on the landing – cold-blooded bastard! We might've jumped him then, but he was hanging on to your hair. Stuck there in the attic we were about as effective as wasps in honey until an infernal din in the pipes gave us the cover to storm the bathroom. John whistled Pansy in through the front door and you know the rest."

Kate slurped the last of the soup, covertly noting signs of the shared nightmare on the man's face.

"When did you know it was Peter you were after? Right to the end I thought it had to be Terry."

"I don't want to overtax you. You can catch up with the rest later. If you've finished, I'm ready to go."

"No. Please. If you have time. A – a ghost has been raised and I must – see it laid to rest again. Please." The Detective-Chief Inspector looked searchingly at Kate for a moment but did as she asked.

"There were various indications it wasn't Colebrook's body we had, though not obvious all at once. It was a very clever set-up, worked out logically on graph-paper you might almost think. Yet there were some clumsy botches that relied for their success on us being fools. The first oddity was that disturbance in the ice and it showed the pond itself had been tinkered with. That thaw the day before you found the body – it allowed someone to free an arm and bring it to the surface. He was ready for it to be found then, you see. The cord looked frayed, but examination showed knife-cuts on two of the strands. Then it froze, harder than ever, and preserved the disturbance of the thin crust on the surface. But for that we mightn't have been so certain that someone was trying to lead us by the nose.

"Then your description of Colebrook's hands didn't fit what we could see. The nails, the relative length of the thumbs. There was the slight indentation of a ring, and Sinclair was known to wear a ring but Colebrook not. You'd better let me have it before I go, by the way. It's the only piece of identification we can scrape up.

"Though that family's faced enough already. No one should be put through that kind of grinder, poor devils. They had nothing to be proud of in their son, but they know he wasn't a murderer and they were sure he was dead when he didn't make his weekly call home. He always said that contact kept him sane, you see, and when you found the body they knew. But there was nothing positively identifiable on the corpse – and nothing to allay their fears either. There was no convenient mole or scar that wasn't just any old mole or scar. This isn't fiction. But we couldn't officially pronounce on his death on the strength of what they told us – not that they told us about that affair two years ago or the subsequent blackmail. It didn't seem likely that Colebrook had killed off that supply of golden eggs. And anyway, we preferred to keep the probability of Sinclair's death to ourselves for a while.

"But Colebrook didn't pass up many chances to incriminate you, did he? Interesting. The ring, and that letter. They found it at the original search of the flat, but only later information on names and circumstances pointed its significance. The assumption then was that Colebrook and Sinclair, for reasons best known to themselves, had gone off together. And actually your Principal believed that Colebrook had hung himself out on a limb and then couldn't face the exposure.

"You heard about this supposed offer from Lethbridge College? His old school? And you all believed him. You made it very easy for him to make fools of you all. But that letter – I couldn't ignore it but it seemed too pat. I was almost sure you wouldn't have been so careless with it if you'd managed all the rest. And no one could confirm any exchange of letters between you two. I reserved it as a clincher if necessary but I didn't want to believe in it.

"And then we heard about Colebrook's watch. Now, the corpse had a very faint summer outline of a watch worn on the *left* wrist. So. Two men had vanished and someone was determined that Colebrook should be certified dead. That obvious someone was Colebrook himself. His clothes, his car, the clumsy burglary of the groundsman's shed and use of the tools were aimed to fix our minds on Morgan's Mount. He'd even slashed the dead thumb to simulate his own supposed injury and clipped on the finger-stall. Obviously easier than trying to blacken the nail when he couldn't have known how the post-mortem bruise would've shown, and well thought out in advance. He's clever, all right. But it was a slash so deep that Colebrook would've needed more treatment than a simple stall if he'd cut himself like that. Dammit, the top joint was nearly off. That's what you were trying to remember, wasn't it? When we collared him I saw the nail and realised. It would've given us additional proof that the corpse wasn't Colebrook's but we were pretty well there anyway."

"I didn't remember till I saw him this evening," Kate admitted.

"Well, I don't like being manipulated so I looked in the opposite direction, at Sinclair. We found signs at the flat and at the wine-bar of his drugs involvement that Gordon Watson later confirmed, and the Drugs Squad should've cleared that little affair up by now. Once they knew Colebrook was alive, in custody and in a position to talk, we were afraid they'd disperse and go underground. It's extremely important that no inkling of tonight's business should be known until we've been given the all-clear. We couldn't even shift you straight to hospital, and you had to suffer the Surgeon-Commander. "Anyway. Where was I? Yes, I think now that Colebrook hoped to cash in on his knowledge of the wine-bar set-up when a later opportunity offered. Meanwhile he diverted our attention to Morgan's Mount and all those supposed suspects. A *crime passionel*, of course, as the wretched *Pioneer* hinted, with a note pointing to you in case we overlooked your charms, the Denham boy and even Miss Nicholls thrown in as a fringe benefit. Enough to keep us occupied until he was ready to set up Sinclair as a decoy. Gordon Watson I'm sure he was reserving as a future nest-egg too and Miss Purbeck – who might've repaid investigation earlier – well, perhaps he didn't know enough about her. I'm sorry you were at the receiving end of our attentions as well as Colebrook's but for a while I was ready to believe you were the manipulator. I'm sorry. But apart from Watson's story, there were times when you seemed to be, if not lying, then skating over the truth and leaving bits out. What was it you held back?"

"Nothing important. At first only that Gordon and Jeff had told me Peter was friendly with the wrong sort of people in the town. And then Jeff didn't admit he'd known Terry Sinclair. But I thought that was their business to clear up. I was more afraid of – of what Elinor might've done. But she'd only been – silly."

"The both of you were silly," the Detective-Chief Inspector retorted. "In the end your friends did you no service. They were quite prepared to use you."

That's what Peter had said, that she'd virtually asked to be used. And yet, she'd taken care not to involve herself. That was an irony Celia would've appreciated. But that Alex McPherson could see her as a manipulator and murderess when – Yet he'd have felt doubly cheated after hearing Gordon's story, Kate realised, and doubly angry. The swing from possibly culpable woman scorned to probably culpable lesbian might well have been more believable in the circumstances than a heterosexual *crime passionel*. And if she herself had known the story in time – Kate turned away from those thoughts.

"So you already knew Terry was dead before all that Bude business? It had to have been Peter."

"Mm. But still not how far you were involved until those clothes were found. Just too cleverly indicated, they were. They had to point to Colebrook setting up his final alibi. So I thought. I didn't spot that as another diversion, this time away from you. I wish very much we could've prevented this further tragedy here. I'm sorry."

We always say sorry when it's already too late, Kate thought wearily. She was unable any longer to bear hearing more of what was for her the real tragedy two years earlier. The ghost had been laid. But there were still things Kate wanted to know.

"How did you find out about my daughter so early?"

"Your Professor Edwards told me that first day. He warned me you could be unnecessarily pestered and distressed if reporters came to know about your circumstances. Naturally he was hoping for as little disturbance as possible at the Department, but he was also concerned for you."

"Thank you for not naming Ruth and me. What happens now? To Peter."

"Remanded for psychiatric reports. Do you still want to call your daughter?" Oh, God, but she was tired.

"I'd better. She ought to hear first from me. Thank you – for everything. I'll come down and see you both off now. I know you'll still be busy when I'm peacefully asleep."

"Will you sleep, Kate?"

"Oh, yes. Surgeon-Commander Bellew was right about me, you know." She grinned awkwardly.

Detective-Chief Inspector McPherson left the room and Kate followed him slowly down the stairs. She found him with W-P.C. Potter in the living-room, gazing at the television.

"No revelations yet," said the policewoman, unhooking Domina from her jacket front and putting her in Kate's arms.

"Thank you for my supper and for looking after my cat."

"They're good people, cats. You'll be okay?"

"Fine. Oh – " Kate rummaged one-handed in the writing-desk for Terry's signet ring and handed it to the Detective-Chief Inspector. She should have felt some pang, she believed. But she felt nothing.

Kate locked the front door, knowing that except for a few formal meetings she would never spend time with Alex McPherson again. Had they both been much older, or much younger, the instant liking each had felt for the other might have developed into an easy, understanding friendship, without one feeling threatened and the other betrayed. But not as things were.

Kate turned to the 'phone, noticing the faint stain on the hall carpet where Anne's dog had lain. Someone had been scrubbing at it. Pansy, she supposed. Kind of her. Kate dialled a long distance number and hooked a chair nearer. Vivvy's voice was the most comforting thing she knew.